Teddy Toddy

S. Burgin

*The topics depicted in this book are of an adult nature.
Contains content that some may find disturbing.*

This is a work of fiction. All the names, characters, businesses, places, events, and incidents in this book are either of the authors imagination or used in a fictitious manner. Any resemblance to actual persons, living or dead is purely coincidental.

Copyright © S. Burgin 2024

Chapter 1

Welcome to the quaint little village of Aviary Avenue. A sweet and simple life for those who reside here. Plentiful in trees and wildlife as nature surrounds the busy yet peaceful high-street. Where you'll find charming cafes and local amenities. Drop by Roy's Tavern for a family lunch or an evening drink to wind down for the day. You'll find everything you need, right here, trust me. I'm sure you've heard all the tall tales about our little part of the world. But come on now, you must realise that the media milked our tragedies dry. They didn't actually know what really happened. It's very unlikely to happen again, I assure you. The news made out as though murders went unsolved, with culprits never captured. Friends, believe me, that's simply not true. Listen, I'll tell you everything. There's a perfectly good reason for it all. Please, allow me to explain.

The story began in our delightful Tavern, formally known as, Roy's. Home to all, the alehouse had been the heart of the community for generations. It'd been in Roy Richard's family, dating back to the early 1900's. It even managed to stay afloat during the war. Meals were rationed sure, but a lovely spam sandwich would never go amiss. Plus, the potential for safety was promised by the underground bomb shelter that the family had built. Now, Roy was a man of simple pleasures. Hardworking yet quick witted. He was the console for those with heavy shoulders and the triumphant gavel for the light fingered.
Mrs Violet Richard and Roy had met after she'd run away from home one evening about thirty years ago. Her widowed mother remarried a cruel man for the financial stability. When old enough to leave home, Violet presented her mother with an ultimatum. Threatening to leave and never return unless she divorced the obtuse man that was her stepfather. Alas, her mother refused. And so, with

no plan, no resources and no confidence, Violet made her way to the only place that people around these parts consider to be as good as home, The Tavern. On approaching the entrance, she observed the enormity of the door towering over her. Darkly painted oak with elongated brass handles, stood between her and fate. Upon opening and entering, she spied a strikingly ample man. He stood weary and tired from a hard day's work as he continued on with the required tasks that his father had assigned him. In one hand was a spray bottle, the other contained a ragged cloth. As he slid the cloth across the tabletop, his glance raised to meet Violet's gaze. They've been inseparable ever since.

Their son, Malcom, however, wasn't one to stick around. He moved into an apartment in the city by his early twenties. Leaving Roy and Violet to run The Tavern. The upper floor was renovated into a three-bedroom flat. With the largest room belonging to Roy's parents before their recent passing. The Tavern was a beautifully classic build. Two slim pillars afront the entrance, positioned perfectly. The gable roof, coated in sleek slate. Walls were gifted with a fresh coat of paint during the spring prior, like that of a colourful seaside house. Though, Roy's palette lacked similar flair, the integrity remained cosy with a burgundy bliss. Inside The Tavern reminded one of a sanctuary from the cold. The same scent that carried charm and comfort through notes of ale and oak, welcomed guests upon their arrival. A scent of which, our leading lady, Esther Petunia was already well acquainted with.

Now, allow me to introduce you to Esther Petunia. Though, plain in her attire, she attracted particular attention. Including mine, at the time. Not in the way in which you may have presumed. She was a peculiar case. Had the potential for a thriving life but chose not to, Esther kept to herself. She occasionally wrote for the About Aviary daily newspaper. Her profession persisted of the acquisition of commissions for small scripts that she would create for advertisements, not only for the paper but for small businesses that would reach out to her too. When it came to her personal life, she had an odd selection of "friends", I would say. And her family, you ask? Well, that was also somewhat of a question mark.

It was the beginning of January 2020. The pandemic hadn't enforced the first lockdown as of yet and the community continued into the new year as they usually would. With empty promises of weight loss, exercise, and self-inflicted restrictions on enjoyment. Perhaps if they had known what was to come later that same year, they'd have been more kind to themselves. Had an extra slice of cake or cheeky glass of wine. Esther hadn't much interest in the resolution fads and so paid her usual visit to The Tavern, just as she had most evenings. She held enough confidence to drink alone, preferably accompanied only by her notebook and pen.

"What are you working on?"

Violet asked.

"Never you mind."

Esther clapped back. Violet playfully threw a kitchen towel in Esther's direction before leaning in to speak to her. Gesturing over to the village's finest underground pharmaceutical salesman.

"Someone's here for you".

She uttered. Esther turned to face George Jameson, meeting his stare as she tipped her head to discreetly greet him from across the bar. As her attention returned to Violet, Esther gave a thankful grin and made her way to the back entrance that led to the beer garden, where she would be greeted by his hand grasped tightly across her shoulder.

"How much do I owe you?"

She asked. George placed his face, far too close to hers.

"Just a quicky."

He replied, perverted in his tone.

"You don't want fifty quid?"

She mocked, not taking him seriously. Taking a step back, he then jokingly grimaced.

"Yeah, fuck it. I'll take the fifty."

She asked if he would stay for a drink, to which he accepted. He wasn't one to turn down a free pint. Upon returning to the bar, Esther ordered their drinks as they found an unoccupied booth to chat. The two met on a night out some years ago, before she moved to Aviary Avenue. They'd spent most of the evening ditching their mates to talk to one another outside, smoking and drinking into the lonely hours of the night until she went home with him. Come morning, they both awoke to the unexpected sight of the other as Esther let out an involuntary giggle before George lost self-control and did the same. It was in that very moment, they intuitively concluded that their relationship was simply platonic. And though life had taken them in different directions, they still made the time, as and when they could to catch up with an old friend. They spoke truthfully, as always. Their bond seemed fleeting to those on the outside looking in, but to George and Esther, it was timeless and unwavering without rules and expectations.

See, here is where I'll give the boy the benefit of the doubt. He wasn't some menace to society, not really. He worked at the off-licence by the hairdressers and in all fairness, minimum wage wasn't a sufficient living wage, so he made his own money on the side. Dealing was a risky game, but the income attained was that of which George believed he would never earn honestly. He wasn't proud of the card he'd been dealt, but he played it as well as he could to survive. That was what Esher felt. The rest of the town, however, perhaps weren't so forgiving.

After Esther had called it a night, George loitered by the bar while enjoying a couple more pints. As closing time approached, he hung his hat for the day and headed off home. He lived in a studio apartment above the pizzeria just off the edge of the high-street, along an elongated row of terraced houses. It wasn't far, as anticipated. Just a quick brisk walk. As he was just a few doors away from his building, George took the keys from his pocket, ready to enter his home when the slam of a car door sounded behind him. He casually turned his glance toward the road, noticing that there wasn't a car to been seen.
Odd
He thought to himself. For those who hadn't drives afront their houses, there was a communal carpark with designated spots for each household built by the end of the pavement. There would be the occasional car parked on the street if residents had visitors staying, and that particular family didn't have additional allocated parking. The nights were typically silent as Aviary Avenue is a small village. The shops close by a reasonable hour during the week, a little later on a Saturday but then they'd close on Sundays. With the exception of the pub and the newsagents by the post office. Earl would open Sunday mornings until 11:00am, just in case anybody needed anything. Toilet roll, loaf of bread, nappies. You know how it is, there's always someone who's forgotten to pick up something before the shops closed. That night was no exception. It felt still, just like every other night. George could hear nothing but the pitter patter of footsteps. Footsteps that resembled that of a large dog that hadn't had its claws clipped. As each pad hit the concrete, the nails would involuntarily slap against the ground. The footsteps reached his door just as George had. Animals often wondered around his building due

to the food wastage that critters would find within the bins from the restaurant downstairs. So, assuming it was just some stray, a fox, or some type of wildlife he couldn't care less about, he pushed the jiggered key left and right until the lock flipped. He then coaxed the handle downwards and opened the door before entering. Still buzzed from the lager, George hadn't thought to close the door right behind him. He opened his jacket, allowing it to slide from his arms before placing it on to the hook. He took off his shoes and then closed the door, locking it for the evening.

12:00am rolled around as Ether settled into her own bed. Her eyes sat glassily and empty like that of a pottery crafted dolly. She drifted into unconsciousness, encouraged by her self-medication.
George tragically, afforded no such luxury.

Chapter 2

Sundays. Once everybody's favourite day of the week. The only places open generally, back in the day were the bars and a few restaurants or cafés. Nowadays, everywhere is open all of the time. I never saw the appeal of 24/7 opening hours. Who on earth is nipping for a pint of milk at 2:00am? Whoever it is, needs to get their priorities straight. Our little nook wasn't anything like that. Even our takeaways closed at 10:00pm. The only place that stayed open late was Roy's Tavern. That wasn't preposterously late either, for a pub. Sundays however, Roy and Violet would picnic by the pond every week, unless the weather dictated their traditional plans. They would serve the Sunday carvery until the late evening before heading off for a pleasant picnic with the ducks in the summer. In the winter however, they'd set on a couple extra staff members, so they could leave before it got dark. Most of their team were in their early twenties. University students that needed flexible hours to fit around their course schedules.

Roy and Violet weren't the only ones with their routines. The lunchtime carvery invited the likes of Mr and Mrs Platt. A God-fearing pair of whom participated in all the villages weekly affairs. Loyal to their faith and the community, Mr and Mrs Platt took pride in their dedication to keeping all in order as they believed it should. Both had been born and raised in Aviary Avenue. They met as teens at the church since their parents were consistent attendees. Both knew their place in society and in their marriage. Righteously unhappy, some would mutter as they passed on the street. Mrs Platt cared for her husband with his unfortunate disability. In the early year of their betrothal, Mr Platt took a frightful fall amongst a flight of stairs. Irreparable damage was inflicted to his spine and confined him to a wheelchair as his lower half became administered with irreversible paralysis. Mrs Platt respected her duty as a wife. The service to her husband's needs had exceeded her expectations of course, but Mrs Platt was strong in every sense. He was her responsibility as say's her lord.

Mr Platt liked a carvery. He liked an extra-large portion, which came with a sausage and another Yorkshire pudding. Whereas Mrs Platt would stock up on the vegetable variety displayed. Strictly prohibiting herself from self-indulgence. She found justification in a hefty dessert so long as she had endured a plate full of gravy deprived vegetables.

"Sure, you won't have Yorkie this time Mrs P?"

Roy toyed as he served out the portions.

"Certainly not, Mr Richard".

Mrs Platt confirmed. She didn't appreciate Roy's wit as others would, but the years had accustomed her to such attributes. That Sunday, however, she was already in a humourless mood.

"She came home late again."

Mrs Platt mentioned in a casual tone but without casual intent, as she dished up her vegetable medley.

"Why would that be, Mr Richard?"

She continued accusatorily. You see, Mr and Mrs Platt had a moderately sized, two-bedroom house. It had a vacant room after their daughter had moved out. Eve, the ripe and virtuous offspring that her mother had tried so desperately to keep from temptation, fell pregnant before marriage. After a shotgun wedding at the Town Hall, Eve moved into a one-bedroom flat above the local hairdressers with her husband and baby boy, Ellis. Mr and Mrs Platt had offered up the room for rent, with utilities included in the monthly fee. A list of house rules had been written with white chalk on twin black slabs hung with thin fraying rope on the bare bricked wall by the front door. One of the rules, encouraged a curfew. Esther Petunia hadn't shown much respect for the curfew. She had lived there for about a year and so became accustomed to the expectations of her accommodation and its enforcers. Obtaining a clean, well-cared for room deemed more attainable than renting a flat on a freelance writer's wage. Writing could prove unpredictable in its substantial retrieval of regular income. Esther thought she had found a way in and out of the house without detection. Inevitably incorrect, as it would seem.

"She did? Sorry Mrs P, I can't think of why she would have".

Roy lied, attempting to conceal his knowledge on the matter. Mrs Platt raised her attention from the plate, up to meet Roy's avoidant glimpse.

"Yes, Mr Richard. She did. But she won't tonight."
She stated as a matter of fact.
"Will she?"
Mr Platt added with an arrogant tone, directed towards Roy as he handed over the meat coated plate to his condescendingly mannered customer.
"No, Mr P. She won't".
Roy grinned, offering up the extra Yorkshire pudding, gripped between a green handled pair of tongs.
"Enjoy your meals".
He finished, relishing in the annoyance he and Esther had inadvertently caused the pair as they ventured to their table. That morning they'd attended the weekly service at the Church. An intimidating spectacle, beautifully lavished with gargoyles guarding its stature. A stain glass window facing the high-street, engraved with the artistic threat of eternal damnation avoided by the Arc in which had saved those without sin. The pews categorised by their unspoken hierarchy. Typically, the longest and most loyal members sat closer to the sermon, this included Mr & Mrs Platt and their daughter Eve, who was still expected to attend regardless of her new living arrangements.

"You've got a stain, Eve. On your shoulder, what is that?"
Mrs Platt observed, as she often would. Her journey to parenthood had its unfortunate hardships. A heart-breaking miscarriage tore the world she'd desperately tried to reach, from the palm of her hand, before miraculously catching grip. Eve's conception meant everything to Mrs Platt. She liked Eve to maintain the perfect image of a child that she had always dreamt of. A beautiful young girl wrapped in a blanket of elegance and decorum.

"It's just a little spit up, Mother."
Eve responded, as politely as she was able. She had lost interest in her parent's faith long before falling pregnant herself. She'd learned about other religions at school. She'd learned about other cultures and their beliefs and values. It upset her to recognise the limitations she was conditioned to as a result of her family's values, with her being a woman. Being a woman who was different to how her family believed women should be. But she also learned that people are going to be whoever they want to be, they'll live their lives the way they chose and believe whatever they want to believe. Sometimes she may not understand it, but she could at least try to respect it. She would abide by her mother's wishes to attend the weekly service, show her respect, in the hopes that eventually her mother would return the

sentiment. It would just take patience, she believed. Her patience was often tested by her mother's abrupt contempt for Eve's choice in formal wear and the quality of its presentation.

"Ellis was fussing, there was a weird noise down the street last night that woke him, so I tried to get him down for a nap before setting off. If I had gotten changed, I would have been late".

She protested, once more as politely as she was able.

"I'll fetch you a spare cardigan next week, in case it happens again".

Mrs Platt concluded, accepting Eve's excuse in frustration.

"Thank you, Mum. That's very thoughtful of you".

Eve added. She would often allow her mother the win, just to avoid the confrontation, especially in public. Her mother had a way of silencing her, occasionally with a hint of a personal issue. Threatening the exposure of something private with a little comment or gesture, to influence Eve's behaviour. The confrontation wasn't worth it, not over a little spit up.

Ellis would be left with his father, Jason, when Eve attended church with her parents. Jason and Eve had met at an ice-cream parlour in town. She'd been out with her friends shopping for the afternoon on a Saturday. He had been at the skate park with his gang of fellow youths. Though they'd attended the same school, most of Eve's friends were either neighbours or people her age from Sunday school. She'd never gotten close to anybody like Jason before. He lacked conformity and structure and yet was compact with understanding and selflessness. The key to a door that Eve had always wanted to open, once insufficient in comprehension, now indulgent in exploration. When they fell in love, both had actually planned Ellis's conception. He wasn't an accident as most had thought, with the two still confined to their teenage restrictions. They wanted to marry. Jason asked Mr Platt for his daughter's hand, to which he was rejected. Eve had hoped that they would be wed before trying for a baby, but she knew that her parents wouldn't get in the way if she were already pregnant. And so, a plan unfolded. Mrs Platt suspected the reality of the circumstances but never uttered a word. Not yet anyhow. She would save that little Chesnutt for a more convenient opportunity.

Jason loved his little boy. When Eve had to go to church, he would usually take him out for a walk. Wrap him up all tight and cosy in his pram and take some sliced grapes in a sealed disposable food bag for the ducks. A worn-out bench sat between the bushes by the pond. On the Sunday prior, Jason took Ellis from the pram and settled onto the bench.

"Oh, look Elly welly, the duckies know we've got their breakfast."

He warned, playfully. The ducks took a slight flight above the water's surface and glided to a gradual landing with their wings outstretched before pulling them in to a close. They landed by the lands edge, waddling into the ground from the waters shore.

"Hello, gents!"

He exclaimed, as he scattered the first handful. The ducks excitedly quaking as they snatched each visible serving from one another.

"And ladies, my apologies".

He added, throwing out another serving, bouncing Ellis on his knee as they both delighted in the clumsy birds causing a raucous.

That particular Sunday however, Ellis hadn't slept well through the night and so Jason stayed home as the baby had a nap. He would usually make a start on dinner later, but as he had the time, decided to make a Sunday roast for when Eve returned from church. The flat could get noisy through the day, with it being above the local hairdressers. The weekends were especially loud, and they were the busiest, so getting the baby to settle hadn't been easy. Jason hadn't heard the noise that awoke his son the night before, though Eve had. She'd described it as someone having dropped something or broken something heavy. Jason didn't really care in all honesty. He just hoped it didn't happen again, as he rocked his son to sleep.

Chapter 3

Esther was regaining consciousness after a night of being dead to the world. The morphine had run its course. Exhaustion pulled at her skin from the beds desperate grasp as she forced herself to awaken. The phone highlighted the notification of a repeated alarm, the next due to sound after three minutes. She took an exaggerated breath while rubbing the temple of her forehead. A quick blink and the alarm screamed at Esther, demanding that she start the day.
"Alright, for fuck's sake".
She snapped, dismissing it. She took a moment to accept that a new day had arrived. The room in which Esther resided was decorated with a powdered olive green. Eve's name was stencilled into a mini heart shaped frame containing an illustration of a lipstick red apple.
"A reminder".
Mr Platt once proclaimed.
"Of the sin we must atone for".
Esther didn't really understand what it meant. She avoided asking questions through a reluctance to indulge in such a topic. The room was soft, quiet, and obedient. The only loud quality, being the red of that apple. Structurally organised with a single bed by the door, a desk by the window and a chest of drawers pushed back against the wall, standing neatly in between. The rooms functional integrity provided an unexpected comfort. The rules however, suffocated Esther, but this way she could write. Had she a flat to pay for, plus utilities, food, and transport, she would be left with no disposable income.

She turned on her computer to check who was online and to her surprise, George wasn't. He would usually be logged in by midday on a Sunday. Esther dropped him a text before going about her business. The ensuite shower was attached to the wall above the bathtub, hidden by a sheet white curtain that exposed nothing but the silhouette of its user. After having gotten washed and cleaned her teeth, Esther checked for George's usually reliable and timely response only to be met with concerning disappointment as the message hadn't even been read.

"Curious".

She admitted aloud. She took a pair of black jeggings from her drawer along with a Gray T-shirt, plastered with the decorative white floral arrangement, Mrs Platt had woven into the cotton. Esther didn't care for florals, but the Platt's had a dress code amongst other dictations, for living under their roof.

"Modest and feminine".

Mrs Platt had once suggested.

"No… tat".

She concluded.

When dressed and ready for the day ahead, she considered checking in on George. Insecure about her lack of invitation, Esther created an excuse for her unintentionally intrusive visit. She switched off her phone and hid it inside of her bra. Her idea was to request for some marijuana to endower herself with. Excusing her lack of having contacted beforehand, with the situation of her 'lost phone'. And so, she put on her longline coat and made her way to his apartment.

The trees were still dead from the cold. Spookily so, I always thought. January is such an in between type of month. Where we're not quite over the events of the year just passed, and we're not quite ready for the year ahead. The intermedial drudgery, evoking the 'go on ahead' voice that life unwittingly distils in us. Anyway, when Esther arrived at Georges apartment. She knocked an appropriate three times before forcing entry. Not necessarily by slamming into the door with such a forceful blow, that it succumb to its lifeless wooden state. No, she simply picked the lock with her hair pin. A skill that George had taught her actually. They'd fancied a trip to the cinema one afternoon. And so, baked in sweet delusion and penny-less from rent, Esther conducted a plan to sneak into the movie and steal snacks from the stock cupboard.

"Who is this deceitful witch?"

George had joked, impressed by the might of her arm as she threw caution to the wind.

"It's locked."

She sighed, stating the obvious.

"Here, let me show you a little trick."

He offered, as he took the pin from her hair. Causing the brassed red fringe, she'd been growing out, to fall on her cheek. For George to then take his hand and delicately fold the loose hair behind her ear.

"Suits you, red".

He whispered in admiration, before checking no one was around to see the crime they were about to commit.

There was no way Esther could have known that the single step taken through George's apartment door would lead her down an unreturnable path. She would find his coat that he had worn the night before, hung on the same very hook it that it had always hung. His shoes placed by the door with the lacers still tied as he'd scraped them off, one foot at a time. His phone and keys, placed atop the kitchen counter by the microwave. All was accounted for, except of course, for George.

"Who are you?"

Esther heard. The whole floor was just one room, with kitchen cabinets adjacent to a simple fridge freezer, in the far-left corner. A small bathroom built into the far right. He didn't have an oven, just a cheap microwave stationed on top of the counter. His mattress lacked a bedframe and sheet covers. He wasn't one to spend money on decorative things, apparently that included a nice bed spread. Next to his bed were two used cans of cider and an unemptied ashtray, accompanied by an opened pack of cigarettes. Alert and slightly afraid by the question she heard, she turned to find a young woman by the open door.

"Who are you?"

Esther questioned.

"I asked first."

The woman demanded, impatiently with concern.

"Ok".

Esther replied cautiously, surveying the person in front of her for a glimpse of a clue. Her features resembled the description of Ivy, the woman that George had mentioned he'd been seeing. Her hair styled with an ash blonde pixie cut, neatly straightened, and maintained. Wide with curiosity, her eyes hid behind false lashes and black liner. Her body deemed undetectable as her green mac, layered with a hoodie and a decorative scarf, hid her figure.

"Ivy?"

Esther asked, confirming her suspicion. The woman stepped back, more so alert than before.

"George talked about you. I'm Esther. I don't know if he mentioned me".

She concluded. The woman's shoulders dropped, as did her guard.

"Oh. Yeah. He mentioned you. Where is he?"

Ivy asked.

"I was going to ask you the same thing".

She answered, disappointed by the exchange. Ivy had popped by on her break from work. The off-licence was closed but some staff were allocated on a weekend rotation to restock and deep clean the store, fresh for the new week ahead. She hadn't time to wait for George to get back from wherever he had gone, so she headed back to work. Meanwhile, Esther made herself comfortable in his desk chair, knocking the mouse as she fell carelessly into the seat. The computer lit up to display a screensaver, a picture of George and Ivy eating chips on a brick wall. The computer had been left on, which wouldn't usually be the case. He would have shut it down before having left. Esther decided to shut it down for him and unplug it, so to not leave it running up the electric bill. She sat back, spinning left to right, contemplating her next move. That's when she saw a slight tear where the carpet had been seemingly pulled at and pushed back into place. She studied it for a moment before removing herself from the chair, taking one step at a time toward it. Placing her knee carefully onto the carpet before reaching for the tare, taking the corner in her index finger and thumb as she peeled the tip.

"Esther!"

A shriek exclaimed. Esther jumped out of her skin. She stood with her back to the wall as her glance darted out through the door that Ivy had left open. Mr & Mrs Platt stood waiting.

"Oh."

She sighed in relief as she approached them, closing the door behind her as she entered the street.

"Quick word, deary".

Mr Platt commanded. She went on to endure the verbal scolding of Mr & Mrs Platts wrath for having disrespected their curfew the previous evening. They interrogated her on her whereabouts, with it being so irresponsibly late. Their rants hardly affected her, but even less so on that day. Mrs Platt observed Esther as her husband continued on about rules and expectations, noticing that she hadn't been paying attention.

"Her head's in the clouds. Don't waste your breath."

Mrs Platt spat, loitering on the pedestal she proudly built for herself.

"You're on drugs aren't you, Miss?"
She accused, persistent in her pursuit of authority.
"No."
Esther insisted, defending herself.
"No, I apologise for having been late. It was Saturday night, people were out, having a good time. I lost track of the hour and I'm sorry about that. It won't happen again".

She lied, in the hopes that her deceit would deem believable. Silence fell as the conversation uncomfortably dropped. Esther took the handles of Mr Platt's wheelchair to assist with the journey home. As they entered the house, the smell of fresh linen hanging from the washing line in the kitchen welcomed them. Mrs Platt assisted her husband into his living room chair before checking if their clothes had dried. A large hickory brown, leather recliner centred the family area, a chair that he'd spent most of his days facing the blindless window.

"So, I can keep an eye out".
He would say. Compulsive in his desire to control the goings on around the neighbourhood. Waiting to pounce on the opportunity to preach etiquette and appropriate behaviour to the kids, playing on the street.

"Are you going out again, today?"
Mr Platt asked Esther, expecting the answer to be, no.
"I think so, yes. I will be. Before Roy closes".
She answered politely.
"I couldn't find my mate earlier. I'm just popping to see if he's at The Tavern".

She continued. Anticipating his lack of empathy, Esther prevented his chance to respond by interrupting him with the offer a cup of tea. Mr Platt's concerned brow clenched tightly as he looked upon his wife. The two exchanged a personally offended stare as he answered.
"No".

Chapter 4

Eve and Jason's humble abode was above the hair salon. An insignificantly small structure of brick, with a display window to the right of the doorway that essentially advertised the service to be expected. Through the window, the public eye would be met with the pleasant sight of customers. People sat, having their hair dyed, washed, styled, and dried as they gossip drivel about neighbours and celebrities. Resting tabloids amongst their laps as they drink instant coffee. The waft of shampoo's, conditioners, and dye's, assault the nostril within seconds of entry. Eve & Jason needn't endure this hair care seduction every time they entered their home as there was an outdoor stairway hidden behind the building that led to the upper floor. Of course, getting the pram up and down the stairs had proven itself a time-consuming task and so Dana would let them keep it in the staff room during opening hours, so long as they entered and left through the back.

What could I tell you about Dana? She hadn't grown up in Aviary Avenue, in fact she was born at home in a flat just outside of the Town. Which wasn't far, technically still a local. The community embraced her with open arms. As we do, all of our newcomers. Odd one though, might I add. She read tarot cards and collected crystals. Communicated with the great beyond and such. Her clothing always consisted of some eccentric colourful pattern, flowing from her bangle covered wrists. Eve had taken a shine to her. She admired her lack of conformity just as she had with Jason.

After Eve had returned from church, herself, Jason, and Ellis sat down to dine on their Sunday roast. The fold-out dining table hid beneath a plastic sheet that Eve had purchased from a discount shop in her attempt to spruce up the place. Two identical plastic garden chairs hugged the table, leaving space for the donated highchair that Ellis received from Violet. She'd kept hold of a few totems from Malcom's childhood, the wood crafted highchair being one of them. Opposite the dining table, stood the bench that Jason and his friends had once stolen from a neighbour's front lawn.

"They never use it anyway".

He'd laughed, justifying his crime.

"I said a sofa, not a bench".

Eve had protested, hoping to encourage him to return the stolen good.

"No. You said that we need something comfortable to sit on. Well, this will be comfy with a duvet thrown over it, add a couple pillows".

He replied, defending his decision. Jason worked late as a delivery driver for the pizzeria. The pay was minimum wage, and his employer wouldn't make a deal for covering any milage, even though he had to use his own car. Eve worked part time for Dana as a cleaner. At 16:00pm, she would go downstairs and deep clean the store, including the office, staffroom, and toilets for two hours a day, on a flexible rota. She would be done in time to get back to Ellis, so that Jason wouldn't be late for his evening shifts that would generally start for 18:30pm.

"Did anybody see you?"

She'd sighed.

"No, don't worry, it's ok".

He'd reassured. Planting a gentle kiss amongst her brow, while they sat comfortably on the stolen bench.

Dana was on a quick smoke break when fate came for her. She was waiting for a customer's colour to take. Leaving some lady with a latte and a magazine whilst she popped out. The smoking area was just the pathway along the side of the building that lead to the back. She'd put out a couple garden chairs, only useable during warmer days. There hadn't been a shelter. So, often she would stand, holding an umbrella for her nicotine fix. Her index and middle finger delicately grasped the decoratively orange filter of her cigarette as she brought it up towards her face, guiding it towards her mouth. As Dana's lips hit, she drew in a deep concentrated breath. Smoke gliding down into her lungs as she released and blew the fog back out. Her pupils dilated and her arm hair erected from the fix that she had been craving since her last drag. Her eyes glazed with mindlessness as she let her thoughts wonder off. This was her five minutes. Her three hundred seconds of uninterrupted emptiness, where there were no customers, no paperwork, and no calls. Just Dana and her cigarette. That is of course until a car door slammed shut, bringing her back to earth. After an irritated sigh and a heavy eye roll, Dana elongated her neck while remining close to the wall, in an attempt to see who had pulled up. Concealing her whereabouts behind the side of the building, knowing full well she would have to cut her cig break short if it were a customer. To her surprise, there was no one there. So, she relaxed her neck and watched burnt ash fall from the extension of her fingers end. The last of which landed next to an unanticipated shape. A foot of some sort. An animalistic foot.

Dana's cigarette was left unfinished. It dropped to the ground, accompanied only by the ash that had been released but a moment before.

"One minute!"

Jason yelled, both friendly and apologetically as a knock sounded at the door. Eve was playing with Ellis in the living area and Jason had gotten started on the washing up, before placing the marigold gloves by the sink to answer.

"Oh, can I help you?"

He greeted as he opened the door.

"Where is she?"

A woman demanded. Her hair, pasted in peroxide at the root. She had a black towel resting on her shoulders, held together with a hair grip. Her eye liner was as heavy as the wrinkles that her foundation attempted to conceal.

"Who?"

Jason answered, confused, and growing increasingly aggravated by how this woman's interruption to their day carried an unwelcomed attitude.

"That flake, doing my hair. This was supposed to wash off fifteen minutes ago!"

She exclaimed, gesturing to her burning, chemical coated scalp.

"What, Dana?"

He asked. He couldn't make heads or tales of the circumstance presented on his doorstep. How someone had convinced themselves that this, in any way, would be deemed appropriate.

"Yes, Dana! Can you tell her to get off her fat arse and come down to finish my hair?"

She carried on, before Jason lost his temper.

"Woah, don't talk about her like that, she's not even here, OK? I'll come help you look for her, just let me put my shoes on and I'll be right down."

He replied, shutting the door on the woman. Door closed, back to the wall, Jason looked upon his wife. They exchanged the same disgruntled expression. They assumed Dana must have gone to the bathroom or had been in the staffroom or office, and this woman just decided to take it upon herself to cause havoc for the sake of retrieving special treatment. Her outburst had upset the baby, causing little Ellis to make a fuss, which his mother had to stay and soothe as his father went to investigate the issue further.

Jason and this infuriating woman walked side by side down the outdoor steps on their mission to resolve all of the hullaballoo. There hadn't been much natural life garnishing the front of the building, however the side entrance leading into the back was heavily trimmed with overgrown bushes, weeds, and dandelions. Just on the one side. The building was semi-terraced to the adjacent structure, harbouring a tattoo parlour. What the alure is with permanent doodles, I will never understand. Anyway, as Jason avoided the overgrown hedges on his way to the salon's main door, he spotted Dana's cigarette on the ground. It had burnt out, only in a way that had been partially inflicted. A perfectly parallel tube of ash was still attached to the bud.

Maybe she dropped it, halfway through?

He thought to himself, as he continued in his search. Dana wasn't to be found on the shop floor, in the office, the staffroom, or the toilets. Jason didn't want her to lose business over this. For all he knew, there could have been an emergency that she had to deal with and perhaps had just forgotten about the customer. Reluctantly, he asked the lady to get comfortable by the hair-wash basin to rinse the dye out himself, using whichever shampoo and conditioning treatment was on the shelf by the tap. He apologised to the lady for the inconvenience and vouched for Dana's good name.

"I promise that this has never happened. I'm assuming she got a call for an emergency or something. But the dye is off your head, and I put plenty of conditioning treatment on your hair so it should be ok. Its up to you, if you want to wait for Dana, or if you want to end your appointment as is, and I'll go get you one of the mini sample packs they have in the back as an apology, what would you like to do?"

He explained, attempting to calm her down.

"Nope! I'm going. Give me my freebie and I'll be on my way. Oh, and in case you were wondering. No, I won't be fucking paying."

She shouted, with her arms crossed as she tapped her foot theatrically.

"So unprofessional!"

She concluded as she stormed out, freebie in hand. May and Olly were on shift that Sunday, but they were booked up with their own clients. Jason had asked for their help, but neither were able to, not if they were to get their own appointments done in time.

"Can't you see, I'm doing a cut and colour myself, if I leave it half done for 10 minutes, the colour will be uneven."

May had protested.

"I'm already behind as it is, and I can't stay late. Our lass' booked us in for a carvery, if I stand her up, I'll never hear the end of it. Just wash it off for us, Jase. Do us a solid, and you can have a fiver out of the tip jar if you do".

Olly had bribed.

Jason returned to the flat to find Eve had soothed baby Ellis for an after-dinner nap. She quietly asked what all the commotion was about, and if he'd manage to sort it. He took a seat on the bench he'd stolen just a few weeks before, wrapped in an uncovered value duvet he'd bought that same day to make it more homely. His shoes remained on his weary feet. Shoes with soles that had lasted the good part of three years but hadn't yet fully worn to a lack of utility. They rested side by side as Jason sat, leaning his elbows atop his knees.

"Well?"

Eve persisted.

"Where's Dana, then?"

She asked, not yet understanding the gravity that particular question held.

"I don't know".

He answered, cupping his exacerbated expression into his open hands, before sliding them downward for them to meet, grasping one another amongst his lap as he rested his back against the hard bench.

"She's just gone."

Chapter 5

The rattle of the last orders bell never seemed enough to herd out the kind of customers who lacked self-awareness. The ones that take their sweet time to suckle a drink through an absorbent paper straw that's consuming their drink faster than they themselves ever could. The ones that declare that last minute trip to the loo, just as the waiters thought they were ready to leave. The ones who dump their plates, cups, and napkins askew on the tabletop, along with damp ring marks next to the coasters provided. Worst of all are the ones who see a bin, and instead, just leave their rubbish on the lid. As the last family exited The Tavern, Violet hurriedly, yet politely locked the door behind them. She was frustrated by the reduction of staff that day. Two had called in sick, so her and Roy weren't able to duck out early to their picnic plans before January took the afternoon sunlight.

She leaned against the door, her hand still clutching the handle, contemplating her escape from the mess she had to clean. During daytime hours, a table is presented by the bar's end. It's displayed with condiments, a milk jug, and wooden stirrers. Additionally, there would be a pile of plain print out pictures for colouring and a small basket of individual 4-piece packaged pencils. Red, yellow, green, and blue. It helped the families to keep the kids entertained during their meal. Sachets of salt, pepper and sugar were savaged open and spread all over the surface as though someone decided to season the table. The milk jug had been tipped over, which wouldn't have mattered had someone not taken the lid off. A sea of milk seeped into the carpet as a fly invited his friends to dive in for a pool party. Colouring pencils were everywhere, one was even in the light shade on the ceiling somehow. Violet got started on the tidying and cleaning as Roy got started on bringing up the stock from the cellar after changing the barrels.

The last table to clean was that of which Mr & Mrs Platt had dined earlier that afternoon. Another booking had sat there after Mr & Mrs Platt left. A table of four, double dating duos. Leaving chewed gum under the table and lipstick stains on the glasses.

"The bloody nerve."

She sighed to herself.

"What's that, love?"

Roy asked from behind the bar, not realising she was speaking to herself.

"Look at this shit tip. They've left gum under the table! I remember their faces though, don't you worry, they won't be coming back here again if this is how they treat the place".

She continued, reassuring herself.

"Fuck'em".

Roy added.

"I've just got crisps and soft drinks to fetch up, then I'll sort that gum out, love. Why don't you go and get a hot bath and pop that new dress on. He'll be here soon".

He suggested.

"Alright, well I won't say no to a nice soak in the tub. Thanks' love".

She replied, appreciative of the relieved workload.

With the tub filled almost full, vanilla cupcake candles ablaze, Violet glazed her foot into the cherry pie scented bubble bath induced water. With a rolled-up towel placed between her head and the tubs edge as she relaxed. Taking soft breaths, in and out, to switch her mind off from the world. Bubbles corroded the surface, her eyes drew a blank, dead in their gaze. Her imagination let loose to gallop in calamity. The background faded as a dragon emerged in bubble form. Its scales pop and crackle as it escapes from the steam on the water's surface. The bubbles erode as it approaches its fate, deluded by freedom but burdened by despair. The bubbles disappear along with its form. It has moments left. It knew, she knew. She watched as it turned to meet her deathly stare.

"Why give me life but disallow me to live".

It plead, as she awoke from her trance. It was nothing but a pile of diluted soap sprawled along the window ledge. Its time was short and desperate, she felt.

A knock sounded at the door.

"Mum?!"

A man's voice called.

"I'm in the bath, hon! Your dad's downstairs, I'll be right out!"
Violet replied, while stepping out of the tub and pulling the plug on her personal hour.

Malcom was the classically handsome type. Tall, dark hair, brown eyes, white smile. He worked in a call centre in the city. A thankless job, dealing with complaints and following up on resolutions he'd actioned. Working 8:00am until 16:00pm, Monday to Friday. Occasionally Malcom would join his parents for a Sunday dinner, had he no other arrangements. He'd made it in time for all the chores completion and so the family sat to dine on the leftovers that the chef had stored from the carvery.

"So, Malcom. Please tell me that you've started seeing someone".
Violet pressed, making her son bashful in his reluctance to discuss such matters.
"No, Mum. I haven't, please tell me you'll drop it".
He answered back, in a direct yet courteous tone.
"Not everyone's as lucky as you and me, love. He'll meet someone eventually, give the boy a little air".
Roy joked, attempting to ease the tension. Violet was old fashioned in a sense; she was concerned that her twenty-five-year-old son hadn't found himself a wife yet. Herself and Roy had met in their teens, whereas in Malcom's teens, he spent his days in his room playing computer games. Violet assumed he was immature for his age, that he'll grow out of it and when he's older, start to take more of an interest in dating.
"Look, I know what you're going to say, but"
She started.
"No! I don't want any set ups or blind dates, Mum. How many more times?"
He cut her off, having had this same conversation, every visit he made.
"Can I just come to see you both without you criticizing me before we even get to dessert!"
He yelled, before getting up to leave the table and heading toward his childhood bedroom. Violet rolled her eyes and looked at Roy for confirmation that her actions were just, only to find him ignoring her as he played with the broccoli on his plate. She accepted that the silence that fell after Malcom left the room, spoke only of her defeat. The meal ended after the main, there'd been speak of apple crumble and custard, but nobody seemed in the mood for it. After an hour or

so had passed, she put the pre-made dish in the oven anyway. Malcom preferred a corner piece usually, because it was crumblier, and he liked the hidden crunch slivered in creamy sweet custard. She dished up the crispiest corner piece into a bowl, along with a single serving jug. Placed it on a tray along with a dessert spoon and a glass of fresh water as she made her way upstairs. Violet then knocked on her son's door and awaited permission to enter, to which she was given.

"Peace offering?"

She asked, gesturing to the pudding she'd prepared. He didn't respond, only sighed as he tried to force a smile. Violet then sat the tray down onto his bedside cabinet before taking a seat for herself beside him on the bed.

"How must it make you feel, sweetheart. All this pressure I put on you to hurry your life up".

She acknowledged, attempting to understand his contempt.

"You know, my life became better the second I met your father. Maybe because it was that way for me, I just keep trying to make that happen to you. I don't know".

She rambled, trying to make sense of her behaviour toward her son. Malcom reached for the jug and poured its contents as it glided out to smother the crumble. He then set the jug back down and reached for the spoon before taking hold of the bowl. The first spoonful overfilled with ripe, piping hot, sugary apple wearing a biscuity coat, drenched in custard.

"Oh, whew".

He expressed.

"Hot out of the oven, isn't it?"

He laughed, blowing on the next spoonful that he scooped. He shared a thankful grin with his mother as he enjoyed the loving gesture she had baked. He took a moment to think, before considering meeting her halfway.

"Who is she then?"

He asked. Malcom knew his mother would only persist until he eventually brought someone home himself. He considered just humouring her at least, that way when it went badly, they could finally drop it. Violet's face lit up like a Christmas tree, she was getting what she had always asked for.

"Oh! You are going to love her, honestly sweetie! She's so beautiful and kind, and she's a receptionist so she works in customer service too. Oh, and she lives just outside of the city so she's not too far away and…"

His mother excitedly trailed on, before he cut her off her once more.

"Just, tell me her name and her number and I'll see how it goes, mum. Don't let yourself get carried away".

He laughed, in a failed attempt to settle his hyped-up mother.

"It's not a marriage proposal, for fuck's sake".

Malcom joked, before she back handed the side of his head.

"Less of that lip, you little shit".

She added playfully. Violet kissed the place on Malcom's head that she'd just clobbered and took his empty dish along with its tray back to the apartment's kitchen, thanking her son for his understanding and expressing how much she loved him, on her way out of the door.

Roy had been at the kitchen table, going over the finances for the bar as Violet walked in. He knew his wife like the back of his hand, every expression she showed and tried not to show had its meaning, and Roy knew them all. He saw straight away that his wife had managed to buy her son's compliance with a beautifully baked bribe.

"It won't work, Vi."

He observed, as his glance never left the paperwork, confidently sipping on a cup of tea.

"You don't know that".

She protested, desperate to get her way.

"I do, Vi. And you do too. If we force this, were going to push him away".

He replied.

"Oh, because you're so sure? How do you know? What if he just needs to meet the right woman, have you thought about that, what if he's just shy or too picky?"

She asked, badgering her husband to get him to change his view on the matter.

"You already know what I think".

He answered firmly.

"Well, if that's what you think then why don't you just ask him?"

She questioned, becoming increasingly immature in her pursuit to win the debate.

"Because Violet, he will tell us when he's ready. We have no right taking that away from him".

Roy snapped, beginning to lose his temper while concealing the volume of his outburst.

"No right? Excuse me Roy Richard, I am his mother".

She argued.

"Then act like it".

His voice raised, having lost his patience, completely unaware that Malcom had heard every word.

Chapter 6

Seemed that some of our citizens needed a little perspective. Don't you agree? There's victims going missing, and all that people can think about is roast dinners and hair appointments. Silly, really, when you think about it. See what they didn't know was that there was a tale of a beast whispered under the breath of those who'd heard its wail. Rumour has it, the creature was born of human flesh. An unforgiven soul was sentenced below upon their untimely demise and begged for redemption. Wanted for nothing but to walk amongst the earth's surface once again. Had they known the terms of such luxury, would they have preferred to stay in hell?

Unfortunately for Esther, she was unable to acquire more information on George's whereabouts. There'd been a rush at The Tavern that afternoon when she went to enquire before it closed. Neither Violet nor Roy had seen him after he left. They hadn't time to really discuss the matter and so asked that she return the next day if he still hadn't shown up.
"Sorry, I know its busy here today".
Esther apologised insincerely, in her attempt to sugar coat her inconvenience as she continued to pester. "Was George busy last night, did he meet with a few people? Who was the last person that saw him?"
She pushed.
Roy was in the middle of serving a gentleman at the bar. The man regrettably ordered a lager shandy as a compromise, since he'd already had a lager with his meal. He knew that a shandy would prevent the inevitable disapproving grunt from his wife back at the table, who hated it when he drank during the day. The glass had only just been placed back on the shelf after having been in the dishwasher. Often the glasses would shatter, for putting cold liquid against the hot

surface too soon. Thankfully this one didn't. Clean water from the condensation dripped down the exterior onto Roy's palm as he tilted the glass below the nozzle and pulled the lever. The fluffy fizzy fluid filtered into the internal dome, growing taller inside the glass before reaching the edge with the foam neatly aligned at the surface.

"Three-fifty, mate".

Roy stated, as he placed the beverage onto the beer mat atop the bar, before turning his attention back to Esther.

"Erm, I don't know, Essie".

He answered, not really trying to remember because another customer required his service.

"Look, I'm sure he's just stopped at his mates. I don't have time. So, either put on an apron or let me work".

He continued. The ultimatum he gave wasn't a joke, Roy had every intention of letting Esther help out if she were willing. Mainly due to the lack of staff he had in that day. Usually, she would help when there was time to. Though she couldn't help but feel weary about Georges unexplained absence. She apologised once more to Roy, this time with genuine intent and left The Tavern.

When George was in his early twenties, he tried marijuana for the first time. He'd tried it at a house party that he'd been invited to. His friend, Pete was at university at the time. Instead of utilising the accommodation provided through student halls, he rented a flat. During a reading week a few years ago, Pete invited a few friends over to play whatever useless video game was popular at the time. He led George to the coffee table where a pick & mix of drugs were presented decoratively, along with all the nick knacks, or must I say equipment required for usage. All that his friends could teach were the basics. Who's selling, how much the going rate was for specific quantities, and finally how to use such recreational pastimes properly. He didn't only see the opportunity for a good time, he saw a chance at a business for himself. Aviary Avenue isn't the type of place that accommodates drug users and alcoholics. It is a respectable community that takes good care of its grounds. George was well aware that such goings on didn't occur here. Instead of respecting that, he chose to exploit it. He saw an open market and grabbed it with both hands.

This particular profession requires a profound level of secrecy and trust. One simply cannot text with the blatant request of cocaine. There is a unique language, and so only those trusted are educated in its translation. The profession also requires safety measures to avoid authoritative detection. This includes the use of a burner phone. Any cheap mobile with a pay-as-you-go sim. Easily replaceable. Customers names abbreviated or altered to protect identities in case the phones are ever confiscated, preventing users from potential prosecution.

Later that night, some friends had left, and some fell asleep on the sofa, while Pete retired to his bedroom. George couldn't sleep. He thought about his life and where it was heading. He thought about his lack of resources, his inability to gain higher education like the friends surrounding him had access to. He thought about his job, and if he would ever feel a sense of purpose, doing what he did for a living. He wondered if he would ever live in a nice home.
Pete's flat wasn't much to brag about. It was filthy due to the occupants being unwashed students. The sink was full of pans that had been used days before, the counter tops covered in toast crumbs and dripped butter. Sugar scattered by the kettle from the numerous teas made without proper etiquette. The coffee table guarding the TV from feet flung outwards, as the lads rested on the sofa. It presented the remaining unused substances ready to be abused. He crept toward its inviting scent, before lowering to his knees to obtain a closer look. Considering his next move very carefully.

Esther took a seat on a nearby bench by The Tavern. Contemplating her next investigative tactic. Roy's dismissive comment weighed on her. Perhaps she had been overly concerned. It wasn't as though her and George spoke regularly. Each of them had their own lives separate to the other. Esther's days were primarily spent writing. The majority of commissions obtained were through independent companies, not broadly recognised. People who worked from home, who needed appealing descriptions for their websites and products. The About Aviary newspaper would contain local advertisements written by Esther also. The pay was fair, but she wasn't one for lavish possessions. Her intentions persisted of the dream to travel. Her disposable income would initially be stored for a future outside of the perceived detainment of a small village life. Her unwillingness to self-indulge often took a toll on her social life. When asked to go out for a meal, she would politely decline. She would listen to the equation whispering at the back of her mind. The total cost that set her back, little by little. With illegal contraband, clearly taking priority.

George however, lived each day as it was gifted. He didn't spend frivolously neither, mind. He fancied himself an avatar of a sort. Challenges presented were game levels to conquer, each with life's reward awaiting. For example, say his journey was to be burdened with a forceful gale. A rain of which, so manipulative that it found its way through George's raincoat, making him push his way through the tough winds on his walk home from work, cold and soaked. His reward, a hot shower. Bubbly, and sweet smelling. Along with a freshly prepared pizza from the takeaway downstairs. All finished off with a movie and some snacks.

George, somewhat like Esther, always admired the idea of travelling. But instead, he usually just took life as it came.

He's probably just busy.
Esther thought to herself, still perched upon the public bench.
Nobody else is here, fretting about it.
She realised, as she began to recollect others that he was close to. Esther considered people that she and George had in common while scrolling through the contacts logged on her phone. That's when it occurred to her. The burner would be in the apartment.

Chapter 7

Have I formally introduced you to Troy as of yet? No? Ah, my apologies. You remember, the hairdresser that had infuriated her customer? Well, she had a son, and his name was, you guessed it, Troy. He went to look for his mother the following day, Monday I believe it was. Dana would have usually been home on Sundays, if not by 16:30pm, then at least by 17:00pm. Not that it mattered anyhow since Troy hadn't noticed his mother's disappearance until the next morning. This was due to him having had a long day himself. Having a game of football in the afternoon and staying out late with his mates at the pub afterwards. Troy assumed his mother had already gone to bed by the time he'd returned home.

On that morning, he got ready for work. He'd been doing some construction job in the city, just a short train ride away. On days that Dana didn't have work, he would pester for a lift to avoid catching the train. Grabbing his keys on the way out of the door as he yelled, directing his enquiry in the general direction of the stairs.
"Mum?!"
He called.
"Any chance of a lift?"
He asked, as no answer was returned. Listening to the silence that his mother's response held before climbing the stairs to wake her.
"Please, I hate catching the train."
He whined as he entered an empty bedroom, realising she wasn't home.

Not all hope was lost, he knew that if she wasn't in, she would be at the office. Troy still had time to venture to the salon to nag his mum. Only, to his surprise the salon was closed. The shutters pulled down and padlocked shut. Olly, Dana's assistant manager, had a spare set of keys. The general rule being, last out locks up. At this point, Troy began to worry. He'd called his mother on the way to the salon, just for there to be no answer. He'd originally concluded that she had it on silent while she did the paperwork. If she wasn't in the office, if she wasn't at home, if she wouldn't answer her mobile, where was she?

Troy made his way around the back of the building to speak to Eve and Jason. He knocked at the door cautiously, uncomfortable with the performance of interrogative probing. He waited impatiently for either of the two to answer the door, until it opened to present Eve with a towel flung over her shoulder, and a Sippy cup in hand.

"Troy?"

She gasped.

"What are you doing here?"

She questioned. They all knew each other in an acquaintance capacity. They'd only ever spoken at the salon or if they bumped into one another in the street. Troy's audience at their home had surpassed the expected threshold that was the foundation of their disconnected connection.

"Have you seen mum anywhere?"

He asked awkwardly.

"Not since yesterday. I saw her doing some woman's hair through the window when I came home from church. Let me ask Jason."

She answered, calling him into the doorway.

"No, I haven't seen her either. Some woman was going off on one about her yesterday, though."

Jason added.

"I don't think she came home last night; you know. I came in late. I assumed she'd gone to bed. Anyway, she's not home, so I thought she must be in the office, but she isn't".

Troy started to explain, as his breath became shorter.

"What woman, what do you mean, what happened?"

He continued.

"A customer came to our door, she was ranting about how your mum had popped out for a cig break while her colour was on, but that she never came back".

Jason explained, reluctant to admit that he hadn't investigated the matter further.

"Who was she, what time was this?"

Troy persisted.

"Erm. Maybe two or three o'clock? I think, I'm not sure".

Jason answered, increasingly desperate to conceal his knowledge on the matter. Realising his error in judgement from the previous day, dreading the potential consequences for his naivety.

"Let me put my coat on and some shoes, I'll come help you look for her. Don't worry. I'm sure she's just shopping or something and left her phone on silent. I'll bet she's perfectly fine".

Jason offered to help, while ineffectively comforting Troy.

Their first thought was to check the smoking area for any clues, since that's supposedly where she was last seen, according to the angry customer that had complained about her. Troy asked Jason if he'd noticed anything yesterday when he walked that same path the day before, anything that stood out as a clue. Jason considered the question while pulling out a cigarette from the box in his tracksuit pocket. He offered one to Troy and they both stood quietly, having a little think to themselves, until he realised. The burned-out cigarette on the floor, the one that seemed unfinished.

"She dropped her cig before finishing it".

He observed. Troy's expression was clueless as to how he should emote, until the outburst was explained with Jason's previous sighting of said cigarette.

"Do you think she collapsed? What if she fell into the hedge and was just left there all night?"

Troy cried, as he threw his cig to the floor, his attention redirecting to the surrounding plant life as he frantically searched for his mother's body only to discover that it was not there. Jason lunged towards him and wrapped his grasp around Troy's shoulders to pull him out from the bushes before pushing him against the wall, trying to meet his viewpoint in order to calm him down.

"Look, she's not there, mate".

He demanded.

"I'll get the police".

He added, as Troy pulled away from his clutches.

"You're going to report me? I'm trying to find my mum, you cunt!"

Troy yelled, while uncontrollable tears crept from his eyes.

"No, dickhead! To find her, let's talk to them to see if they can help. If somethings happened, which I'm not saying it has, but if it has, the sooner we get help, the better".

Jason tried to get through to him. Troy agreed that informing the police was the best strategy for retrieving his lost mother. He and Jason headed off to the local station.

See, they were too busy looking down on the ground for Dana. Had he looked upwards, Troy would have witnessed the outstretched lifeless arm of his mother hanging from the rooftop just above their heads, waving goodbye as her son walked away from her corpse. What a terrible shame. That being said, it was probably for the best that Troy didn't discover the body himself. What would such a thing do to the mind, I wonder.

Chapter 8

Tuesday came with a heavy fog that pressed on the chest of those that stood watch. A collection of residents, incapably grasped for air as the community wept. Blue and red flashes of unsightly light, glared amongst the entirety of the crime scene. Ugly yellow tape scraped across the perimeter from post to post, disallowing common civilians' passage. Troy, isolated within the crowd, locked his stare onto the black sack strapped to a wheeled bed, that was pulled from the rooftop.

Grief stricken people all find their own ways of processing tragedy. Jason was riddled with overpowering guilt for having not tried harder to find Dana back when the opportunity had presented itself. No amount of consoling from his doting wife could rid him of that realisation. She and Dana were friendly. Dana offered the apartment above the salon when she learned of Eve's pregnancy. Having known Mr and Mrs Platt as neighbours for so many years, she'd anticipated Eve's need for her own space to raise the baby. It used to be a spare room where Dana herself would stay when she started up the business. She'd been granted a hefty loan, which required a heavy repayment plan. It was crucial to use every day wisely. Some days Dana wouldn't finish setting up, filing documents and contracts, decorating and such until gone 02:00am. Often Troy would just come home to the salon instead of the house as there was a bed for him too. As a single mum, she was determined to build a substantial career to support her only son. And that's what she did.

The village was in an uproar. Devastation developed into disgust. Anguish consumed the community like a plague, as the rumours flared like a pirate's flag. Dana had been murdered. An autopsy was to be expected, but from first glance, officers deducted foul play.

Tongues began to wag as the conspiracies unwound. Not before condolences were offered to Troy while he was still present, as it would be perceived as poor taste. He hadn't heard them, mind. He wasn't even there. His body was, of course, but his thoughts were with his mother.

"Can you pick up some shampoo?"

He shouted from the couch as she was heading out. Troy would often use shampoo and conditioner samples from the salon when he'd ran out. He'd been lounging around the house that morning, watching TV before planning to meet with his friends.

"Alright, love!".

She replied, closing the front door behind her.

He stood still like furniture, as people rested their heads and their hands upon him to console the poor boy. They apologised for his loss and prayed for him in the middle of the street. He wasn't listening. No, he wouldn't hear. Instead, Troy replayed that last memory in his head, over and over again.

The witch hunt was afoot. Not soon after the police had arrived, did the shops close one by one. The fear distilled was shared throughout the village. Our villages' good name had been compromised, and so the people took it upon themselves to hold a meeting. It was agreed to be held at the community hall. Roy & Violet would host. They suggested setting up a table for attendees to bring food and beverages to share as they'd no inkling of the meetings potential duration, with it being such a horrifically delicate topic.

The next day's paper would read of a mysterious midday murderer. A demented killer, so confident that they took a life in broad day light without anybody noticing. Esther wouldn't look, through fear that George had suffered a similar demise. Amongst the villagers, Esther was also motionless. Her hands hung hidden within each pocket. One palm holding her keys, and the other, her phone. The commotion that had unfolded around the salon encouraged her grip to tighten. No longer was she second guessing herself. George was a missing person. And so, Esther vowed to find him or die trying.

Chapter 9

Mr & Mrs Platt invoked a new curfew at their home. Disregard for the curfew was, as usual, strictly prohibited. Esther was to abide for her own safety, they stressed. The community meeting was arranged for 15:00pm that same day. Some felt it too soon to be expecting attendance after the incident itself. Others wanted it to be sooner. Adamant that something must be done.

They'd made their way home for lunch time. Mrs Platt prepared some quick chicken paste sandwiches for herself, Mr Platt, and Esther. Offering a chocolate bourbon with a cup of tea for afters, while she got started on cooking a pasta bake for the buffet table. Bringing the swirled pasta to a boil, Mrs Platt poured a ration of blended chopped tomatoes into a pan atop the burning gas fired hob. She then threw in some sliced fresh basil, half a clove of garlic and some chopped chives, right before sprinkling it with grated mozzarella. After draining the steamed water from the cooked pasta, she married it with the sauce before nipping in a dash of salt and pepper. The food was laid out into a cooking tray, ready to go in the oven for fifteen minutes, before they had to set off. Once fully cooked, the dish was carefully wrapped in kitchen foil to preserve the heat. Esther offered to carry it between two tea-towels serving as oven mitts, on their way to the community hall.

The hall was plain, beige, and dry. The floor outstretched with cheap wood replicating lineal. The perimeter of which, curled from its base where the plastic ground met the wainscot. Inside a storage cupboard rested a pile of metal foldable chairs. The padding on the seat and back rest consisted of a simple cobalt blue. As the time reached 14:45pm, residents of Aviary Avenue began to filter into the room. The table had been set up by Violet who had arrived just a few minutes beforehand, but chairs were still left untouched. People grabbed their own chairs as they came and seated themselves, as and where they wanted. Placing down the snacks and dishes they brought along with them, onto the table. The rows deemed askew due to the lack of preparedness. Each person had their own ducks to align before attending the meeting. As a result, the room was barely set up. By 15:25pm, Roy decided to get started. They'd waited for any possible latecomers, but concluded that who ever was going to come, would have already gotten there by that point. He started out by thanking everyone for coming.

"Now, I don't know how to even begin with this. I can't seem to figure out the right words to describe how this morning's events have affected me. Affected my wife, and my son".

He began, speaking loudly and clearly as the acoustics of the hall carried his voice like a microphone.

"But what I want to say is, this should not have happened".

He stated as the audience would nod respectfully in agreement.

"Dana's son won't be with us this afternoon. Obviously, he won't be in any condition to come. I'm going to ask if him if they would like any help with the funeral arrangements, but they might just want it to be a family affair. Perfectly understandable if that's the case. So, if we could all just take a moment of silence, please. To express our respect now, while were all together".

He paused. The room became weighed down by the descended hearts of those who knew and loved Dana, as a heavy silence spoke volumes. When a minute passed, Roy took a deep breath, preparing himself for what he was to speak of next. The residents sat on the edge of their seats in anticipation.

"There is a killer in our home".

He stated, with an infuriated sigh.

"We need to come up with effective preventative methods, so that nothing so devastatingly horrific ever happens to anyone else".

He carried on.

Mrs Platt was the first to blast off from her seat, her arm flung into the air as though squatting a fly. Roy turned to her with an agreeable tilt of the head to welcome her response.

"What about a neighbourhood watch? I've been thinking that if we all chip in, we could buy hi-vis jackets, body alarms, whistles, and torches. If we get enough volunteers, we can have them on a shift rota type basis".

She enquired, knowing others had been discussing the same idea, but she wanted the credit.

"Yeah, that could work. What time would people be staying out until? Where would they be stationed?"

Roy asked, agreeing with the notion but trying to work out the kinks.

"Well, I suppose that would depend on who volunteers, wouldn't it?"

Mrs Platt answered defensively.

"How do you mean?"

He pressed.

"We need some muscle, Mr Richard. I'm happy to volunteer, but unfortunately, I don't see myself as much use after dark, as I myself would just be in danger. Perhaps if people like me could take the day shifts, and those with a bit more meat on their bones can take the later ones. The more participants that sign up, the more area we can have covered".

She finished, taking back her seat as it rested between Esther's chair and Mr Platts wheelchair.

Eve stayed at the hotel with Ellis when Jason attended the community hall gathering. His determination outtrumped anyone else in that room. He was fully aware of the mistake he'd made and fully prepared to make it right.

"I'll volunteer".

He offered as he rose from his seat.

"This happened right outside my doorstep. I could have just as easily been the one found on our rooftop".

He explained, keeping his more primary motive a secret as he didn't want the village to know how he could have saved Dana, but didn't.

"Whatever it takes to keep my wife and my baby safe. I'll do it, I'll do the late shifts. I finish work usually for half ten. I can head straight out after that, until early morning if you need me to".

Jason plead.

Malcom was sat by his mum. He filled his pockets with mini sausage rolls from the buffet to sneakily nibble on throughout. All the remaining dishes were covered as social protocol dictated that the food be consumed after the meeting concluded. He hadn't eaten all day due to the shock from that morning's news. The sausage roll stealing could easily be perceived as disrespectful, but it was the resolution to the interruptions that his stomach growl would inevitably cause.

"I'll do it".

Malcom contributed, chewing on the pastry.

"I can move down here for a few days, if that's alright with you?"

He gestured to his mum and dad listening.

"Well, ok. Thank you, son. Why don't we move on to some more ideas? Whoever wants to sign up for the neighbourhood watch, just write your name on the spare paper that I'm sure Violet will have in her purse, thanks".

Roy avoided giving his real answer. Both him and his wife shared a concerned look of agreement that Malcom would not be getting involved. Roy himself was committed to the cause, but he would not put his son in the line of fire. Neither would Violet, especially during the shift with the highest risk.

Mr Platt extended his curfew from the house to the village. He suggested earlier closing times to prevent citizens form having to return home when its dark. A suggestion that encouraged a lot of push back. People argued how alternate opening hours would affect their income. That it could cause disruptions for delivery routines and employment rates. Others argued that they would have to rethink their whole business's expenses to accommodate the loss of revenue. Mr Platt refused to accept the outcry of the disobedient crowd.

"Have you all just forgotten why we're here? A woman has been killed. A mother, a real-life person, who was going about her daily life, was snatched in broad daylight, and brutally murdered! Now if this killer can accomplish that during the day, without being detected even in the slightest, what on earth do you think they're capable of when its dark? When there are less people around to hear you scream for help, more places for them to hide and pounce on you when you least expect it? We need to be realistic here people. Ask yourselves if it came down to it and you had to choose, what is more important?

Mr Platt asked. He paused, knowing that he held the room in his hands, as he delighted with the weight of it.

"Your livelihood or your life?"

He finished. Mrs Platt took hold of his shaking hand.

After the meeting, people scattered. Some made their way home, and some stayed for the buffet as they discussed the goings on amongst themselves. The volunteer list was filled with names, one of which was Malcom's. He mentioned to his mum & dad that he was nipping to the loo before they set off back to The Tavern. Once out of sight, Violet subtly picked up the list, seemingly to write notes while scribbling out her son's name. Roy pretended to be distracted by loudly complementing Mrs Platts pasta bake.

"This is delicious Mrs P! What's in it?"

He boasted.

"Its just a standard pasta bake, Mr Richard. Don't you offer three types of pasta dishes at The Tavern?"

She interrogated.

"Yeah, but not like this one, this tastes as though it came straight from Italy! Can I take a plate home, do you mind?"

He carried on as his wife gestured that her mission was complete.

"Yes, I suppose you may. There seems to be plenty left if you would like the remainder. I expect my basin returned promptly".

She offered sternly.

"That's brilliant. Thank you, Mrs P, I'll return it to you first thing in the morning".

He promised.

"Very well. 9:00am will be most suitable. Good evening, Mr Richard, Mrs Richard. Thank you for hosting todays gathering".

She replied, putting an end to the evening.

When Roy, Violet and Malcom reached their home, Violet got started on crafting a collection container. She sought out an old shoe box and sliced out the middle to resemble a letterbox. In the back of her closet lied a decorative case filled with acrylic paints, brushes, and sketch paper. The colour palette she felt most appropriate would be similar to that of uniform which spoke of authority and security. While at the same time, standing out enough for passers-by to notice. She painted the box a safety helmet yellow and expressed her calligraphy with the words, Neighbourhood Watch Donations, in a navy blue. She placed the box on her bedside cabinet to dry before stationing the collector to its work location by the bar, first thing in the morning.

Chapter 10

Detective Inspector Michael Jones' Tuesday morning started much like any other when he was home alone. His husband was away for the week on a lad's holiday. A holiday that he wasn't in the mood to attend and so used work as an excuse to bail on. A friend of his, had recently gotten engaged to a woman he'd met at work. The holiday was supposed to be some sort of week-long bachelor party, something that Mr Jones considered himself too far old for, or at least too tired for. His husband Toby however believed age is just a number and you're never too old for a good time. Sounds like a mid-life crisis to me, but what do I know. That morning, he started his day with a large latte. Michael didn't believe in leaving the house for someone else to prepare things for you that you could have just as easily have prepared at home. That being said, he wasn't one for an instant coffee. As a wedding gift, he and Toby received a single use coffee machine with a grinder built in for convenience, along with a milk steamer. The portafilter rested upside down on the sink drainer, having been rinsed and ready to use. He took a measurement of fresh hazelnut roasted coffee beans and portioned it into the machine before switching it on. The sound of beans grinding as the scent of hazelnut induced caffeine slid into his mug. His senses enlightened, relieving his reluctance to wake up. He then poured full fat cows' milk into the stainless steel, temperature-controlled pouring jug. To then place the steam nozzle in as it frothed the milk into warm silky liquid satin.

Just as he sat down at the kitchen table, wrapped in his dressing gown, latte in hand, a notification alarmed on his phone as a call interrupted his breakfast.

"This better be good, I've just sat down".

He joked while taking a sip.

"Michael... brace yourself for this one".

Jones was advised. His grin subsided.

"Where am I heading?"

He asked, dropping his humorous tone. He'd become accustomed to the lifestyle by this point in his career, he was confident that he'd seen it all. That is, until he came to our village.

"Aviary Avenue".

Detective Inspector Michael Jones first saw Dana from afar as he approached the salon. An officer pointed out the body's arm hanging from the rooftop.

"OK, how do we get up there?"

Jones asked casually, assuming there was a set of stairs built inside or outside of the building. His initial suspicions were that she was on the roof with somebody. That it was an accessible aspect of the facility. She was accompanied by possibly an abusive partner. An argument gone horribly wrong.

"That's the thing".

The officer started.

"There's no way up. Whoever did this, somehow threw her body up there".

He answered, as he walked away to proceed with taping up the restricted area. DI Jones considered his view for a moment. The structure wasn't excessively tall, but he thought surely, no matter how strong a person is, it couldn't be possible to throw a human body that high. As he proceeded to step closer, he noticed there were no signs of blood. Not on the concrete, not on the brick wall, not on the plants, nowhere.

Maybe strangulation?

Jones deduced. He continued on toward the back of the building. There stood a staircase that led to Eve, Jason, and Ellis' flat. Placing his black leather shoe on the first step with a gentle caution, one foot followed the other as the metal staircase rattled. The un-oiled joints of steal screeched and squealed with each movement. Had the killer used the stairs, the residents of that flat would have heard.

The top of said staircase's surface area provided enough space for the police to place a step ladder to assist them onto the rooftop. It was a simple wooden fold-out that lacked paint. It confidently situated itself by the top step, watching DI Jones embark upon his next move as he climbed.

What would usually happen during the morning while Toby was away, would be that he was the first to call. He would ask Michael how he'd slept, then discuss their plans for the day. Michael planned to get the shed painted that Tuesday. He'd been meaning to for a while, but something always came up. He liked pastel colours, so his final choice on the matter was to paint it in a matt summer cloud grey with white boarders. It would look seasonally sensible regardless of the time of year, he felt. In that moment, he wished that he had missed the call. He wished that he had left his phone switched off. He wished that he was painting the shed.

Dana's jaw had been torn from her face and left to dangle across what was left of her neck. The back of her tongue stuck outwards beneath her front teeth, missing its tip as it had been seemingly gnawed off. It was as though a bear had ripped her apart for dinner, to then change its mind and leave its scraps. Her eyes were frozen in fear, locked in a desperate state of a life preserving plea. Her body looked like a ragdoll that had been dropped mindlessly by its preoccupied holder.

"What the fuck!"

Jones exclaimed aloud to himself, before flinging himself toward the opposite edge of the rooftop to vomit. His surroundings started to waver, everything around him doubled as he dropped to his knees. His hand pressed firmly against his mouth, preventing the howling wail that his soul hoped to cry.

The officer from before had climbed the step ladder not long after DI Jones, arriving just as he began to pick himself up to leave the crime scene.

"You, OK?"

The officer asked with a heartfelt concern, having just experienced his own first glance of the body beforehand.

"Yeah".

Jones answered.

"Just get me the fuck off of this roof".

Exiting the crime scene, DI Jones noticed the people gathering. Most residents were circling around a young man in his mid-twenties, mindless as though the life had been drained from his skin. Some people were still in their dressing gowns and their slippers, sipping coffee from mugs they'd brought from home. All of them watched the police investigate the scene like they were watching it through a television screen. All of them but for one. A young woman. Her fox-red hair was scraped back into an uneven ponytail. Wearing beige pyjamas underneath her winter coat and knee high, faux leather boots. Her attention was drawn to a house down the street, holding a heavy make-up-less expression of worry and guilt. That is until her head turned back toward the salon, and her eyes met with his. He studied her attire, her mannerisms, and movements before she left, feeling uneasy from the unwanted attention. DI Jones thought to himself.

Let's start with you.

Chapter 11

Across the duvet cover on Malcom's single bed, lay three outfit choices his mother had selected while he was in the shower on Wednesday. Not that he had asked. In fact, he specifically pleaded for her not to do so. Violet had entered the room without Malcom's knowledge while he was in the shower.

His full black beard was trimmed to shape his strong jawline and slightly crooked nose. Prone to acne, he typically exfoliated his face with a scrub and a face cloth before stepping into the shower. The tropical steam, opening his freshly cleansed pores as the pineapple and mango face & body wash, rinsed away the excess dirt. He then focused on shaving his thick and unruly chest chair. He'd received mixed opinions on the level of attraction such a sight encouraged. But, because he planned to wear a V-neck shirt, Malcom felt it best to tidy it up. After washing his body, he finished with shampooing his short, layered hair. Hair that held the same thick, rich, deep velvet shine and texture to that of tar. Upon stepping out from the bathroom, wrapped in a white daisy decorated towel that his mother had picked out, Malcom entered his room to find the outfits that were chosen for him. Two included tailored trousers. One was black, one was ash grey, and the third choice was that of a navy-blue chino. The black pair matched with a white dress shirt and vest to wear underneath. The ash grey trousers were presented with a baby blue polo shirt tucked into a matching grey blazer. And finally, the chinos were to go with a red, blue, and white stripped polo shirt. An outfit to which Malcom felt would make him look like a little sailor. He himself had planned to just wear a nice pair of jeans and a pristinely white, long sleeve V-neck T-shirt that he'd already ironed to use. Reluctant to get into a feud with his mother over the trivial matter, Malcom went with the grey trousers and pastel blue shirt.

Meanwhile Roy was downstairs in the office of The Tavern. It was a quiet day, with most people feeling safer staying at home. He'd told his staff members that if anybody didn't feel safe enough to come through, they wouldn't have to. Unfortunately for some, that wasn't an option as they had their own expenses and commitments to respect. So, Roy offered to give those who didn't have their own transport, a lift home to make sure everyone got home safe after work.

As he was the self-appointed leader of the Neighbourhood Watch, it was his responsibility to assign duties and keep record of which volunteers went where and at what times. He'd started out by forming a list of the equipment needed for each person and the costs involved. Nineteen people had put their name down to participate, which implied that they required reflective vests, torches, whistles, and body alarms for each of those nineteen people. It proved difficult to collect donations to fund the project due to the lack of traffic coming in and out of The Tavern since the news hit. So, he would have to go door to door. In addition to the shopping list, he wrote out a procedure's protocol sheet to hand out to volunteers on shift. It would detail instructions of the body alarm along with encouragement to take photos using flash, to then finish with advice on what to do if danger presents itself. Violet cleared a few tables on her way down to the office, not that there were many to even clean.

"How are you getting on, love".

She asked Roy as she entered the door with a cup of tea, made just for him.

"Not so great, I'm afraid. I don't know how we're supposed to fund this without going around, pestering people for cash".

Roy answered. Violet took the seat opposite the desk. The office was small, unpainted, undecorated, with safety advisories on the wall alongside a sign-up sheet for a now cancelled staff outing. Filing cabinets filled the far wall and the rest of the space was crowded by a simple pine desk with an accompanying swirling chair either side of it.

"I've been thinking that we could have a quiz night, you know. That ought to bring a few punters in, I recon".

Violet suggested. Roy took a moment to consider, though he hadn't taken much convincing. Anything would be better than having to go door knocking, he felt.

"Oh?"

Roy replied, requesting more context.

"We could have prizes for whoever comes in 1st, 2nd and 3rd".

Violet continued, excited about her idea.

"What do you have in mind, love?"

He asked, pulling her from her chair to sit on his knee.

"Well, the top prize could be a bottle of whiskey from the cellar, 2nd could be a bottle of wine and the 3rd, maybe a family meal token for a free carvery?"

She answered, confident in her suggestions. She knew that Roy wouldn't be too fond of the notion of giving away free alcohol, but they both knew that if nobody donated, then the expenses from the much-needed donations would inevitably fall on their lap. It was cheaper to give away some alcohol then have to pay outright for nineteen peoples worth of Neighbourhood Watch essentials.

"How are we going to get them to donate, though? You can lead a horse to water, but you can't make it drink, can you?"

Roy added, concerned that their plan had a hole in it.

"Daft egg, we'll have an entry fee. £5 for individual players, £10 for teams of three. Nobody will want to pay a fiver just to take part, but they'll split a tenner between three. We'll get enough to cover the Neighbourhood Watch stuff. And we could split it, give the rest to Dana's family?"

Violet concluded, relieving Roy of his worries.

"You're not just a pretty face are you!"

Roy joked as Violet got up to leave, with him giving her bottom a pat on her way out.

"Give over!"

She laughed, as she left to check the pub floor.

Malcom stopped by the bar for a little Dutch courage before heading out. His flavour leaned toward a merlot typically, but a spiced rum held more promise. At home, he would delight in an evening drink from crystal glassware. Its sharp design cut through the atmospheric glimmer of Malcom's bedroom harder than the liquor it supported.

His mother emerged from the stock room, carrying an opened cardboard box filled with crisp packets, chocolates, and other confectionaries. She set them aside to feast her eyes on her blushing boy.

"Oh, look at my beautiful hansom son! I'm so glad you chose that one, those colours suit you right down to the ground, let me get your father, sweetie".

Violet exclaimed, not allowing Malcom to respond. He took another jolted shot of spiced rum before his mother returned. When she came back, she rushed towards him, dragging Roy in from behind as she coaxed him unwillingly into the conversation.

"What do you think?"

Violet asked Roy.

"I thought you said you were wearing jeans and a top?"

Roy asked Malcom, ignoring his wife's persistence. Malcom was vexed.

"Mum put this on my bed".

He answered shortly, as Roy turned to her, irritated.

"Do you want to help him when he needs a piss too, Vi".

Roy snapped.

"Don't be that way with me Roy Richard. He looks smashing thanks to me, so I'll have less of your lip".

She snapped back.

"Oh, and you're welcome, Malcom!"

Violet whimpered, stomping off upstairs in a huff.

Roy looked to his son apologetically, he worried that his wife's behaviour emasculated Malcom. That she took advantage of the power she had over him, knowing he would never speak back as she would feel disrespected if he had. Roy suggested that Malcom should get changed. He would feel more comfortable on the date if he felt like he could be himself.

"If I could be myself, Dad, you know I wouldn't be going on this date".

Malcom said in a solum voice. Roy took a moment to think of the right way to reply.

"What are you trying to tell me, son".

He asked delicately.

"Nothing".

Malcom answered. He'd pictured it in his head a thousand times, the day he would tell them that he wasn't single. He would tell them that he'd been seeing someone in the city on and off. That he'd been having relationship problems. He couldn't ask his father for advice, nor could he seek comfort from his mother. Malcom was aware that his father knew of his homosexuality as he'd heard a fight between his parents. Somehow, knowing this actually hurt more. This was because it robbed Malcom of his safety net. He was always scared to find out if his parents love was unwavering. The argument allowed him to see that his mother had a clue of his true identity. Yet alas she had still wanted to change him. This inevitably confirmed Malcom's greatest fear. The fear that perhaps his mother's love was in fact conditional.

"I better head off."

Malcom finished, as he left his father's inquiry hanging above the bar.

Chapter 12

Dust had accumulated throughout George's apartment, by that same Wednesday. The items discovered before had remained untampered with. The last visit had been brief and interrupted. And so, a more thorough investigation was required. Esther made a start in the bathroom. If one could even describe it as such. On the ground was a none-slip, waterproof flooring with a plug hole in the left corner and a shower head fixture hovering above it. The toilet sat opposite on the right, accompanied by absolutely nothing. Not so much as a toilet seat, lid or a tissue paper dispenser. The toilet roll was placed on the side of the inadequate sink, alongside a bar of 17p value soap. Floating above the sink was a shelf supporting a plastic disposable cup as it carried an unbranded toothbrush and toothpaste. Next to that was an opened, three-quarter full packet containing disposable razors. The towels were folded and kept on the sill beneath the faded-out window. She found the smell surprisingly delightful as she noticed an air freshener hung on the doorknob. The type that is usually intended to hang on the mirror in the interior of a car.
Cute.
Esther thought to herself as she lifted the air freshener closer to her nose. Bubble-gum candy floss flavour, yellow and pink stripes in the shape of an unwrapped sweetie.

Her mind travelled back in time to the day they'd broken into the cinema. Once they were in the building, Esther and George weren't sure where to go next. They were in the back, where only staff were permitted. Unlike the customer area, there weren't any signs advising direction. Somehow, they'd managed to find the sugary snacks stock room in their lolli dally state. They filled their pockets with share bag chocolates and crisp packets before realising the lack of hydrating essentials in this cinematic survival mission.

"We need pop, Esther".

George whispered, putting mini peanut bags into his socks.

"Ah, shit. Where's the drinks?"

Esther asked, looking around the room multiple times before realising she had searched the same spot four times.

"Must be in another room".

George answered, as he popped his head out of the door to see if the coast was clear. That's when he'd noticed the break room door was not only open ajar, but also unoccupied.

"Leave it with me".

He commanded sincerely.

The staff room had a pile of two brand new uniforms by the kettle and toaster. Both uniforms had newly made name-badges resting on the packaging. Two names, Hillary, and Max.

If this isn't a sign, I don't know what is.

George thought as he smiled to himself. He went back into the storage room and gave Esther, Hillary's uniform as George changed into Max's. They put their own clothes into Esther's tote bag and hid it behind the outdoor bins next to the door they'd entered from. Once in Character, Hillary and Max set out to look for the beer cellar.

In movies, daringly dangerous drug dealers tend to hide contraband in sealed airtight bags inside the back of the toilet. Perhaps such a common place, deemed it slightly less effective. The towels seemed too easy, but it was worth a try, Esther had thought. Unsuccessful, she moved onto the kitchen. The cupboards proved uncooperative also, she even checked the fridge freezer. The microwave however wasn't empty. It had inside a bag of salted popcorn, fully popped, yet left cold and untouched.

They hadn't stolen popcorn that day at the cinema if you would believe. When the general manager was done with her office work, she came out to the floor to check on how the team was getting on with the busy period. She noticed right away that Max and Hillary didn't look how they had when they'd been interviewed for the position. In fact, they sounded rather conspicuous as well, especially when the bottles of lager they'd stuffed under their belts, crashed together as they walked. Sorry, ran, out of the building as security chased their criminal behinds. This occurring after they'd already managed to sneak into three viewings whilst the manager had been in her office. None of the movies they'd caught were from the beginning, mind. They'd snuck into random screenings mid film.

Esther took the stale popcorn from the microwave, tore the paper bag open and reached her hand inside its buttery contents to eat a piece. It'd tasted fine so she continued to graze as she surveyed the room until remembering the rip in the carpet on her first visit. It still appeared to be slightly raised in the corner by a plug socket. Now that she'd noticed, the plug socket also appeared loose. The gap was too thin for her to get her finger in between. With the additional threat of an electrical current invading her autonomy, it'd been illogical to use bare hands. A wooden spatula made an appropriate tool. Esther pried the socket from the dry cracked wall, only to find that there was no wiring connected to the house within. Instead, was a hidden hole where George's stash was stored, along with some pills and the burner phone.

A knock startled Esther, causing her to drop it. She remained noiseless, weary of the visitor, discretely replacing what she had found, along with the socket to disguise its contents. Another knock sounded. This time followed by the thunderous temper of woman scorn.

"George, why aren't you texting me back? If you have another woman in there, I swear you'll be sorry!"

Ivy yelled. Esther rose to her feet. She had every intention of ignoring her by committing to quietness, hoping that Ivy's own impatience would ware her down.

"I can see you, whore!"

Ivy screeched, banging on the window that was revealed by curtains undrawn.

"For fucks sake".

Esther sighed, as her eyes rolled backwards like balls on a pool table. She approached the door to open it, reluctantly welcoming Ivy into the apartment. She barged past Esther like a bull avoiding branding. The veins in her forehead resembled that of the missing electrical wiring, charging her with jealously and rage.

"Are you fucking my boyfriend?"

Ivy asked, demanding an honest answer. Esther pushed her away from her personal space as she mocked the absurdity.

"No, I'm not. He's not really my type".

She answered, insulted by the accusation. Ivy's rage subsided unwillingly before it was replaced by humiliation, hidden by a slight disbelief.

"Oh".

Ivy said as she released an embarrassed smile.

"Where is he then?"

She asked. Esther thought about how she should answer. She needed help finding George without involving the police. If they were to find him first, he would be carted off to prison. Then again, she didn't know Ivy well enough to bring her in the loop. Esther allowed the question to float in the air between them for an uncomfortable minute.

"Is he ok?"

She continued, growing increasingly agitated with the time Esther was taking to respond to her simple question. Ivy then took a step toward her, locking eyes in a threatening manner to demand she share her knowledge on the matter at hand.

"I don't know."

Esther gave in. She went on to explain to Ivy how she had last seen him on Saturday night. That he'd also not responded to her and so she came to check for any clues at the apartment as to where he may have gone, but the place looked as though he hadn't even left.

"What! Let's call the police then, fuck! Why didn't you just do that as soon as you knew he was missing? He could be fucking dead like… like Dana!"

Ivy shouted, as she pulled the phone from her pocket, dialling 9-9…

"Woah, give me that!"

Esther exclaimed, snatching it from her manicured hand.

"And will you shut the fuck up yelling, Jesus Christ. You know he's a dealer, dickhead. Do you want to send him down?"

She continued, trying to shout under her breath. Ivy grabbed her phone back from Esther, asking what they were supposed to do if they cannot seek the authorities help.

"We find him".

Esther stated, as a matter of fact.

"We're not the fucking Hardy Boy's. Have you even found anything yet?"

Ivy questioned. Esther kept the burner phone to herself. It was too valuable an asset to her investigation to treat so carelessly. She maintained confidence in the concealing of the socket she'd recently discovered. However, if Ivy was to start snooping, she would notice the carpet anyway. And so, Esther casually explained to her that she had noticed the corner looked as though it had been pulled, but she hadn't had a chance to look at it properly as of yet.

Though both young ladies recognised the slight abnormality to their observation, neither could have predicted the horror held in such a simple clue. Ivy dropped to her knees, supporting her upper body with her right hand on the ground, using the left to pull the carpet out to reveal what laid underneath.

Can you guess what they found? Go ahead and have a try. Could you have anticipated the sight bestowed on our friends Ivy and Esther, because they definitely hadn't. Who could have possibly possessed the might to drag George from his feet as he gripped the carpet so tightly that he'd pulled it out? Who could have cleaned up the horrendous view to such precision? Who could have committed a sin so secretly, leaving barely a trace? A murder so malicious *must* be cast by that of unearthly life. A soul returned to honour a deal. An eye for an eye, a soul for a soul. Tell me, how far would you go to gain back what you'd lost? Our beast, my friends, knew no bounds.

Chapter 13

The police still hadn't permitted Eve's family to return to their home because the forensics team required the entire premises. Unfortunately, the hotel they'd stayed at couldn't sustain a long-term solution. Other guests had complained to reception regarding Ellis's crying. The unfamiliar environment unsettled him and so he'd been up most of the night unable to rest. Both Eve and Jason felt it best to leave the room for an hour, for some fresh air. Perhaps a ride in the pram would calm Ellis, they thought. It was an inexpensive room, containing the bare basics. A double bed, ensuite toilet and shower, a wardrobe possessing a mini-iron & board and an old TV paired with an un-sanitised remote. The beige ceramic lamp balanced on a single bedside table that matched the wardrobe.

One of the drawers carried a worn-out bible. Eve considered it for a moment. Wondering why a hotel would put a bible out for guests? She wondered if it was intended as a condescending reminder for adulterers that brought their mistresses for a night of guilt-soaked sex. Or maybe it was for weary travellers passing through, lonely in their journey and so seeking comfort in the company of their lord. It could have been there to convert people during their stay, bored with the minimal entertainment that the television provided, turning toward an inquisitive read. The bible caused discomfort in Eve. It represented the grip that her mother and father held. The discouragement towards seeking answers to questions that her bible didn't want her to ask. Questions that her parents didn't want her to ask. The memories that drawer's bible forced Eve to recollect were of the sermon stood affront the cattle. The stale hall with rows for the plenty as he became ever so passionate in his knowledge of demons and hell. How confident he was to save them from such fates. She would be met with the stare of an unwelcoming, well-dressed army when she wore a short skirt, not understanding the crimes associated with its length. Perhaps army was too bold, though it attempts to describe the hostility. She found that their good intentions hid agendas that Eve wanted no part in. No, she would keep that drawer closed.

January forced another mist amongst the village. The sky lay a sheep wool blanket over the inaudible Tavern. The air was dense in vapour as the clouds tried to refrain from release. Water droplets filled with anxiety and caution seeped into Jason's eyes as he wearily sought out the entrance door, just as Malcom walked out. Roy was at the bar watching his son leave when Eve, Jason and Ellis entered. After they'd ordered some drinks and meals, they asked Roy to join for a chat, if and when he had the time to do so. Roy and Violet were like a pair of un-appointed Mayors. Both knew all the ins and outs of the village's goings on. Far more than the likes of Mr and Mrs Platt. Though the Platt's knew of all the daily occurrences, the gossip, and the news. What they weren't aware of was the underbelly of their so-called home. The deals, the drugs, and the discrepancies from average existence. The Richard's on the other hand, were well informed. So, when Eve and Jason discussed finding a more reliable roof to refuge, they knew Roy and Violet would be the people to turn to. Nothing was particularly wrong with the hotel, only the cost per night was cause for pause. Fortunately to their surprise, the Richard's offered up their own apartment. Only two rooms were occupied with themselves and their son Malcom. The third was originally designated to Roy's parents. Since they passed away, the room was left untouched. He let them know that he just needed a couple hours to wash the sheets and spruce up the place but informed them that they were welcome to stay a few nights until the police permitted their return.

Eve, Jason, and little baby Ellis's home had been ransacked by the authorities armed with a warrant. The victim's blood soaked through the ceiling and dripped onto the cot's fresh linen. Officers invaded the cupboards and cabinets, bagging anything deemed suspicious and obtaining DNA traces. Photographic evidence was taken from every nook and cranny throughout the outside and inside of the building. The victim's body had been thoroughly examined by Detective Inspector Michael Jones. That is when his stomach settled. He found that the lower jaw had been physically pulled out. The inner gums had indentations replicating that of a large hand with sharp, possibly claw like nails. Bite marks were presented along the rim of the tongue where the tip had been gnawed off. Bruises had flared along the arms and legs representing a struggle. And lastly, the torso also had bruising yet far more severe. DI Jones deduced that the victims rib cage had potentially been shattered.

Upon closer inspection, he found a short red hair by the victim's blood-soaked foot. After sealing said hair in a contamination proof plastic bag, DI Jones thought back to the woman stood by the crime scene when he first arrived. The woman with fox-red hair, that had an uneasy way about her.

Once Eve's family had finished their meal, they stayed for a coffee while Ellis took a nap in Jason's arms. The clouds released their gasp, spewing out heavy salted rain onto Aviary Avenue. A rain that soaked Jones upon entry to The Tavern. The customer toilets were on the lower floor, down a set of carpeted stairs. The men's room consisted of three stalls, three sinks, five urinals and two automated hand dryers. Above the sink displayed a row of mirrors dimly lit by a decorative brass sconce. Jones undressed from his longline basil-green mac to reveal a charcoal grey fitted suit and black tie. He rolled the fresh toilet paper into a hefty bundle in an attempt to dry the rain from his face and hair. His dark blonde, newly trimmed style remained damp. Though he thought it appeared more professional than leaving it so drenched that it dripped onto his broad shoulders. He then folded his coat along his right arm and made his way back upstairs toward the bar.

Detective Inspector Michael Jones approached Eve's table. He started off by apologising for the interruption and formally introduced himself before taking an uninvited seat. He took out a hand-sized flip notebook and pen, ready to take notes. Jason explained his side of events. He informed DI Jones of the customer that ruined their afternoon with a complaint about Dana skipping out in the middle of a hair treatment, a bleach root touch up to be more specific. He added that he went down into the salon to check the toilet, the office, and the staffroom to find that Dana wasn't there and that her co-workers were also unaware of her location. Olly and May informed him that she had gone out for a break. Finally, he let Jones know that the only clue he found was that of an unfinished cigarette left on the concrete of the smoking area. Whereas Eve simply stated that the customers behaviour at the door was unpleasant and aggressive, but that when Jason had gone to rectify the situation, she stayed in the flat with Ellis. The last Eve saw of Dana was when she walked by the salon window on her way toward the flat but hadn't noticed anything out of the ordinary.

DI Jones then questioned Jason, asking why he hadn't reported her missing there and then. Jason placed his coffee mug onto the table as his hands trembled. Tears crept from the crevasses of his wide jade green eyes as he choked out the words, I'm sorry. He defended the decision by explaining that he assumed she'd gotten an emergency call, that perhaps she had something personal to attend to. Nothing so devastating had happened in Aviary Avenue before. It hadn't even crossed his mind that she could have been in danger. Jason expressed his regrets, promising to help in any way possible to catch and punish whoever did such a despicable deed. The couple were then informed that it could potentially be weeks before their family could return to the flat. So, Eve updated the detective on their new temporary living arrangements, this way he would know where to find them if he had any more questions.

DI Jones casually mentioned having seen people standing watch when the crime scene unfolded and how he was looking for a red headed woman, wondering if they knew of her. Eve spoke to him about how her parents rent a room to a young woman who fit the description mentioned, but that it wasn't likely to have anything to do with her.

"You're on about, Essie?"

Roy butted in, offering his unwelcomed input in the conversation.

"She was here when it happened anyway, mate. Can't have been her".

He pointed out, expressing a tone that encouraged the conclusion of the detectives visit.

"Well,"

Jones began, arrogantly.

"I'll be on my way, then".

He grinned.

Chapter 14

Miles of woodland surrounded the high-street. Trees grew plentiful, hiding the British burrows carefully crafted by critters. The winter sun hadn't yet obtained the might to motivate flowers to bloom. Instead, the cold covered the lifeless plants with incoherent despair. A foot path from the high-street led to the pond. A vast mass of natural water, painted with mouldy looking moss and patches of crinkling cracking ice wrapped around a minuscule patch of land. Otherwise known as the island. The island was inaccessible to people, it was where the ducks, geese and other bird life would go to nest. It was a sanctuary of peace and seclusion away from the hustle and bustle of busy bodies. Esther often wished she knew of a place like that for herself. Where her every move wasn't monitored and criticized by anybody. That afternoon, she had ran from George's apartment. Sat by the pond, directly on the ground, she stroked the dirt, burying it into her fingernails as she gripped each handful to bathe her skin in its scent. Esther adored the smell of dirt, grass, and all things natural. It soothed her, but her addiction delighted in the smell of smoked tobacco slightly more so. A more artificial relaxant. A fog of cigarette smoke dissipated around her as she turned to find Troy towering above her.

"Can I cadge one?"
Esther asked indiscreetly.
"Sure".
Troy replied as he slid a single cigarette from its packaging, offering for her to take it. Once lit, the smoke glided down her neck, danced on her lungs until escaping through her mouth and nose.
"Can I take a seat?"
Troy asked.
"Sure".

Esther answered. They sat speechless for a few minutes, watching the ducks waddle on their island.

"Your mum cut my hair super short once".

She mentioned, breaking the silence. Troy's lips raised to a slight grin, if just a little.

"Yeah?"

He replied.

"I thought I'd try a bob".

Esther said. Her tone trickled with humility and humour, indicating her regrets for getting such an unfitting haircut for her frame.

"Oof".

Troy replied.

"That's how your mum reacted".

She mocked. Esther chuckled, as Troy allowed himself a smile. Her pun provided the first smile that Troy's face was able to express since his mother's death. He'd had plenty of people gifting their condolences and offering up their deepest sympathies, but no one had yet said anything pleasant about his mother. No one had shared with him a memory of happiness of their own, not until just then. Not that enduring a terrible haircut was a happy memory for Esther, but she felt it may be a decent anecdote to break the ice.

"So, I know why I'm here avoiding the world."

Troy stated.

"Why are you?"

He asked candidly. His heart was too heavy to carry his grief, let alone carry the pressures of conversational decorum. Esther closed her eyes. She could see George's blood scraped across the floorboards beneath the torn carpet. The ripped wood and loose chippings where he clawed for freedom with his bare hands, searing his nails into the splintering ground. She could hear Ivy screaming down the phone to the emergency services. As Esther opened her eyes, she began to weep. Troy tried to place his hand upon her shoulder for comfort as she pushed him away.

"I'm sorry. I am, I'm sorry. I know you're just wanting to be nice but if you comfort me, I wont stop crying. Just give me a sec".

She snapped, raising to her feet. Taking in deep breaths to exhale them, choking on her tears as she calmed down. Troy lit another cig as a distraction, holding back his own pain. While the pack was still half full, he offered up another cigarette to Esther for her to take as she sat back down beside him. She explained to Troy about what she had just seen, believing that George's death was likely carried out by the same person who killed Dana.

When heavily pregnant with Troy, Dana and May visited a Christmas market. A jewellery stall caught her attention. Cluttered with colourful scarfs and dreamcatchers, ornamental dragons, and trolls. A glassware hand-shaped jewellery tree presented a dazzling bracelet. A delicate white gold chain with rose quartz crystals imbedded within.

"Ah, good choice, dear. That particular one will bring you unconditional love".

The salesperson advertised.

"Good! I could do with a new bloke, my last one sodded off with a leggy blonde".

Dana joked. She hadn't taken the lady seriously, but the bracelet was pretty, so the sale was made regardless. She presumed, as many would, that such love would come from a dashingly hansom man. She was wrong. That same day, Dana went into labour. Four weeks, too early. Her premature child miraculously birthed with no complications. A healthy baby boy was born. His newly opened eyes looking into hers.

"This is going to sound ridiculous but, just, I don't know. Humour me".

Troy started, fiddling with the rose quartz crystals dangling from his wrist. He began to detail his experience with that of his mother's teachings. Dana owned a set of tarot cards to which she would carry out readings for close friends and family. Knowing most people don't believe in occurrences of that nature, Troy hesitated to present his suggestions. He informed Esther that his mother had studied the use of crystal ball's and connecting with those beyond the grave. Whenever she had carried out these rituals, it was to communicate with lost relatives to confirm they had travelled to the other side successfully. To assure that their souls were resting in peace. He'd intended on trying it for himself, to reunite with his mum one last time. Too embarrassed to admit to the dread preventing him.

"So, like, we talk to the dead?"

Esther asked suspiciously. Her reluctance was persuaded by her detest of all things supernatural. Her stance on the matter was that it wasn't real, but in case it is, don't mess with it. She shook her head to every desperate reasoning he swung in her direction, unable to make herself clear as he continued to beg. Troy argued that he'd seen his mother perform the rituals a thousand times. That it was perfectly safe and there was nothing to threat over. Continuously protruding his case regardless of Esther's refusal.

"No!"

She finally snapped. Troy stopped mid plea. His shoulders dropped along with his persistent pursuit. His blank stare got lost in the sky as he lowered his trance to meet Esther in the eye. Both motionless, but a meter apart.

"I miss her".

He spoke. Troy took his first step towards walking away from the pond, away from Esther. She raised her arm out wide, to stop him in his tracks.

"Ok".

She said, admitting defeat.

"No harm in trying, is there?"

Of course, that's what they thought! Naïve and reckless, what admirable qualities. It's a wonder she hadn't been killed yet, being so stupid. I'd have stopped her myself. Yet, alas from here, I can only observe events. I can't interfere with them. It's so aggravating I must admit. If only she'd have sought help, informed others of the tragedies unfolded, things would have turned out so differently. They say don't poke the bear. Wise words from the experienced and educated. Some, however, will happily poke the bear just to prove that it bites.

Chapter 15

When Mr & Mrs Platt heard of Eve's new living arrangements, neither was best pleased. They found that shacking up in an alehouse was beyond distasteful. Worst of all, with her being a young woman. Mr Platt appalled himself by the thought of what the congregation must have believed. He wouldn't have a daughter carelessly destroy his stature within the church. No, it simply wouldn't do, they agreed. It wouldn't be ideal to have all three live under their own roof but for appearances sake, it would have been more appropriate. The issue was Esther. Mrs Platt had her reservations toward her. Never had Esther flared a keen eye untoward a gentleman to her recollection. Her male counterparts persisted platonically. Fortunate, in one manner, as her taste in companionship lacked class.

They had noticed her behaviour alter progressively, since before the hairdresser's murder. Esther's attention often fleeting, appeared frail. Her appearance lacked preservation, with grease creeping from her scalp onto the deep-rooted red of her hair on most days. Wearing the same jeggings and hooded sweatshirt day in, day out. Make-up enhanced her delicate features only as and when required. For example, during video chats with clientele, or if called in to meet with advertisers in person. Yet, this occurred less frequently over time. Therefore, raising the Platt's suspicions.

Esther had set off out earlier that day to George's apartment and hadn't yet gone home. After having returned from the crime scene of Dana's death the day prior, she hadn't left her room until the following morning. The Platts' took it upon themselves to search her room while it was unoccupied. Convinced they would locate evidence of illegal contraband. Mr Platt perched himself on the adjustable stair lift by the top step where a tall, thin window overlooked the driveway. He did so to watch for Esther's return home so that he could warn his wife to replace the possessions tampered with. Meanwhile Mrs Platt made her way throughout her daughter's old room in search for information. She started with the basics, ransacking cupboard drawers, the desk, under the bed. When unsuccessful, she tore off the pillowcases and duvet cover. Flipped over picture frames on the wall and rummaged through jacket pockets. Growing increasingly impatient, Mrs Platt started on the bin. She hadn't a proper bin set out for her garbage as there hadn't been much space to place one. So, Esther would typically place an empty carrier bag over the door handle. She never needed to push the door handle down as the latch had broken some time ago. Fortunately, the carpeting was thick enough to hold the door to a close with the assistance of a doorstop as and when needed. She would never use the handle, just so to avoid the bag dropping onto the floor on her way out. Mrs Platt proceeded to empty the bin bag's contents onto the floor. Picking through papers, wrappers, and unfinished food before heading for the pile of mail she had emptied from the desk. Filing through, she read Esther's bank statements, medical appointments and personal letters but found nothing illegal.

"She must have hidden them somewhere else".

Mrs Platt deducted from her search. As she sat in the mess, she had caused for herself, Mr Platt called over to her. Esther was walking down the street towards the house. In a furious panic, Mrs Platt asked her husband to go back downstairs and ask Esther to help him back into his living room chair, thus buying her time to reset the room. Firstly, placing all the rubbish back into the bin bag and placing it back over the door handle, to then recover the duvet set and pillowcases. Finishing off with placing the mail back into Esther's desk and closing all the cupboard drawers. Mrs Platt inspected the room thoroughly before exiting, to assure everything was as it was, when she heard Esther finishing up with her assistance given to Mr Platt and coming up the stairs. Mrs Platt quietly but quickly crept from Esther's room into her own, delicately closing both doors behind her.

When Esther entered her room, she knew instantly that someone had been in it. Everything was as it had been when she left, all but for one bin bag that had fallen to the floor. Someone had used the door handle. Her bets were placed on Mrs Platt being the obvious culprit considering Mr Platt's condition. Understanding that the time she had just spent accommodating the favour he'd asked of her, was a distraction to allow Mrs Platt more time. Before confrontation, Esther recognised she had to confirm what had been tampered with and deduce what they were trying to accomplish by going through her things. The most obvious conclusion was that the Platts were looking for her stash. She headed to her chest of drawers and pulled out a pair of ankle boots from the bottom drawer. She then tip them upside down, emptying the contents which consisted of pills, weed, cigarettes and a match box.

Time to move guys.

Esther thought to herself. She then pulled out the stash from Georges hidden plug socket. While Ivy was on the phone to the police, Esther cleared its contents into her pockets. She told Ivy that she couldn't be in the room anymore, the sight was too upsetting, so she ran. Esther knew the police would be round to question her soon. She had to hide the stash somewhere that the police wouldn't search for it. That's when she heard Mrs Platt head back downstairs.

"It'll have to do".

Esther told herself, as she took the entire boots worth, plus George's stash, into Mr and Mrs Platt's bedroom, gently closing the door behind her. Their bedroom's décor hadn't differed much to a Victorian setting. Gold ornaments of various animals were presented among the windowsill, either side a thin hourglass vase of daffodils in a fake floral arrangement. The bed deemed crisp and pristine in its accurately folded linen, supporting decorative pillows of plenty, unnecessarily scattered throughout the head of the bed. Esther ventured towards their wardrobe in search for Mr Platt's wellington boots. He never really worn them, but his wife bought them as a precaution, in case he ever was in the need. She stuffed the wellies until the stash was hidden deep past the sole of the boot. After placing them back, exactly as they were, she closed the wardrobe door and returned to her room.

The kitchen and dining room were adjacent in the Platt household, essentially the same room only separated by the arrangement of dining essentials. The table overlooked the patio that sat opposite the double-glazed sliding double door, decorated with ugly worn-out garden gnome's and plants they never actually cared for.

"Where have you been?"

Mrs Platt asked, fully expecting a definitive answer.

"I needed some fresh air. I've been for a walk by the pond."

Esther answered, if not with a slightly vague honesty. Mrs Platt studied her. Esther's fingernails held trapped dirt beneath them, and her clothing smelled of smoked tobacco.

"You look and smell foul."

Mrs Platt stated with no remorse.

"You know we do not eat with dirty hands at this table. There is a nail brush underneath the sink. I expect you to take it to the bathroom upstairs, get washed and put on some clean clothes."

She commanded. Esther, reluctant to do so, tried to protest by apologising for her attire and requesting that she washes after dinner, with it being a hot meal. Mrs Platt placed two plates on the table, both filled with a cottage pie sided with green beans. One placed in front of her husband, and the other, herself, as she took her seat at the table.

"Dinner starts at five, you know that. So, I expect you to freshen up now. Preferably quickly. Because, as you said, it's a hot meal."

She confirmed. They bowed their heads as they began to pray, thanking their lord for the meal. Esther, still stood by the table, watched as they ignored her. Her meal was prepared and plated atop the kitchen counter. Steam elevated from the buttery fluff of mash potato protecting the stew of fresh vegetables, gravy and mince cuddled underneath. Her patience wavered along with the structure of the room. Her blood fizzed as her nerves elated, beneath her skin was the sensation of popping candy just as it hits the tip of the tongue. The words were reaching the surface, yet she refrained. She closed her eyes, gripping her fingers within her fist. She spoke out of turn once more.

"I don't have the energy to get washed and redressed right now".

Esther persisted. Mrs Platt stopped eating. She placed her knife and fork parallel on her plate as she looked up toward Esther.

"You're being incredibly disrespectful. This is not your house, it's ours. So do as we ask, and don't you dare talk back".

Esther lost her temper. The weight of the day had proved to be overbearing. Her ability to endure the patronising prance of the Platt's audacity had thinned significantly. She snatched Mrs Platts plate from her and threw it into the kitchen wall. Mash, gravy, and vegetables splatted throughout the room, coating the surfaces, cabinets and flooring as the plate shattered dramatically. Mr Platt grabbed a hold of Esther's arm and pulled her face to meet his level.

"How dare you! Mental girl?!"

He yelled, still gobbling a forkful of dinner while tightening his grip. Esther escaped his clutches as she fell backwards, regaining balance by gripping the dining chair.

"Go to your room!"

Mrs Platt commanded with a raised, threatening tone. Esther looked upon Mrs Platt with confused contempt of her condescension. She decided to confront her, regarding the invasion of her privacy. She exposed her awareness of their room raiding ransack. How they constantly disrespected her, yet they expect a higher treatment for themselves than what they are willing to offer others. That Mr and Mrs Platt's behaviour was contaminated with self-riotousness, control, and entitlement over other people's opportunity to express free will.

"You are high right now, aren't you?"

Mr Platt asked in an interrogative manner, exhausted by Esther's incoherent and disobedient rant. Esther decided to no longer endure the perceived toxicity that poisoned her every day under their roof. She left Mr Platt's question unanswered and cleaned up the mess she had made, before retiring to the bedroom to pack her things so that she could leave the following morning.

Chapter 16

Eve assisted Violet with the arrangements for setting up, ready for quiz night. They'd selected a theme for the questions which was the 90's. Staff were asked to attend work in fancy dress as a celebrity or a character from a film/sitcom based in that era. As they chatted, Violet offered Eve some work for the hours that Jason would be home for the baby. She suggested that Eve could work 09:00am to 15:30pm, three days a week on a flexible rota, and so was welcomed to start that same week.

"Thank you so much, Mrs Richard. I honestly wouldn't know what I would do, without yours and Mr Richard's help".

Eve said, expressing her gratitude.

"Well, I mean, there'd be no room for all three of you at your parents now, would there?"

Violet responded, hoping to successfully coax a little more insight on the situation.

"No, but that's not really the only issue. I understand where she's coming from and all, but Mum doesn't really let me raise Ellis my own way. She kind-of intrudes, and I wouldn't have a leg to stand on if I were under her care".

Eve continued, careful not to speak out of turn as she let down her walls, just slightly.

"Neither I, nor Jason would have room to make any decisions. We get on better when I have my life and they have theirs".

She finished, second guessing herself, cautious over having revealed too much.

Violet couldn't help but take Eve's confession to heart. It encouraged her to consider her relationship with Malcom. She wondered if she was intruding, and possibly disallowing him to make his own decisions. See, Violet remembered her father fondly. A strong and hard-working man. His death came with no concrete explanation, but she always had her suspicions. A flamboyant man in the 70's, a time where such a personality was considered offensive. All Violet could recall of his death was the officer arriving at the door. Usually when bearing news of that nature, the informant would remove his hat, and place it respectfully upon their chest. The officer at the door that day, hadn't taken his hat in respect. He hadn't even flinched as her mother wept at hearing the words; your husband is dead. Violet wondered if times had changed enough for her son. She feared that if she let him be, would an officer someday arrive at her door. Hat still atop their head as they utter the words, your son is dead.

Malcom spoke casually of the date that he endured. Him and Mai hadn't any more in common past their occupations, but it seemed easier to convey a reality his mother preferred than to expose the truth. Mai was fair in her looks. The curls of her mid-length layered brown hair fell effortlessly amongst her shoulders. Her slim hourglass figure fit snug in the eggshell white, bodycon dress that she wore that evening. Paired with a low heeled, leathered ankle boot and gold studded earrings. Her face contoured professionally around her lined, plump lip. Mai was striking when presented in all the bells and whistles. Still beautiful in a plain ensemble. Yet, her physical perfection was of no interest to Malcom.

Eve sat comfortably within a booth by the bar, Ellis amongst her lap as she proceeded with wrapping cutlery. After Malcom had finished stocking up the bottle fridge, he joined Eve to assist with the task at hand.
"I heard your date went well".
Eve started, intending to create simple small talk to pass the time.
"Yeah? Well, that's the word isn't it, I suppose".
Malcom responded, accidentally revealing his contempt.
"Oh, sorry. I was just chatting, I didn't mean to pry or anything, sorry".
Eve apologised.
"No, you don't have to say sorry or anything, it's me, I'm just tired. I probably sounded more serious than I am. Erm yeah, it went ok. She's really pretty and nice, so".
Malcom explained, trailing off as he lied.

"That's great. Yeah, your mum was telling me about it. She's been boasting about you, successful in the city and now you've found a nice lass. You're her favourite subject".

Eve joked, trying to lighten the mood only to accomplish the opposite.

"Oh, I'm aware, don't worry".

Malcom snapped, misplacing his anger toward his mother onto Eve. He left her to finish the cutlery as he went out to the beer garden to smoke.

Eve continued to wrap cutlery and entertain Ellis as she helped set up. She folded the napkin into a cootie catcher and drew pictures on the folds. Each fold had a different picture drawn, including a pirate flag, a flower, a smiley face, and a puppy dog. The enclosing fold, read of different things she'd written to Ellis, such as, "what a pretty day" and "mummy & daddy love you". She would ask Ellis to pick a picture, so she would open up the fold and read him the message. That is until he put the napkin in his mouth, dribbling all over and accidentally ripping it.

"It's OK sweetie, how about we get you a biscuit?"

Eve said, in a soft and comforting tone.

Jason had tried to get in a quick nap later that day once the room was ready. Sleeping at The Tavern proved more comfortable than the hotel, but it still held an uncomfortable presence. Memorabilia of Roy's parents guarded the room with ornaments and photographs, confirming the temporary nature of their stay. A grandfathers eyes followed him in his every step. Eyes that knew of the guilt carried, pressuring the admittance of failure. Failure as a husband, as a father, and as a friend.

Jason called Troy, intending to request that they met to talk, only he hadn't answered. Once getting dressed after his unsuccessful nap, Jason made his way downstairs to speak to his wife.

Eve chose not to confront Jason regarding his lack of self-care. The grease on his hair stretched an inch with bits of dry skin clung to the roots. His gingerbread brown beard, mis-shaped and unruly, hid the grief that his pale skin advertised. While the clothes, both ill fitted and poorly matched, hung loosely along his frame. He smelled of must, smoke and sweat. Roy and Violet had only a humble bathtub that lacked shower facilities. Sufficient sure, but Jason was preoccupied with the disassociation that was his new norm. Instead, carried out a minimal cleanse with a splash of soapy water to the face and armpits.

"Want to help us wrap cutlery?"

Eve asked her husband as he approached their booth.

"Sorry, love. I'm going to see if Troy is in. I just want to check to see if he's alright".

Jason answered.

"Ok, well keep your phone on you, let me know when you get there safely".

She said, anxiety riddled.

"And be careful".

She instructed. Jason's demeanour was new territory for Eve. Her concern for his wellbeing increased, unaware of the correct words to use to ease his suffering. Fortunately, the move into The Tavern was beneficial in more ways than one. To give credit where credit was due, Violet was wonderful with Ellis. Granted, Ellis wasn't able to talk back to her as much as her own son could.

"Is he not staying?"

Violet asked Eve, watching Jason exit through the front door.

"No, he's got stuff to do, he won't be out long".

Eve replied, uninterested in discussing it further as Violet pressed the matter. She sat opposite Eve with her arms outstretched, gesturing for Ellis to come and sit on her lap. As the baby was passed over, Eve tried to change the subject.

"So, 90's night, what are you going as?"

She asked.

"Oh, you know I couldn't afford a proper costume or anything, so I'm improvising. I was thinking, Sporty Spice".

Violet answered.

"I've got a nice set of tracksuit bottoms that I got for the Zumba class I meant to go to, and I could just wear a vest and do my hair like she did back then".

She continued, explaining herself.

"Oh, that's such a good idea. I'm not sure what I'd go as, but Ellis already has a pink and yellow spotted onesie, so he's going as Mr Blobby! Aren't you, sweetie?"

Eve laughed, playfully baby talking to her son.

"What time is it starting again, did you say nine o'clock?"

She asked. Ellis had begun to reverse cycle, so he would have been up late regardless. Eve had been trying to regulate his routine as it was before, but the disruptions to their lives caused complications.

"That's right, love. Nine o'clock".

Chapter 17

A single lit candle surveyed the wallpaper with a weak glare that flickered at the slightest movement. Accompanied only by the shimmer that crept over the gap above the curtain rail, sprinkling from the streetlamp. There'd be no interruption due to the police tape wrapped around the apartment like a present, poorly packaged. A mysterious missing man allowed the morbidity of the street to remain mute. They would enter undetected with the aid of Esther's cunning capabilities. Invasion of a crime scene, both illegal and nonsensical but Troy insisted the connection take place where a soul was taken. Dana's body was out in the open, in the middle of the villages highstreet. Detection would have been inevitable. George's apartment, newly sealed off, promised privacy. Jason brought over a box of plastic hygienic gloves that he took from the first-aid kit by the bar, along with hair nets and face masks. DNA could be used against them in court, obviously. To intervene with a crime scene, lacking in anticipation for potential consequences, makes me question if their entitlement was so elevated it extended past the restrictions of the law or if they were simply stupid.

On Thursday, a few hours before breaking into George's apartment, Troy had been at his house, rummaging through his mother's prized possessions. Her tarot cards were worn out from over-use. Dana referred to them regularly during times of uncertainty and spouts of her independence's occasional decline. Seeking guidance on her life path, requiring confirmation of difficult decisions. Desperately seeking validation for choices that she made, resulting in unhappiness. She'd bought a pretty set. The borders palleted heliotrope illustrations intertwined by the top right and bottom left corner. The images that represented each cards meaning looked hand drawn, as though delicately water coloured. She'd had the pack for as long as Troy could remember. His friends often mocked him for his mother's behaviour. Referred to her as a witch, a freak, an unusual loner. He loved his mother, although he avoided that side of her, burdened by embarrassment from his past schoolmate's harassment.

That same day, a knock sounded at the door. Upon opening, Troy found Jason on his doorstep. Jason's eyes were clung to the floor as though unwillingly anchored. His hands hid in his pockets while the jacket slouched over his hungry frame.

"Hi, I can go if you don't want me here, mate. I just, I just need to see how you are".

Jason stuttered, holding back tears.

"Shit".

Troy answered with insincerity.

"Oh, well yeah, obviously. Sorry".

Jason replied, realising he'd wasted his time.

Troy took in the fresh air that he'd avoided since last shutting his door. As he exhaled, he decided to drop his attitude and invited Jason inside.

"You want a beer?"

Troy offered.

"Nah, best not, Eve wants me to go to that quiz tonight. We've got Ellis to watch, and he's not been sleeping so... Plus, I just think if I have a bottle, with the way I feel, I won't put it down".

Jason confessed. Troy said nothing, he gave a gentle nod to confirm his understanding and instead poured Jason a glass of water with orange squash. He watched Jason gulp the juice almost instantly, taking in his dirty hair and clothes, before looking down at his own appearance. Troy realised that he also hadn't been taking care of his own hygiene, unable to recollect the last time he'd even slept.

"What's all this?"

Jason asked, gesturing to Troy's mother's possessions cluttering the living room, as he finished up the glass of squash. Troy looked at the mess, then toward Jason.

When the police found his mothers hand dangling from the salon roof, Jason averted Troy's gaze from the ghastly sight. He turned him to face the other way, promising that no matter what happened, he wouldn't be alone.

"Did you mean what you said?"

Troy asked ominously, providing no context behind his meaning.

"What I said?"
Jason replied.
"I wouldn't be alone".
Troy answered. Jason placed the empty glass onto a side table by the sofa, giving Troy his undivided attention.
"Absolutely. I'm here, whatever you need".
He confirmed.

Dana had decorated her living room with the intention to illude masculinity for her son's sake, but unwittingly flared femineity through fluffy throws and pretty paintings of prickly plants. The cushions consisted of a lavender scented fabric as they stood attention on a three seated sofa. The elephant grey seating, pressed against the wall by the front house window. The carpet was as simple a beige as any, covered by a handcrafted rug embedded with carefully woven stars scarpered around a crescent moon. A moonlight pallet mixed with early dawn pastels that engulfed the rugs primary colouring. The wallpaper paint stokes were of a midnight blue, with photographs placed steadily throughout the room. Photographs of the family, together on trips to the zoo, the beach, and the park. The living room served as the perfect shrine to withhold Dana's intact memory.

"My mum was into some weird stuff".
Troy started, figuring out his sentences fleetingly as they came out.
"She used to communicate with, I don't know the right word, the beyond?"
He trailed, embarrassed of the wording used. He brushed himself off and told Jason to forget it, he hadn't the emotional strength endure embarrassment.
"No, it's ok, just ask what you want to ask. I'm not going to judge, I swear".
Jason plead, desperate to make amends by any means possible.
"I'm going to try. Well, I'm going to figure it out first, the way to do this shit, then I'm going to try".
Troy continued to ramble.
"Try what? I don't understand what you're asking of me".
Jason asked, attempting to understand.
Troy went on to explain his urge to speak with his lost mother, if at least for one last time. Existing in an empty house felt like the whole world was empty. The company he kept was that of his sorrow and despair sat either side of his shoulders. Whispering threats of the never-ending cycle, swallowed by fear of rejection and lack off

connection. He wondered how he would even converse, now with a heavy humidity from tears of air gasping cries, suffocating every topic. Reluctant to admit vulnerability all while clinging to any opportunity to be so.

Chapter 18

That same Thursday, Esther finished packing up her belongings after her immature outburst with Mr and Mrs Platt. She received a call from an unknown number. She selected to answer the call but stayed mute, intending to hang up before sixty seconds passed, preventing her phone from being traced. On the seventh second, a voice spoke.
"It's just me, dickhead. You don't have to act all mysterious. I'm not with the bobbies, they took a statement and sent me off".
Ivy spoke, irritated.
"What do you want?"
Esther asked, uninterested in pursuing the conversation any further due to her reluctance towards her own accountability.
"What do I want? Are you serious? Are you insane? We saw blood, arsehole, and lots of it. You should have called the police when you first noticed him gone. Oh, speaking of which, they would very much like to talk to you!".
Ivy yelled.
"No shit".
Esther snapped.

As she hung up the phone, the front door knocked with the force of a fist. Blue and red light flashed through the net curtain hiding the windows view. Esther quickly shoved herself into the shower, grabbing her own nail scrubbing brush on her way in. She washed any remaining scent of dirt and cigarette smoke that lingered on her hair and skin from the day prior. It bubbled down the drain in a musty coloured foamy liquid. Within minutes, she dried herself off and threw on a pair of denim, high waisted jeans and a freshly washed, plain white crop top. She ran back into the ensuite to mouthwash and brush her damp and unruly red hair, when another knock followed, only now it presented itself at her bedroom door.

"Just in the bathroom, I'll be out now, one second!"

She shouted with an inpatient politeness.

"That's alright Miss Petunia, I'll be downstairs when you're ready".

The officer called back.

Shit.

She thought. Esther shoved the clothes worn on Wednesday, into the bottom of her suitcase, underneath all of the other belongings she had packed so far, before sliding on her slippers and heading down the stairs. The top step was the largest. A pit of a step, deep and dangerous as though filled with great white sharks. Beyond that was open waters, she was easy prey, prime for the taking. The first thing she noticed about the policeman was that he wasn't dressed in the correct uniform. Not to conduct an interrogative interview at a suspect's home, one would think. His figure hid behind a standard charcoal suit with a tie that landed on his crotch as he sat in Mr Platt's living room chair.

He won't be happy about that.

Esther thought to herself, as she looked to see Mr Platts swallowed rage, seeping from his brow, agitated over the occupied chair. When the policeman noticed Esther enter the living room, he rose to his feet, extending his hand to introduce himself. She looked at his hand and then back at him, directly into his eyes as she asked what this was about. He pulled back the 'hung-to-dry` handshake, amused by Esther's initial reaction to his presence. It hadn't occurred to him that she knew he would be trying to obtain a fingerprint from his visit. So she wasn't to touch anything in the room that he could discretely take and have analysed. A handshake was pushing on paranoia, but she was taking no chances.

"It's nice to meet you, Esther Petunia. I'm Detective Inspector Michael Jones. I know that's a mouthful, so you may call me DI Jones, if you'd like".

He grinned, rather presumptuously.

"Nice to meet you too, Sir. What can I do for you?"

Esther pressed, in no mood to play whatever game he had going.

"It's regarding a call we received yesterday, Miss Petunia. The young lady who called mentioned that you were at the scene with her but left abruptly when she contacted the authorities".

DI Jones stated confidently.

"That's correct."

Esther replied, throwing off his scent. The inspector was expecting her to deny the allegation. Set back by her admittance, he enquired as to why she would leave before the police arrived.

"I... it was a sight, Sir. I couldn't bare to look anymore. I had to come home".

Esther continued, before Mrs Platt butted in.

"What's this about?"

She intervened.

"This young lady lives under my roof, Detective Inspector. I have a right to know what kind of trouble she brings back here".

She demanded.

"Of Course, ma'am. Unfortunately, I'm not legally permitted to disclose any details on the subject. Its up to your tenant to decide what she wishes to share with you or not share with you, I'm afraid".

DI Jones stated, perceptively disrespecting her authority.

Esther kept her packed suitcase to herself. She thought it more convenient for the police to assume an incorrect location. She hadn't had time to deal with George's burner as of yet. She feared that the blame for George's demise could fall far too easily on her drug deprived head. She hadn't even informed the Platt's of her planned escape from their *hell house* as she would call it.

"I'd appreciate if you came by the station tomorrow, Miss Petunia. I just have a few more questions that I'd like to ask you".

Jones concluded as he showed himself out. Esther replied with a polite, albeit regrettable smile as confirmation for her intended attendance.

"You have some explaining to do, young Miss".

Mr Platt commanded, with a gaze that instructed Esther to take a seat. Esther walked over to the sofa that sat opposite his chair. A two seated leathery contraption that also reclined, as part of a matching set. Mrs Platt stood behind her husband's wheelchair, resting her bony un-manicured hand upon his wicker looking waistcoat's shoulder padding.

"The friend I mentioned, who I couldn't find".

Esther started, pushing the words from her emotionally beaten chest. The words were right there, as though in the atmosphere yet unattainable. Swarming around her mind, teasing her. Taunting to be caught so that she could throw them towards Mr and Mrs Platt, and away from herself.

"His girlfriend was helping me look. There was... blood".

She stuttered, unable to force any more speech. The Platts shared a look of concern, not aimed for Esther's wellbeing, but for their own.

"I see".

Mr Platt said.

"So, this is the reason for your behaviour".

He asked.

"Yes".

Esther answered. She could sense her mental health's plummeting decline. Detached from the conventions of normalcy. Impatient and infuriated by expectations of conversational decorum and manner. The energy usually spent on expressing polite physical mannerisms and pleasantries in both tone of voice and pretence of interest had already been spent. What remained was the chilled and echoed cave, hesitantly buried underneath her light cotton top. The delusion invoked by her drug use, drinking and avoidance untoward the world, sought more safety than that of reality. She was separate. Her mind, her body, herself, her entirety.

Mr Platt excused Esther, requesting that she went up to the bedroom so that they could discuss how to move forward from the day's events. Both Mr & Mrs Platt agreed that such a trauma would inevitably trigger more disruptive behaviour to which they had no intention of being held responsible for. They cautioned the possibly of more required visits from the police and expressed their distaste in enduring potential public humiliation. They'd suffered enough, they believed. Firstly, with Eve's disregard to their guidance. Participating in premarital relations as though she were the likes of Mary Magdalene herself. They revolted in their daughter's promiscuity, eternally grateful for the wedding having taken place before the birth. They never felt any promise for potential in Esther's future either. Writing her off a lost cause, they decided she was to vacate the premises, and so Mr & Mrs Platt planned to evict her the following day.

Chapter 19

"Hi everyone! Welcome to our Tavern's first official quiz night. As you know, we're here to raise some money for a good cause. So, I'd like to say thank you to everyone who came tonight. There's a drop-box by the quiz-sheet pile, so if you can, we'd appreciate some donations. This money is not only for the safety equipment for our patrol volunteers, but the rest of it will go directly towards Troy and his family. So, once again, thank you everyone for tonight, you're support goes a long way".

Roy announced, microphone in hand. He'd found a cheap wig online that he purchased for next day delivery. It resembled the long straw like locks of a rock 'n' roll lover. With baggy jeans ripped at the knees and a checked shirt jacketing a plain white T-shirt, attending the event dressed as Garth Algar.

"Right on, so ground rules. Cell phones off, if I hear a phone vibrate, see a screen light up or catch anyone trying to sneak a glance at their phones, then you will be disqualified!"

He stated, as the crowd groaned disapprovingly.

"I know, I know. But, c'mon, rules are rules people!"

Roy laughed as he commenced with the quiz, beginning to ask the prepared questions.

When the customers had herded into The Tavern that Thursday night, they were greeted by staff dressed as various 90's references. The condiment table presented a pencil holder filled with blue ball-point pens and a pile of paper with the numbers from one to thirty typed vertically within the margin. A member of staff dressed as Johnny Bravo greeted the guests, taking entry fees from participants and welcoming them to the event. The kitchen had already closed, but chips were still served due to the simplicity and efficiency of the dish for the busy night ahead. The majority of participants were sat in their teams, three to a table. All with their own team names, most of which kept up with the theme. One group named themselves the Macauley Could-wins, while another went with, 10 things I hate about quizzes. The drinks flowed as did the conversations amongst friends and acquaintances alike.

Eve had attempted to put Ellis down for the night, intending to disinvite herself from the evening's festivities if successful, though unfortunately, she was not. Once presented in his pink and yellow onesie, Ellis was tucked into his car seat, wrapped in a puffy security blanket. This way if he felt sleepy, Eve wouldn't have to disturb him by putting him to bed. She liked the idea that Violet had, attending the quiz night dressed as a Spice Girl. As Eve had elbow-length, Whisby blonde hair, she looked in the wardrobe for inspiration, hoping to find a nice little number that could pass for something that the popstar, Baby Spice would have worn. The closest piece of clothing that remotely resembled what she had in mind, was that of a silk under skirt in a pearl white. She pulled the elastic waistline up above her chest, transforming the ankle-length skirt into a knee-length dress. She brought in her curves with the thin cotton belt from her powder blue dressing gown, tying it into a bow at the back. She hadn't a denim jacket herself, but Jason had one that he'd left sprawled on the floor. She rolled up the sleeves to meet her elbows then tied her long locks into Baby Spice pigtails. For her makeup, she used a blue sparkled eyeshadow, similar in shade to match the dressing gown belt, along with a Barbie pink lipstick to finish the look. Though she didn't have any platform trainers, what she did have was a pair of plain white pumps.
They'll suffice.
She thought. She'd arrived early to secure a booth at the back, assuring space that was a little cosier and out of the way for Ellis to settle. Jason had promised her beforehand, that he would be there for 20:30pm at the latest to enjoy the quiz with his wife and son. As 20:30pm turned into 21:00pm, he still hadn't arrived, and the quiz commenced without him.

"This seat taken?"
Malcom asked Eve, while holding two half-pints of lemonade.
"No, evidently not".
Eve answered, embarrassed for having been stood up. As Malcom took a seat opposite within the booth, he pulled a carton of Apple & Blackcurrant Juice out of his back pocket.

"Here you go, little man. Don't think I forgot about you!"

Malcom exclaimed, passing the juice-box over to Eve, before placing one of the lemonades her way as he took a sip from his own.

"Lovely, he could do with a drink".

Eve thanked, opening the juice box for Ellis.

"Jason working tonight then?"

Malcom casually asked.

"He wasn't, but I'm guessing he picked up an extra shift and just didn't tell me. He's been a bit off, these past couple days. Well, I mean, everyone is I guess".

Eve answered. As reluctant as she was to over share, Jason's recent behaviour had encouraged her increasing loneliness to pour out. The opportunity that Malcom presented for consolidation was definitely appreciated.

"He was there though, wasn't he? Like, he was the first to see. Did he actually see?"

Malcom asked, confidently over stepping. Eve was taken aback by the abrupt nature of his enquiry. Not only due to its candour, but also because she didn't know. Jason hadn't told her whether of not he saw the body. He merely stated that they found her, and so hadn't shared any more.

"I don't know. In all honesty. I shouldn't think so, it… Sorry, she, was on the roof".

Eve answered, stunned by the speed of severity the topic's progression became.

"Are you on the clock tonight?"

She continued, trying to change the mood, politely indicating her desire for him to leave her and Ellis to enjoy their evening.

"Yeah, well, kind of. I'm not on the bar tonight or anything, I just said that I'd help clean up afterwards. So, how would you like a teammate who's a wiz at quizzes, and will more than likely win this bad boy?"

Malcom joked. He'd picked up on how he'd accidentally made her uncomfortable, and so was happy to stick to lighter things, hoping to make it up to Eve by winning her the top prize.

"Sure, why not?"

Eve answered shyly, slightly reluctant.

At question fifteen, Roy called for a quick ten-minute break so that the customers could get another round of drinks in for their tables, use the facilities, or go outside for a quick smoke. While Malcom went to bar, Mr & Mrs Platt approached the booth and seated themselves comfortably. Eve's stomach felt as though it had been dropped into a pit as her throat began to dry up.

"Mum, Dad? I didn't know you were coming by tonight".

Eve said, masking her discomfort.

"Yes, we took a table by the window. We want to contribute. Mr Richard does right to raise money for the Neighbourhood Watch. I actually think this was a good way to pull the community together to work toward a solution".

Mr Platt answered.

"I couldn't agree more".

Eve stated, surveying the room. Waiting for them to get to the point as to why they approached her.

"We don't have long until the break is over. So, I'll get straight to it. We have discussed it, and we would prefer you move back home".

Mrs Platt started, knowing that her daughter wouldn't protest in public.

"That's kind of you to offer. But may I discuss it with Jason first?"

Eve answered quickly. Her answer was no. The only issue was that saying no to her parents never sat well with them. Though, on occasion, Mr & Mrs Platt would respect a no. Only when it came from Jason, with him being the husband and therefore the *man of the house*. Mr Platt appreciated that his daughter respected Jason's right to a final word. After all of her previous disgraceful behaviour, he considered her recognition of a woman's place somewhat commendable. Realistically the dynamic he believed his daughter and husbands relationship held was a fabrication to avoid pursuit of condemnation. Jason saw his wife as his equal partner. They made decisions together as a team, and if Eve wished to say no, he would show respect for that. Both Eve and Jason feared that if her parents were aware of the true nature of their relationship, they would no longer accept Jason's word and their possessive control over her would just worsen. Jason was all that stood between Mr & Mrs Platt, and Eve's freedom.

"I suppose that would be acceptable".

Mr Platt answered shortly.

"We expect a call tomorrow regarding your answer. Don't waste our time. As you're aware, we have a tenant to deal with, to make room for you all".

Mrs Platt added.

"I'll speak with him when he's home from work, and yes of course, I'll call you tomorrow".

Eve concluded, hoping that her answer was sufficient.

They'd returned to their table as Malcom returned with the drinks, wishing the Platt's a good evening as they passed.

"Surprised to see them here, tonight".

Malcom observed. Eve politely laughed to brush off his comment, not wanting to discuss her parents any further.

As the night came to an end, the winners were announced.

"In 3rd, with twenty-five correct out of thirty, we have got the Macauley Could-wins!"

Roy announced, as a group of three men raised their pints to toast their win.

"In 2nd, it's the Absolutely Fabulous at Quizzes, with an excellent twenty-seven out of thirty! Here you are, ladies, congrats!"

He continued, passing out the prizes as the championed tables stood to cheer and claim their winnings.

"And finally, with an impressive twenty-nine out of thirty, it's, Mr Blobby!"

Roy announced, searching through the crowd for the winner. Eve stood to her feet, waving nervously to Roy as she walked towards him to collect the gift bagged bottle of whisky.

"Ah, here you go, love. Don't let him drink it all at once!"

Roy joked, gesturing to Ellis.

Malcom asked if Eve would have liked to stay up to toast their winnings, but it had gotten late, and she needed get Ellis's upstairs where it was quiet. He'd miraculously gone to sleep so she didn't want to push her luck. The two retired to their room. Eve tucked herself into bed and placed Ellis's car seat with him inside, right beside her bedside on the carpet. Falling to sleep facing her tired little boy.

If only Jason was here.

Eve thought to herself as she drifted. The clock had gone past 23:45pm. He would have usually been home by that time. Eve had dropped a text to inform Jason that she and Ellis had called it a night and gone to bed. Asking him to get home safe and to text her back as soon as he was able. Only, what she didn't know was, he hadn't been at work.

Chapter 20

"She'll be so pissed. I'm supposed to be at the fucking Tavern".
Jason complained. Earlier when the quiz had commenced, Jason was otherwise occupied. The three had illegally entered George's apartment as a part of their effort to communicate with the other side. Troy and Esther had gotten cosy on the floor. Sat, legs crossed, as she placed a single lit candle in the centre of the room.
"Just sit down, it won't take long".
Troy snapped, impatient with Jason's bellyaching.
"You said you'd do this. If you don't want to, then go, I'm not stopping you".
He carried on. Jason walked towards them both and took a seat for himself on the spare bit of carpet that hadn't been pulled out. Rummaging through his mother's spirituality books, Troy had found that connecting with the beyond was far more effective when carried out at the place of death.

"Ok, I know, I did. It's just freaky being here. Like, a guy died in here".
Jason blurted carelessly.
"George".
Esther stated, offended by the ignorant tone he used.
"His name is George".
She pointed out.
"Ok, fuck, I'm sorry. Look, I'm not trying to be a dick, but just… cut me some slack. I'm trying my best, but I mean, fuck. I'm allowed to be uncomfortable, you know".
Jason whined, defending himself.
"Can we just crack on and get this over with?"
He demanded.
"Ok. What do we do now?"

Esther asked Troy. He pulled out the deck of tarot cards from his pocket.

"I think there's a ritual you have to do, to bind the cards to their user, but maybe it'll still work because their owner was my mum. We're bound by blood, right?"

Troy suggested as he began to shuffle the deck. He wasn't particularly well informed on all the formalities involved, though that didn't demean his determination. He clarified that as far as he was aware, the cards that fall from the shuffle are the cards chosen.

"What, like, just when a card drops, it means a spirit picked it?"

Esther asked, trying to understand.

"I think so, yeah".

Troy answered. His lack of assurance effected Esther and Jason's confidence in is ability to perform the reading. Regardless, Jason's guilt required sustenance and Esther's grief needed confirmation.

The first card fell, facing downwards, landing on the soiled carpet. Troy placed his hand on the lifeless card, using his thumb and index finger to flip it, revealing the first image. The illustration was of an upright medieval jester, decorated with bells and ribbons as it seemingly pranced through a water painted meadow.

"The Fool".

Troy announced. Jason rolled his eyes back into his throat.

"Even the spirits think we're being dumb".

He complained. Esther ignored his outburst, asking Troy if the card had another meaning. Curious as to whether a metaphor hid beneath its initial stance.

"Erm, yeah. It means new beginnings".

Troy informed them.

"It's a way to say that your life is about to change somehow, in some unexpected way".

He concluded, shuffling the deck to release the next card. As he did so, behind him, the computer switched on. A noise they were all obviously familiar with but hadn't quite anticipated.

"Did either of you turn that on?"

Jason asked, as his sense of awareness increasingly elevated.

"No, I wouldn't worry though. Knowing George, he would have it set up for some automatic system reboot or updates or something".

Esther said, consoling Jason's impending apprehension. While Troy glanced at the computer monitor, the top card on the pile slipped from his grasp. He raised it to view the image. Completely unprepared for its ghastliness.

On the card was the reversed hangman presenting itself before him. The sinister hand-drawn sight of a man hung from a noose, his face hidden behind a woven sack and his hands roped to his feet forcing the hanged man into a foetal position. Troy threw the card away from himself as he jolted to his feet.

"What? What's it say?"

Esther pressed, reaching over to see the card for herself.

"No!"

Troy demanded, pulling her away from it.

"That's not mum's card! I swear she would never keep something so disturbing. I don't know how that got into the deck but I'm telling you, it shouldn't have".

Troy cried, conflicted by his trepidation and agitation, as he believed that someone may have tampered with his mothers' belongings, most likely as a practical joke.

"Ok, fine, but what does it say? Tell us".

Esther pried, trying to get a hold of the situation. Troy explained the illustration along with its possible meaning.

"Punishment?"

Jason asked, forcing the words from his emotionally weakened voice. The bottom left corner of the computer monitor had a red light, indicating its standby mode. As silence fell amongst the three, the red light turned yellow.

"You were at my house, earlier. Did you fucking pull this shit?"

Troy snapped, accusing Jason.

"What? Of course not, why would I do that to you, Troy? I would never even go near your mum's belongings without your say, let alone fuck around with her most cherished stuff. Do you really think I would fucking do that?"

Jason lashed out, incredibly insulted by the insinuation.

"Then who did?"

Troy replied, not fully believing Jason's defence. Esther ignored the two's bickering as her attention clung to the self-activated computer. She watched as lists of data configuration scrolled independently along the screen like a conveyer belt.

"Er, lads?"

She spoke. The two had heard but chose to ignore her as they were equally engulfed in their enraged accusations. The computer screen then stopped. The caret flashed. Esther unwittingly stared with an unwavering focus, locked in time, as it began to type.

```
HELLO TROY_
```

"Oi!"
Esther snapped, breaking them loose from their petty dog fight.
"What? For fuck's sake!"
Jason whined.

She said nothing more, instead, just pointed at the screen. Jason and Troy both retreated as all three stood at a focus. Awaiting explanation, as if from thin air. Trying to rationalise how the screen could independently type. The backspace key pressed inwards by itself, deleting the text. The caret continued to flash, as though contemplating its next thoughts, considering what to say next.

```
TEDDY TODDY MOVES IN THE LIGHT
```

"What the fuck?"
Troy muttered under his breath.
"Shh".
Esther whispered, reading each letter as it appeared.

```
TEDDY TODDY IS SEEN IN PLAIN SIGHT
NO NEED FOR THE DARK
FOR IT TO EMBARK
INTO THE DEPTHS OF YOUR FEAR IN THE NIGHT_
```

See, people presume that their lack of belief on these particular matters, automatically gifts them with correctness. Tis is not better to consider potential possibility, for the sake of avoidance to blind sighted threat. The beast typically thrived on undetectable solitude. Experiencing the arousal of the hunt, only during times of its sacrificial feeds. Maybe Esther and Troy's persistence of pursuit brought about something new for the beast. A thrill it had not yet encountered. A game to play with an untampered mind.

Chapter 21

The following morning came with an unsettling dread after their silly séance. DI Jones awaited Esther Petunia's arrival in anticipation. The interrogation room had been thoroughly cleansed in preparation for the questioning. Judging by his recent encounter with Miss Petunia, DI Jones suspected that obtaining her DNA for the case may prove more difficult than he'd originally thought. In his diligence, he had a case file with evidential photographs and interrogative questions at the ready. Planning to disturb her in order to provoke a more truthful response.

Esther hadn't slept. Her stash was still hidden in the wellington boot of Mr Platt's wardrobe. Regardless, access to it hadn't made any difference. It'd been hardly wise to venture into the likes of a police investigation, intoxicated by drug paraphernalia and lack of self-awareness. The events of the night before, left Esther somewhat disoriented. Trying to keep her mind on track by completing the task of packing up her belongings, preparing to move out from Mr & Mrs Platt's humbly deprived abode. There was no sense in taking packed suitcases along with her to the police station. So, she was to leave them by the door on her way out, to fetch later on when the interview had concluded. Not before she padlocked the zips, locking them for safekeeping, denying access to the nosey Platt's.

Esther dressed presentably. Braiding her hair into a tight and tidy plait, gluing down loose strands with a strong-hold hairspray. She dressed in office black, straight-cut trousers with a plain white, buttoned-down shirt tucked in. The outfit finished with a pair of freshly polished, mid-heel brogues. After applying a modest make-up look, she intentionally selected her lighter layered rain jacket, as opposed to her winter coat. Thus, legitimising an excuse to maintain use of her gloves and beanie hat, once inside. All too aware of the lions den she was to unwillingly trail into. The carcass in the police's sights, being that of her DNA.

"Ah, good morning, Miss Petunia".

DI Jones greeted with a grin fuelled by arrogance.

"This way if you would. Thank you".

He continued, gesturing to a closed door as they reached the end of the corridor. Esther refused to take the bait, keeping her hands tucked into her pocket.

"Colder in here, than it is out there".

She commented, leaving an awkward wait in the atmosphere before DI Jones gave in and opened the door. The parameter of the room would resemble that of a walk-in closet. A simple rectangular, stainless-steel table placed between two metal crafted folding chairs. The walls were of a sickly and lifeless green, paired with a navy-blue carpet, distastefully matched. Along the back was the famously known, ominous two-way mirror, outstretched above the lower half of the disgustingly painted wall.

"Please, take a seat".

Jones suggested as he pulled out the chair that was opposite to the mirror, for Esther to use. He then took his own seat across from her, as he lay atop the table, a case file.

"How are you today, Miss Petunia?"

DI Jones asked with an eery intrigue. Esther got comfortable, crossing her legs tidily as she rested her gloved hands upon her lap, leaning back into the chair.

"I'm well, thanks. And yourself?"

She replied casually. She felt confident that they hadn't found any more drugs in George's apartment. Even if they had, she was sure that there'd be no proof tying any contraband to her.

"I'm well, thank you. Although I am a little confused".

Jones teased.

"Oh?"

Esther enquired, playing along with his unusual ploy.

"See, I've been asking round. And as it goes, you were near the salon when Dana went missing".

He stated, dangling the lead like a carrot on a stick.

"So, could you tell me what you were doing that Sunday, between twelve and three o'clock?"

He asked, happy to catch her off guard.

"Wait, what?"

Esther paused, confused by his tone.

"What is this?"

She asked, her guard raised as did her temper.

"It's a simple question, Miss Petunia. Please answer it".

He responded, enjoying the trouble he was about to cause.

"You asked me here because of the call made about George's apartment. Why are you bringing up Dana?"

Esther pressed.

Detective Inspector Michael Jones was a *proof's in the pudding* type of man. He never extended the invitation for an interrogative battle of evidential ammo, without having a strong hand to play. And so, he opened up the case file. He held up a contamination controlled plastic bag containing a single, two-inch-long red hair.

"Look's a lot like your hair, doesn't it?"

He asked rhetorically.

"I'm not the only ginger in the village".

Esther pointed out.

"No, of course not. But, as I said, you were near the location at the time. You were on your way back from The *Tavern* I believe".

DI Jones continued. Esther considered for a moment, how he could have known that. Assuming that Roy or Violet must have said something.

"You were only at The Tavern briefly though, as I understand it. So, if you didn't go for a nice carvery, why did you go?"

He asked. Exaggerating about how much he really knew; he placed down his bluff.

"I was looking for George".

Esther responded shortly.

"So, let me get this right. You've been aware of Georges disappearance since Sunday and chose not to inform the authorities".

He stated, his tone becoming more commanding, his eyes locked onto hers.

"Why?"

He asked demandingly. Esther didn't answer, she simply stared him down in a roulette of stubbornness and refusal.

"Ok, fine. Don't want to talk? How about we just look at some pictures of what went on as you were *passing by*?"

He snapped, as he pulled the image of Dana's brutalised corpse from the file and slammed it in front of Esther. The gruesome nature of the view caused Esther to rise theatrically from her chair as it fell on its side. Her fortuitous fall cushioned by the ugly wall. Vision, under a bolted lock by that of her crinkled eyelids. Clinging to air, clutching her neck, as she involuntarily vomited onto her blouse. The ground felt disused as though she embodied the sensation of the earth rotating. Esther's fragile mind, distancing from reality, on the cusp of consciousness.

"Shit."

Jones exclaimed, realising that he'd sabotaged himself, and potentially his own involvement in the investigation.

Hours had passed before Esther found herself in a hospital bed. Jones sat in the visitors' chair beside her, patiently waiting for her to awaken. She'd been gifted a private room, one of which smelled of disinfectant with a tint of vomit.

"Hey, you're up. How are you feeling?"

He asked softly. The unanticipated surroundings hadn't deterred her. This due to the relaxant administered upon her arrival, evoking ease.

"What are you doing here?"

She asked DI Jones calmy, in her artificially contented state.

"I wanted to say that I'm sorry. I jumped the gun. I just wanted to make sure that you're ok, before I left you be. So, you're, ok?"

He answered, looking for confirmation. In fact, he cared little for her disillusionment. The Detective Inspector hoped to obtain more information, regardless of her incoherent state.

"Perfect".

Esther muttered sarcastically; drug addled from the relaxants.

"Just fucking perfect, like, I mean, what the fuck is actually happening".

She continued to ramble.

"What do you mean, Miss Petunia?"

Jones pressed.

"What?"

He badgered, trying to get an answer before she fell unconscious once more. Esther inevitably dropped to sleep, leaving DI Jones to relish in his imbecilic impatience once more. He surveyed the room casually until noticing a box of cotton buds by the sink in the ensuite toilet.

"One for luck".

He said to himself. He took an individual bud and used it to the swab the dribble that leaked from Esther's chapped bottom lip. He then wrapped it in the unused napkin from her bedside tray and slipped it into his inner jacket pocket.

He was to give up in his pursuit for direct information from Esther for the day. On his way out from the ward, he considered her admittance. Contemplating what she could have meant. Once outside, he took a menthol cigarette from his almost empty packet, along with the lighter obtained from a multipack sold at the hospital gift shop. As he smoked, he watched as cars drove in to the parking lot. People walking into the entryway and others strolling out from the exit. Friday had brought the village another dreary afternoon. Stuffed clouds and ashy skies, absorbing colour from the architecture, vehicles, and persons painted in the picture of his sight. He recollected Esther's reaction earlier that day, tyring to make sense of her involvement in the case. She may not have killed, he thought. But he intuitively presumed her to be intertwined. Knowing that once sober, extracting further information from her would present an unwarranted challenge. All that he had was his assumptions, a saliva sample, and a single strand of what he believed to be Esther's hair.

Chapter 22

The phone enlightened by the notification of an incoming call. It vibrated repeatedly until exhausting itself, leaving an answering machine message from a number titled, Work. Ivy was expected to inform her employer of absences. Not that it mattered, as he would often guilt her into working regardless. Answering the phone induced anxiety in her. It didn't only mean answering the phone. It meant conversing, expressing appropriate manner and begging for time away from the store to collect herself. It meant being informed of the busy periods, and how the reduction of staff affected potential sales. It meant being reminded of how '*Stacey* broke her arm last year, and it didn't prevent *her* from commitment to the job.' Answering the phone would be work in itself that Ivy wasn't prepared to commit to. And so, she left it be.

Unsure of the time, or even the day of the week for that matter, Ivy poured herself another tumbler of rum, straight. She liked a dark rum, smoky yet smooth. Quality that glided down the throat and warmed up the chest. The discrepancies in her memory, coated by the ooze of alcoholic arcadia, momentary in its coddling. Desperate to forget the blood. Clawing at the chance to remove the recollection. The last time she held her phone to her ear, forcing herself to utter the words.

The last outfit she'd worn remained crumpled up on the floor by the foot of her bed. The smell of sweat and bad breath coated the condensation that masked the windows. Her complexion greased as did the roots of her hairline. Her body odour was wrapped in George's T-shirt. Ivy, engulfed by her desire to wear nothing else while in mourning. Refusing to wash the scent her lost love from such cloth.

When Ivy met George, she'd been preparing for an interview. She'd listed tasks to have completed by the night before. Tasks that included, shopping for a new pair of black trousers, shirt, and shoes.

Exfoliating before applying a moisturising face mask. Researching commonly asked questions in retail interviews, and scripting out appropriate answers that could potentially gain her good favour with the interviewer. Finally, she was to obtain a fresh haircut. The local salon formally known as "Dana's Delicious Dyes". They specialised in colour transformations that presented a slogan, promising irresistible hair.

Ivy had been working on the vegetables market stall with her aunt for a decade. As the years passed, many locals would attain their weekly veg from the supermarkets instead, thus affecting business. Her aunt couldn't afford to pay her anymore; however, she did allow Ivy to continue her work until gaining a new source of income. After enquiring throughout village for job openings, checking the About Aviary newspaper daily, and reading the message boards left up in the general store, she found an advertisement for a retail assistant at the off license.

Her hair typically fell short as an above the shoulder bob. A pallet of blonde tones blended from dark daffodil to light lily pollen shades. Her usual routine was to trim the ends when they surpassed her shoulders. That day however, she felt an opportunity arise for a fresh start.

New job? New haircut.

She thought to herself. Ivy considered a bolder look, a 'pixie cut' as it's apparently called. Her aunt often mocked girls who dared to wear short hair.

"It's for lad's"

She would say, stuck in her old-timer ways. Ivy anticipated her family's mockery, yet it hadn't fazed her. Confident in her stride, she entered the salon, ready to take on the world.

"Hiya, love. How are you, you ready for tomorrow?"

Dana asked, inquisitive in nature.

"Yeah, I've near enough sorted everything. I'm doing a face mask when I get home, after I've done here, but other than that, I recon I'm ready to go".

Answered Ivy in a cheerful mood.

"That's grand, that is, love".

She started.

"Right, now, you're booked in for a restyle appointment. Am I right in guessing you want to change that to a simple cut and blow?"

Dana asked. She'd grown familiar with her regular customers, knowing what they would typically aspire for, each time they attended their appointment.

"Nope, I actually want to go short".

Ivy answered, with a twist to her routine.

"I'd really like a pixie cut. I just feel like I'm starting a new chapter in my life, and I want to start with a new look."

She continued.

"Oh well, look at you! Little miss dark horse!"

Dana joked, surprised by the change up.

"I love it, sure let's go short then, yeah? Mind, I can guess what your Aunty Cathy will say".

She pointed out playfully.

Ivy felt the fresh air on her neck as though for the first time. Dana had styled her a beautifully soft pixie cut, layered delicately to showcase the texture of tones in Ivy's natural blonde. Her first step taken outside the salon's pathway led to a bright and beautiful afternoon, suddenly interrupted by a passer-by. A man, seemingly out of no where walking directly into Ivy, causing her to drop her phone.

"Ah shit!"

Ivy exclaimed, instantly reaching out her hand towards the concrete to retrieve her phone, displaying a shattered screen.

"Brilliant".

She sighed, rolling her eyes impatiently.

"Sorry, I wasn't looking where I was going. I'll pay for that fixing if you want?"

The stranger plead apologetically.

"Well, actually if you want it doing for free, I know a guy".

He offered, candidly.

"No thanks, it's fine, don't worry about it".

Ivy answered. She hadn't anticipated that the man be a gentleman. She'd expected him to deny fault, along with refusal to assist in her damaged property's repair.

"Ok, fair enough. Well, if you change your mind, here's my number. Let me know if you want".

The stranger said, as he pulled out a pen from his pocket, along with a used paper bag that had previously contained a sausage roll from the bakery. He passed over the pastry bag to Ivy, gifting a gentle smile as he walked away. She held the greasy written note to see a phone number below the words that read, 'Hi, I'm George.'

A gentle knock alarmed at Ivy's bedroom door as a woman in her late fifties entered her bedroom.

"Sweetheart, It's just me".

Ivy heard. She clenched in a foetal position on the bed as a hand stroked her arm carefully.

"What if he's dead, Aunt Cathy?"

She choked as her aunt lay down beside her, wrapping Ivy in her warm embrace.

"Shh, I'm here. I'm here, sweetheart. It's going to be OK".

Wednesday had been the worst day of Ivy's life. After pulling the torn carpet out, the floorboards in George's apartment revealed a splatter of blood, seeping into the wood. Its structure had been scraped by what appeared to be the clawed residue of human fingernails. She cried to the receiver, after dialling 9-9-9, screaming, distraught. The call ended and the receiver dropped the line. The request for police intervention had been carried out. All that there was left to do was to wait. Esther had gone, Ivy was alone.

The police bombarded the apartment, carrying equipment, wearing PPE, and warding off the street outside. The first to enter had asked her how she came to find the blood. She paid no attention. Ivy's eye's fell empty. Unable to move, speak or hear, she remained motionless. Moments later, a medical professional took her under their care, and escorted her from the premises. Leaving the authorities to investigate George's home.

Forensics discovered a number of clues; some were undetectable to the human eye, including that of sampled saliva. It spread across the bed, carpet, and desk chair. They collected scattered objects for the analysis of fingerprints, including the bag of popcorn that Esther had left half eaten. It became apparent that there were no signs of forced entry, nor were there any possessions initially tampered with. Including that of Georges clothes and shoes that he had worn, the last time anyone had seen him. There was however a gap in the wall where a plug socket sat. Gently pulled at, it came loose, and the false plug socket stumbled out, completely empty.

Irritably awake; Ivy's mind locked into sleeplessness. Her aunt's efforts proved in vain as she lie wide awake for the duration of her visit.

"You shouldn't be going through this alone. I absolutely hate that you were alone when you saw what you did. I wish I'd been there with you".

Aunt Cathy ranted.

"I wasn't alone".

Muttered Ivy.

"What?"

Cathy asked.

"I wasn't alone, some girl was there".

She answered, vaguely.

"What do you mean, some girl was there?"

Cathy pressed, trying to understand.

"Esther. She's a friend of Georges, she was there before me. She left when we saw…".

Ivy trailed off, not fully answering her aunt's insipid questioning.

"She was there before you? And, what?"

Cathy badgered, not letting go of the potential for a hunt. Ivy thought about her queries for a moment, recollecting the events.

"Come to think of it, she pointed it out. She said she hadn't seen him for a couple days, or something. She was looking for him, then she pointed out the tare in the carpet".

Ivy recalled aloud. Unaware of the damage that particular memory was to cause.

"Right. When you're back on your feet, we're talking to the police".

Cathy stated, like a captain raring to set sail.

Chapter 23

Now isn't Miss Esther Petunia in quite the little pickle. The finger must point somewhere, mustn't it? Conclusions leaped forwards like a sugar glider onto the most realistically reliable branch. But I have not omitted to enquire as of yet. What does your conclusion persist of? The sensational palatable nectar that is the feeling of being right. Wouldn't that be sweet?

Come Saturday morning, Eve was to start her new job at The Tavern while Jason stayed in the apartment upstairs with Ellis. He'd woken up to feed the baby, but otherwise hadn't muttered much. Only spoke to whimper of how tired he'd felt.

"Alright, don't complain to me this morning, Jason".

Eve snapped, as she applied her mascara using a compact mirror.

"I already said I'm sorry for missing the quiz. How long are you going to stay mad at me for?"

He apologised with a slight sincerity. His sympathy lacked acknowledgment due to his rattled state.

"I get that you have to work late. You know I do; we have a baby to provide for. All I ask for is a heads up".

Eve ranted, frustrated by his behaviour.

"I just got busy; I didn't think. I don't know what else to say. I am sorry, though".

He continued, as he tried to wrap his arm around her shoulder.

"Can you not? *I'm* busy".

She snapped, pushing his affection away.

"Yeah, sorry. I'll let you get ready".

He apologised once more before lifting Ellis from his highchair to sit in the bed with him as he switched on the telly. Once ready to go, Eve gave her boy a kiss on the cheek before heading downstairs to start her training.

"Good luck. You'll smash it".

Jason blurted. Eve paused to look back, reluctantly releasing a grateful grin as she closed the door behind her.

"Right, sweetie. What experience do you have with working in hospitality?"

Violet asked while she restocked the chocolate and crisps.

"None, I had Ellis after college, and I've been cleaning for the salon since".

Answered Eve, embarrassed.

"That's fine, love. I'll teach you everything you need to know, don't you worry".

Violet offered supportively. She started out with the till. Each selection had its own section on the touch screen. The options displayed menus such as confectionary, soft drinks, alcoholic drinks, adult meals, kid's meals, and sides. She went on to explain that all employees have a till code that is their own and must not be shared. This being because the process allowed Roy and Violet to keep track of who carried out which transactions in order to resolve any issues regarding discrepancies or customer complaints. After providing Eve with her unique till number, she guided her to into the office to pass on a clean unlabelled apron for the day. Violet had ordered a new one for Eve with her name embroided by the top left corner, just as the other staff had in their positions. Only, it hadn't arrived as of yet. She went on to show her where the storage room was and the beer cellar, teaching Eve how to change a barrel before they moved on to the front of house.

"It's as easy as it sounds, love. Just keeping it clean and tidy, asking if people need anything and all that jazz. You won't be taking table orders, obviously you already know we take food orders at the bar and there's numbers signed across all of the tables".

Violet went on, pondering on what she should teach Eve next.

"Oh! Fire exits. Main entrance, there's one in the kitchen, another one by the back here. The last is downstairs by the toilets".

She stated, informing Eve of the safety procedures while showing her where the first-aid box was along with telling her the names of staff who had first-aid training, including herself and Roy. Violet then set up an account for Eve on the computer to participate in the induction videos for food hygiene, health & safety, manual handling, diversity & equality, employee standards and the emergency protocol. At the end of each tutorial, Eve was to sign a declaration to provide proof of her newfound knowledge. The training filled out the majority of her shift, by 14:00pm she was ready to serve her first customer. Eve placed herself by the shelfing to clean the surfaces, with her back to the bar. It had been a productive day and she felt that she had gained a considerable amount of insight already, therefore excited to practice what she'd learned.

"May we have a pot of tea for two".

A voice asked. A particular woman's voice that she recognised, all too well. Eve dropped the task at hand to face the bar, only to find her mother dressed in what she considers to be her 'comfies'. The outfit consisted of looser fitting chinos and an elbow-length, plain polyester T-shirt.

"Mum, I didn't expect to see you here".

Eve said cautiously.

"I didn't expect to see you working here".

Mrs Platt replied in a back-clapping manner.

"Mrs Richard was kind enough to provide some work. Since I was out of a job".

Eve protested patiently.

"You believe this to be appropriate?"

Her mother baited.

"I'm sorry, Mum. I can't fully discuss this right now, I'm on the clock. Did you just want the pot of tea, or would you like to order food too?"

Eve evaded, redirecting the conversation. Mrs Platt confirmed that the tea would suffice and went on to badger her daughter over having not called to provide her definitive answer.

"Jason took a last-minute shift; he'd not come home until I'd already gone to bed. Plus, I've been preparing for my first day at this new job. I'll ask him when I'm done, and we'll call you when we've discussed it".

Eve stated. Her etiquette coming to an impending decline. She usually obtained the ability to endure her parents perceptively obtuse personalities when previously informed of their potential visit. Yet this had been the second occasion in a very short time span that her parents had intentionally intruded. Both events having taken place in public, thus avoiding Eve's predictable protest.

"Your father and I will be perfectly happy to wait here. The table by the window has a lovely view of the shops and goings on in the village".

Mrs Platt toyed.

"I expect that my grandson is just upstairs with your husband. Am I right?"

She asked confidently. Eve responded with nothing but a defeated expression.

"We're OK to wait. Not too long, mind".

Mrs Platt finished, making her way to the table she'd described as Eve's father waited for his wife to return. The remainder of Eve's first shift dragged on until 15:30pm. Her parents peered in her direction as she vacated the bar and travelled upstairs to speak to Jason.

Chapter 24

On Saturday evening, the village had once again arranged a community hall meeting. This time it focused on the arrangement of the Neighbourhood Watch. Roy came prepared with a Filofax filled with forms that he had written up himself. Each form held multiple copies to hand out to the volunteer patrollers. The first being the initial consent form. It started with a listing of the responsibilities to be carried out. They were to partner up with another volunteer and stay within their pairs on shift in their designated areas. Additionally, they were expected to take photographic evidence with the disposable flash-cameras provided, of any abnormalities and suspicious behaviour. Instructed to blow on the whistle at any sign of trouble.
I consent to participate in the role of a patrol volunteer for the Aviary Avenue Neighbourhood Watch. I accept the responsibilities listed above and am aware of the risks and hazards potentially involved.
The form read. Another was a signing off sheet for the equipment each volunteer was to use. It wrote the selection of a hi-vis vest, whistle, torch, body alarm and disposable flash-camera. This along with the date, time and name of user stated next to it. There were nineteen essentials' packages, all of its contents were coded with numbers going from A-01 to S-19. The last sheet was a timesheet. It expected the name, equipment code and location assigned. Ending with the start and finish time of the shift.

Roy Requested that everybody be seated, so that the meeting could commence. This time, Eve and Ellis attended with Jason.
"Right, so".
Roy started, as Violet handed out copies of the rota he'd written up, along with the other forms and black ball-point pens.

"I've tried to keep your work and family lives in consideration while making this up, but if there are days and times that you're set to patrol, and you know you can't make it, please let me know sooner rather than later and I'll adjust it accordingly".

He announced.

"Before anything else I need you to read the consent form and only sign it if you definitely want to participate. Also, you'll find another form detailing the equipment you'll have on your person before starting your shift. We need to confirm that you have it before you venture out. And we'll be keeping a record of who starts and finishes their shifts, in whatever streets they're assigned to, and on which dates. The equipment is coded so we can keep track of who has what, because this shits expensive people, once it's gone its gone".

Roy stated, concluding his informative speech.

"Said my peace, any questions?"

He asked the group.

Earlier that same Saturday, long before the meeting, Esther discharged herself from the hospital and returned to the home of Mr & Mrs Platt. Her luggage remained as it was, padlock intact. The house was upside down from Mrs Platts overhaul. Carrying out a deep clean and tidying, while Mr Platt surveyed Esther's person.

"Were you arrested?"

He asked, failing to hide his smirk. Esther's primary intention was just that of retrieving her belongings and leaving. She would offer her thanks and goodbyes out of common curtesy. Anything beyond that, felt nothing short of unpaid labour. Instead, she bypassed his snarky remark and avoided his attention, drawing it onto Mrs Platt as she stood by the entry hall holding a feather duster.

"Would you like me to clean Eve's room before I head off?"

Esther asked emptily.

"No, that's quite alright. I have a handle on it".

Mrs Platt answered firmly.

"Eve's currently in the need for a more sustainable residence. Her old room may be a squeeze with the baby, but it should suffice".

She stated, confident in her efforts to retrieve Eve and Ellis.

"Where would Jason sleep?"

Esther asked, aware that the Platt's more than likely hadn't cared enough for Jason to accommodate him.

"Everything is yet to be determined".

She answered vaguely.

"Do you have everything?"

Mr Platt interrupted, hurrying Esther along. She requested one last check before she left, to assure that she hadn't forgotten anything. Mrs Platt went back to her cleaning and Mr Platt sat impatiently in his wheelchair by the door. Esther discreetly took her and George's stash from the wellington boot where it hid. She then took a quick glance at her old living space, both the bedroom and the ensuite bathroom, to find nothing of hers was left. As though she had never been there at all.

Troy had woken late. He'd drank himself to sleep the night before accidently, after originally just pouring a short whisky to take the edge off. His nightstand carried the air-filled bottle, empty of the nightmares it subdued Troy's unconscious mind to endure. The rug supporting his bed, clogged with vomit and tears as he stepped over it to excrete more of his stomachs lining into the toilet bowl. The shower was then set to warm up, while he brushed the night from his teeth and tongue. Too weak to stand, he sat nakedly in the tub. His arms hugged his legs as the piping hot water scolded his neck and upper back. The water pressure penetrating the skins surface, conducting unwarranted heat through the nerves like an electric bolt. Allowing the pain to purchase him. That is until his phone vibrated. He'd left it in his jean pocket which lie crumpled up on the bathroom tiles. Unclogged from his acidic bubble, he switched off the shower and dressed in some comfortable jogging bottoms and a sweatshirt.

"It's me".
The phone voiced, as Troy took the call that had been ringing non-stop.
"I want to know if you're OK".
The caller continued.
"OK?"
Troy sighed.
"No, Jason. I'm not OK".
He stressed, reaching his hand toward his shoulders to rub the scolded skin.
"I don't know if I can come over today. I'm in enough bother with our lass as it is, but I don't want you to be stuck on your own. You should come over to The Tavern".
Plead Jason. Troy didn't answer. He craved companionship through his organ clenching heartache, only he lacked the courage to experience unwarranted attention. After his mother's demise, passers-by felt compelled to intervene with this daily activity when

seen on the street. He couldn't so much as buy a pint of milk without strangers expecting his polite gratitude for their un-asked-for grievances.

"See if Esther isn't busy, she could walk with you".

Jason suggested, after reading Troy's silence rather accurately. As strongly as Troy's reluctance regarding the forced outing deemed, it sought more stability than seclusion.

"OK, I'll text her".

He gave in.

Esther entered Troy's house, suitcases in hand.

"Before you ask, don't. I'm going to stay at the hotel, everything's sorted, let's move past it".

She snapped.

"OK".

Troy replied, unbothered.

"Jason want's me to go to The Tavern. I don't fucking want to, to be honest".

He informed Esther.

"Let's fuck it off then, order some food and crack a film on. I just want to switch off anyway".

She suggested.

"Yeah, fuck it".

Troy agreed. He texted their plans to ease Jason's mind, as he put the kettle on and poured a hot brew.

During the meeting, Jason and Eve sat together on the second to last row of seats in the community hall. Ellis's pram was parked by the end of the row as he chewed on his teething keys. Eve raised her hand before standing when Roy gestured for her to speak.

"What exactly is it that you're looking for?"

She asked. A question open to the room.

"That's an excellent question, Eve. Well, the issue is that we don't know what were dealing with here. Who this person is, where they come from or why they're doing such horrible things to good people. But whoever this bastard is, we'll come together as a community and bring them to justice".

Roy declared passionately, as Eve awkwardly took back her seat.

"So, to answer your question, love. We need to keep a look out for people loitering by themselves in secluded areas. Maybe people that look like they're up to something, you know, like keeping their faces hidden. Watch out for any potential clues. For example, signs of blood, footprints, or anything weird. Taking photos of these things could be the difference between the perpetrator being caught and them getting off without so much as a slap on the wrist".

He answered, in a long-winded way.

"How long are the shifts?"

A gentleman by the front voiced.

"And when do we start?"

He asked.

"Shifts are two to four hours, give or take. Depends on what you're available for. Take this week as a practice run, we'll work out the kinks and figure out how the timetable works out for everyone as we go".

Roy answered, recognising that the question was voiced by Henry, the local butcher.

"Roy, mate. While I've got your attention, Can I just say thanks on behalf of everyone if that's alright? You've pulled this off, both you and Violet. You've done a cracking job. So, honestly, good on you both, really".

Henry boasted, starting an agreeance within the meeting amongst other residents. A woman seated in the middle section of the rows, started a nervous yet infectious clap as the rest of the Neighbourhood Watch members gave a calm and steady applause for Roy & Violet Richard. Roy raised his hand, delicately requesting that the applause to come to an end so that they could proceed with the discussion at hand.

"I appreciate it. Thanks, Henry, for the kind words. Thanks to everyone for that, Violet and I are just doing our bit. Looking at you all sat here, ready to patrol the streets, just goes to show how ready you all are to do your bit as well. Which is brilliant".

He finished, passing the crowd onto Violet.

"Right, I've set up some coffee and biscuits on the table. It didn't make sense to do a full buffet again, since a lot of it went to waste last time. So, help yourselves and let's get those forms filled in".

Malcom remained solemn throughout, his name having not appeared on the rota simmered a trickle of betrayal. He assumed his mother's involvement, only he hadn't anticipated his father's compliance. Malcom held the rota upright, displaying it to his dad who stood opposite the tea and biscuit table. He needn't speak, for his demeanour was loud enough. Malcom left the rota on the table and vacated the hall without offering a goodbye. Roy placed himself against the wall, angrily gripping the guilt he held for undermining his sons' noble efforts.

Chapter 25

Jason's comprehension of perception had broken. When Eve had gone off to carry out her first shift, Jason was left to his own devices. The respect for his life partner compelled him to confront her on the occurrences that had taken place on quiz night. These virtuous intentions inadvertently evaded for consideration over Eve's first day jitters. Refusal of succumbing to illogical conclusions, Jason distracted himself with the TV. Watching shows throughout the day that accompanied Ellis's merriment. Mid-morning, he took it upon himself to contact Troy. Seeking comfort from another to which experienced the same bewildering cursed threat. To his dismay, Troy became otherwise occupied. Leaving Jason alone with his thoughts.

He and Ellis had been snacking on rusks after the baby had his morning bottle. Come 12:00pm, the two settled into Roy and Violets kitchen for lunch. After placing Ellis in the highchair and providing a colourful plastic bowl brimmed with carrot and sweet potato baby food, Jason made a start on cooking a meal for himself.

I can't be arsed.

He thought to himself, as he dragged his brittle body over to the fridge. A pack of six, large, free-range eggs called to him, advertising their simplicity for a quick and effortless cook. Cracking two eggs into a glass measuring jug, Jason whisked the yolk and whites until its contents were light and fluffy. He then dropped a dollop of sunflower oil into a medium sized frying pan, setting the gas fire on a low heat to soften the grease. As the eggy mix pushed its way into the oil, the grease popped and burst, ever so delicately. The mix simmered as it solidified, realising a 'start of the day' aroma. Familiar and homely in its easily palatable grace. Once complete, he slid the omelette onto a clean plate, decorating the dish with the crackling of grounded salt and pepper before taking a seat at the table.

"Smells eggy in here".

Roy observed, entering his kitchen.

"Hello, love. What you got there then?"

He asked Ellis playfully.

"You've got some carrot and sweet mash, haven't you Ellie wellie?"

Jason answered, prompting a silly giggle from his son. Roy took a couple eggs from the opened pack and prepped an omelette for himself, re-using the unwashed frying pan that had been left on top of the inactive gas oven.

"Looks nice that does, lad. I think I'll join you".

He complimented.

The uncomfortable quiet of the kitchen was disturbed by the noise of two men chewing on their squishy eggs. Jason's unkempt physical demeaner became more apparent with each passing day. A delicate topic required a delicate approach, Roy felt.

"We haven't really had a minute to talk, have we? Both of us, being so busy".

He started, treading lightly.

"No, I know. Just been a weird week though, hasn't it".

Jason replied rhetorically. His performance of stability was nothing short of frail, but Roy recognised a man's burden of pride. Empathetic in his observation.

"Whatever it is, Jason. I'm all ears. You know that. I can tell somethings not quite right with you lately".

Roy offered, with genuine concern.

"Yeah, I appreciate that. It's just..."

Jason thanked, trailing off.

"There's something not normal about this".

He blurted, causing Roy's inevitable intrigue.

"Well, no. It's not normal for someone to do this shit".

Roy replied, thinking that he understood.

"No, I know. That's not what I meant".

Said Jason, further confusing the conversation.

"Then, what do you mean?"

Roy pressed, holding on to his sensitivity. Jason had been consumed by all of the uncertainty. Failing in his ability to remain distracted and avert confrontation on the matter.

"OK, I'll tell you, but before you get mad, just let me tell you the whole story first".

Jason began, preparing the admittance of his guilt. Roy, answering with an inquisitive raise of his left eyebrow.

"A customer came to our door, complaining that Dana had gone off in the middle of an appointment. I went to check, and she wasn't anywhere. Her staff were no fucking help and I ended up finishing the hair wash for this random woman".

He explained, bracing himself.

"And then... I just went back upstairs. I didn't call the police, I didn't report it, I just fucking brushed it off like a bloody idiot and ignored it".

His tone increasingly became abrupt as his confession unleashed.

"Troy came the next morning, practically begging me to tell him where his mum was. But, what? What could I do by that point. She... she was already dead apparently".

Jason held in his protruding sob. His sinuses involuntarily excreting mucus and salt-soaked tears, as he caught his breath to continue on.

"There's nothing that I won't do to make up for what I did. I fucking mean it".

He plead.

"Is that why you joined the Neighbourhood Watch Patrol?"

Roy asked softly. Jason avoided his gratuitous gaze, focusing his viewpoint onto the empty plate displayed before him.

"That's why I broke into George Jameson's apartment on quiz night".

He whispered.

"What? Why the hell would you do that?"

Roy argued, distraught over recklessness of the unstable young man sharing his home. Jason defended his actions with the timeline of events including that of Troy and Esther's involvement. Stressing of his desperation to give Troy one last moment with his lost mother, if at all possible. Informing Roy of how they exercised caution, so to not leave any fingerprints or forms of DNA at the scene upon their exit. He confessed it all, but for one crucial part. The introduction of the spirit they contacted.

"I'm not going to pretend that what you did is OK".

Roy exclaimed.

"But I will say that I understand".

He concluded, taking a cold beer from the fridge as he passed it onto Jason once opened.

"Are you going to tell Eve?"

Roy asked in a tone that suggested Jason should have done so.

"Yeah, I will. It's just, her first day, you know? Let her enjoy it for now at least".

He answered.

At 15:35pm, Eve burst into the bedroom, agitated, flustered and alert. Plastered against the door as a barricade, she confronted Jason about their need for prevention of her parent's plans.

"I've been thinking about it, and there's a few things you could say to ward them off".

Panicked Eve.

"What's going on?"

Jason asked, not yet caught up on the situation.

"Mum and dads downstairs waiting to hear your answer on their *offer* to move into my old room".

She explained.

"Absolutely fucking not".

He chocked. His apprehension fuelled by exhaustion. He began listing reasons in his head, of how he could explain to them that it was better if they were to stay put. For example, how their family now resided with the head of the Neighbourhood Watch Patrol, which gifted them all with more protection. Plus, their newfound accommodation provided an increased income, an accessible and convenient opportunity. Jason assured Eve that he would sort it.

"Mr and Mrs Platt, hi. Eve mentioned that you wanted to speak with me?"

Jason reluctantly greeted.

"Ah hello, son. Take a seat".

Instructed Mr Platt.

"I understand that you've been forced to vacate your flat due to the dreadful circumstances that occurred this week".

He began, leading up to his proposal.

"Yeah, but we landed on our feet. Roy and Vi will keep us safe. So, we're doing OK, Sir".

Jason insisted, rushing the conversation.

"Regardless, we'd like to offer Eve's old room. We can have everything ready for tomorrow once it's all cleaned".

He continued.

"I'm confused, sorry. I was under the impression that Esther Petunia was living there".

Jason stated in an accusatory sense.

"Miss Petunia moved out, she found alternate living arrangements".

Contributed Mrs Platt. Hardly believing her blatant falsehood, his enthusiasm to hurry the performance along, encouraged him to brush past her lie.

"OK well, Thank you. That's so kind of you but I'm going to have to turn it down. We've settled in nicely here. Ellis is getting his sleep schedule back to normal, and yeah, we're enjoying it actually".

Jason answered, happily displaying his rejection.

"You're saying, no?"

Mr Platt enquired. Jason remained undeterred.

"I'm afraid so, but that's not to say that we don't appreciate your kindness. I hope I haven't offended you?"

He replied. The couple locked their stare onto the boy that married their only daughter, like a lion would a gazelle.

"No. Of course not".

Mrs Platt answered, relieving the tension before they redressed into their winter coats to leave.

Chapter 26

Detective Inspector Michael Jones had kept himself rather busy. After his liaison with Miss Esther Petunia, he paid a visit to the morgue. The hall-like ward forced the scent of metal and disinfectant, frozen flesh, and copper. Its solitude held the soberness of life's end. Dana lay stiff on the chilled slab that her body had been slapped onto. An identity tag clung to her stone hard toe. The autopsy report suggested a range of ailments befallen to the victim upon their instantaneous extraction from life. The rib cage displayed extreme breakage, as did the rare sight of the half-removed jawline. Predicted to have been carried out by a perpetrator that was quite possibly six to seven ft. With an estimated body weight, varied between at least seventeen to twenty stone. Indicating that the killer had to be physically large with immense strength to illustrate a murder so brutally conducted.

Jones received a call, confirming the results of Esther's samples to find there was no match. Although he was informed that the lab had discovered additional debris that was picked out from beneath the corpse's fingernails. Though, still under analysis, the samples were presumed to be traces of skin scraped from the killer as the victim clawed for freedom. Perplexed to discover the depth of his inaccuracy, he was left to ponder about who next to abuse his power toward. The best lead being that of the victim's son, Troy.

That Saturday afternoon, Troy answered the door with a slice of pizza in hand to see the detective on his mother's case. The pizza's top was coated in a rich tomato and basil marinara sauce, with a duvet thick layer of mixed cheeses where a scattered portion of grilled chicken and sweetcorn swam. It dripped from the boy's chin as he drivelled a drunkard greeting.

"Hiya, mate. What's up?"
Troy asked candidly.
"Who's that?"
Called Esther from the other room.
"That bobby".
He answered back. She'd been helping herself to Georges left over weed. A considerable way to be rid of the evidence, she felt. Esther smoked it in the back garden of Dana's house, so not to leave a stubborn stench that would inevitably take siege of the living room's fabrics. Moderately perceptive, sure. Unfortunately, the marijuana had rendered her incomprehensible, and so, the compulsion she possessed to confront DI Jones on his lack of professionalism had to wait, Esther instead invited herself to remain upstairs. Excusing herself from the confrontation under the illusion of consideration for their conversational privacy, reluctant to face consequences for being high.
"Who's that?"
Asked the detective.
"My mate. So, what do you want?"
Troy responded plain and simply.
"I've received more information regarding your late mother's autopsy report. I can come back another time if you'd prefer?"
DI Jones suggested.
"No, no. Come in, I'll make a pot of coffee".
He replied, inviting the detective inside. Jones cautiously minimised the information he provided. Leaving out the gory details to spare the boy his sanity. Focusing more on the physical attributes of the killer, enquiring as to whether Troy was aware of anyone in his mother's life that fit that particular description, to which he was not.

Dana's staff, Olly and May had been interviewed by officials. He'd had a brief encounter with the two at the station upon his initial questioning on the day that Dana's body was discovered. Security footage secured the accuracy of their alibi. The video saw the victim vacate the shop floor via the customer entrance at 14:07pm on that Sunday. The front pathway CCTV hadn't presented any proof of entry for an individual of that calibre.

"How about your dad?"
Enquired DI Jones.
"What about him?"
Troy sighed.

"Has he reached out since the incident was broadcasted, have you heard from him?"

He continued.

"Nope. Well, I suppose he might have. There's like a hundred messages on the landlines answering machine from a bunch of rando's. Possible that he could be one of them. I doubt it, though. He left my mum before I was even born. Didn't want a family, had no interest".

Troy answered, irritated by the topic, scorn by the abandonment of his father.

"I'm sorry. I'm sure this is uncomfortable to have to talk about. I hope you understand, I'm just trying to cover all bases here. To get to the bottom of all of this".

Jones empathised, treading carefully.

"Yeah, I know. It's ok, I get it".

Troy rushed, avoiding vulnerability, reluctant to let his guard down around the detective. DI Jones requested for any photographic imagery or home videos that included Troy's father. Thus, considering the possibility that the victim's former sexual partner could potentially be the culprit. What if he was bitter about her carrying the pregnancy to term against his wishes? Or if the boy's interpretation of event's could be a fabrication invented by his mother? What if the man in question didn't know about the child? Maybe she gave birth in secret, took the infant away to keep for herself and the father only recently discovered the deception over his only biological child? All these questions swirled around the detective's mind like the sugar cube that he stirred into his coffee.

"Mum didn't keep those kinds of things. She didn't believe in holding onto negativity. All I can give you is his name".

Toyed Troy.

"And what would that be?"

Asked Jones, playing along with his pen and paper in hand.

"Zachariah Hayes".

Answered Troy, sharing no further information. Regrettably unaware of his own father's whereabouts, appearance, profession or even, birth date.

The pizza and beer concocted a mixture that churned the innards of Troy's stomach lining. On the verge of vomiting, he hurriedly pardoned himself to the upstairs lavatory to relieve his insides of the saturated fat, dairy induced alcoholic potion. Meanwhile DI Jones waited studiously within the confine of his notes. A blinding flash of reflected sunlight pulled him from his thoughts as he sat impatiently at the kitchen table. The entry way into the kitchen of Dana's house displayed a row of coat hooks that were illuminated by the daylight shining through the slim vertical windows built into front door itself. One hook in particular gripped onto what appeared to be a woman's longline coat. The reflective glare beamed from a mobile phone screen; half hugged by the pocket hid within. The persistent plop of ejected stomach acid and undigested food continued to symphonise from the upper floor. DI Jones took the vacancy of his surroundings as an opportunity to disrespect his unsuspecting host's hospitality in order to retrieve more personal information. Inside the pocket laid an outdated, barely functional, buttoned mobile. It lacked the technology and ability of a touchscreen smartphone, locked by a three-digit code.

The toilet flushed and the sink activated as Troy finished up to return back downstairs. Stealing the phone as he returned to his seat, DI Jones pretended to stir his coffee.

"Any better?"

The detective joked sympathetically.

"Can we do this some other time?"

Troy requested, ignoring the comment in its uncalled-for humour. Exhausted, and defeated by his meal.

"Sure, here's my number. Call if you have any questions or if you find any more info for me".

DI Jones instructed, handing over his business card.

Upon returning to the station, he was called in for a meeting with his superior, Detective Chief Inspector Douglas Danes. Jones had heard rumours in circulation regarding an infliction of disciplinary action following the interrogative questioning carried out on Esther Petunia.

Politely giving two patient knocks on the door, the troublemaker was welcomed into the lion's den.

"You wanted to speak with me, sir?"

Jones asked, unwavering in confidence.

"Correct, Michael. Take a seat".

Commanded the Chief.

"I called the hospital to check on the patient you had admitted. Fortunately, she is back on her feet again. Supposedly she'd discharged herself".

He began, easing into his tyrant with a slow birth.

"That's good to hear".

Michael relieved.

"Yes".

DC Danes agreed. A tone as flat as his disposition.

"I wanted to speak to you personally, Michael. To ask you what was going through your mind when you showed evidential photographs of an extremely vicious murder, to a civilian that's completely unrelated to the case? A murder committed by what could quite possibly be an actual giant! If by some miracle it was carried out by your suspect, she would have to possess magical powers, would she not?"

Ranted the Chief Inspector sarcastically.

"Sir, please allow me to explain. There was red hair found on the victim's body".

DI Jones exclaimed, defending himself desperately.

"Yes, I'm aware. You got the hair tested against a saliva sample of Esther Petunias, and what a surprise, they weren't a match".

He yelled with his impatience impending.

"What on earth possessed you, Michael?"

DC Danes asked accusingly.

"Sir, with respect. When I saw her amongst the crowd at the scene of the crime, she was the only one looking elsewhere. She was looking down the street towards our next victims house, George Jameson. A missing person of which she knew had disappeared, well before it was reported. Let me make myself perfectly clear, Sir. I don't believe that Esther Petunia committed the murder, but I feel strongly that she has some level of involvement. She knows more than she's letting on. And yes, the tactic I used was too forthright, I know that. I apologise, it won't happen again".

Asserted Michael.

"I know it won't happen again, Jones. You're on thin ice!"

The Chief yelled, barging his way back into his hierarchy.

"I've heard enough".

He barked.

"But Sir".

Protested Jones.

"I said, enough! Get back to work".

DC Danes dictated.

Chapter 27

Alright, alright. Give me a moment to collect my thoughts. Because yes, I know what you're asking.
"Whose Troy's dad supposed to be then?"
Well as I recall, Zachariah Hayes was an automotive mechanical engineer. He'd moved to Aviary Avenue after tiring of the fast-paced and chaotic days fuelled by city life. The garage he worked at was located uphill from the local butchers, right around the corner by the fish & chip shop, otherwise known as the 'Chippy'. Zach and Dana met one evening when she brought her car in for its annual ministry of transport test, failing due to the vehicles exhaust pipe having been rendered insufficient by corroding rust. He first laid eyes on her as she entered the MOT centre office. Zach sat by the computer, his skin covered in oil and grime from the days labour.
"Hi, I'd like to book in for a repair please".
Dana spoke. Her golden auburn ringlet hair framed her cocoa powder eyes and dendrobium orchid lips. Zach's insecurity gripped onto his shoulders tightly, holding him back from delighting in the embrace of her aromatic summer-fall radiance. He, himself was a rather striking man. His muscular strength packed into ill-fitted overalls. Shoulder length layers, lit with tones of blonde and ash folded behind his ears. Eyes of candelabra cactus green watched as the sunlight beamed onto the future mother of his child.

DI Jones' pursuit of tracking Troy's father was surprisingly more fortuitous than he'd expected. The data-base exampled plenty of individuals under the names of Zachery or Zach Hayes, within a five-mile radius dating back twenty-five to thirty years. Only one stood out, displaying the lengthy name of Zachariah alongside the Hayes surname. The man in question was registered to a three-bedroom house uphill from the Aviary Avenue high-street. The rental agreement fell under the category of a bedsit accommodation, ending his contract in 1995. His employment status was registered as full-time at the MOT centre and car repair garage known as, "Melvin's Motors". The personal details proved to be outdated as DI Jones attempted contact. However, the next of kin information detailed his mother, Arabella Hayes, and her telephone number above the home address. The first half of the phone number consisted of the five-digit area code assigned to the city. DI Jones dialled, with little hope of an answer.

"I don't know how you got this number but we're not buying anything, so lose it".

An abrasive elderly woman yapped.

"Hello? Is this Mrs Arabella Hayes?"

The detective formally enquired.

"How do these vultures get people names?"

She muttered, seemingly to the person beside her.

"No, Mrs Hayes. My name is Detective Inspector Michael Jones. I'm calling in regard to your son, Zachariah Hayes".

He clarified.

"What! Oh my god, what's he done?"

She exclaimed theatrically.

"There's a detective on the phone, Zach! What the hell have you been up to?"

Yelled Mrs Hayes. Suddenly, realising that Zachariah Hayes was on the other side of that call, DI Jones quickly and respectively requested that she pass the phone onto him.

"Yes, this is he. What's it to you?"

Zachariah spat.

"I am Detective…"

Jones began.

"OK, Mr Detective. Stop cold calling my mother with whatever scam this is!"

Scolded Zach. The conversation dropped along with the call. DI Jones took in a deep aggravated breath, releasing an ineffective patience inducing exhale.

"For fucks sake".

He blurted, considering the telephone number. Since that was accurate, he thought it seemed fair to presume that the home address would also be valid.

A structure of tan-orange brick, unevenly shoved between the neighbouring terraced houses, presented itself to Jones upon his arrival. The streetside garden possessed nothing but a potholed pathway guided by poorly placed cobbled stone. It's lawn, far overdue for mowing as little sparrows pranced within the uncared-for grass. The Detective knocked at the poorly painted dingy door with a preparedness for an unwarranted confrontation. A gentleman, presumably in his late forties or early fifties answered, slender in his over-sized hooded sweatshirt and jeans. A jawline, gentle and soft. Framed by the waves of sun kissed, dandelion layers hiding strands of silver and brass.

"Are you Zachariah Hayes?"

DI Jones beseeched.

"Who's asking?"

The recipient replied.

"I am Detective Inspector Michael Jones. I've been trying to locate and contact Zachariah Hayes to discuss a recent death".

He informed. The man's demeanour dropped; his legs wavered as he steadied himself by the wooden doorframe.

"I need you to confirm who you are, before I discuss the matter any further".

Pressed Jones.

"Yes, sorry. That's me. Who died?"

Zach answered fleetingly, inviting the detective inside to take a seat. He was informed of the brutal death that Dana endured, along with the rough idea of a suspect's physical attributes, and finally of the wellbeing of his son. Well, to his own knowledge. Proceeding to request for proof of Mr Hayes' alibi in the form of witnesses, preferably accompanied with CCTV footage.

Chapter 28

Cathy had been caring for her niece for the entire week. Coaxing her to get washed and eat, cooking her favourite meal of meatballs and mash after a thorough tidy and clean of the flat. She was a boisterous woman, owning the room that she deigned to enter. Her years of calling customers over to entice their tastebuds with her freshly grown vegetables allowed Cathy a strong sense of presence. A confidence to take up space with pride and self-worth. A value she instilled into her niece, to disallow anyone from making her feel that her presence is nothing but a blessing. A life lesson that Esther seemingly was never shown. Alternatively, her avoidant social presence gave the impression that her upbringing had been presumably dismissive and uninterested. Perhaps she likely agitated others by her acts of authenticity. She stayed out of people's way, conditioned by the distorted mirror of needless disapproval and dishonestly that life reflected. The two young women completely contrasting in their ability to connect, battling head-to-head in their efforts to protect George.

Aunt Cathy had been baiting Ivy over the involvement of the police, dangling the threat of lawful consequences that were at bay for withholding information critical to the case. Ivy argued that there were complications that she wasn't yet ready to share. Complications that required a discussion with Esther before taking issue with the police.

She'd acquired Esther's mobile number from Roy after they'd been in George's apartment together. That Saturday, Ivy rang Esther. Her last call ended unproductively with Esther hanging up, unwilling to converse. Ivy hadn't much hope that the next attempt would differ as the phone rang.

"What?"

Esther answered perturbed, while Ivy rushed to initiate the interaction.

"My aunts making me go to the station. I'll have to tell them shit, Esther. Can't you just meet with me so we can figure out how to deal with this?"

She angrily begged, only to be met with no response.

"I'm not sure what the best way to help George is. This is a whole new territory for me. But what I do know is that I don't want to go into this blindly. I'm pretty sure that you don't either. So, I'm going to The Tavern later tonight around eight. Meet me, don't meet me. Balls in your court".

Commanded Ivy, as she hung up the phone.

She sat by the bar, Kraken in one hand, her phone in the other. She hadn't met Eve as of yet, that being the first introduction. The two had gotten into casual topics, while Ivy waited for Esther to show up. General matters including that of the weather. It was due to snow heavily that evening. The news issued a yellow warning, encouraging preparedness for conditions to alter or worsen. A burnt tobacco-ash smoke fogged up the sky. Greyness poured over the lid of the village, ridding streets of the atmosphere's amiable warmth. The Taverns entry door opened, inviting an unwanted chill. Esther arrived, bundled in knee high boots, a blush white scarf & gloves, and her longline coat zipped all the way to the neckline.

"Let's get this over with".

She sighed, passing Ivy on her way to the ladies' lavatory downstairs. The cubicles were empty, and the windows shut, securing privacy. Speaking quietly to assure their voices didn't carry.

"So, what exactly are you wanting from me?"

Asked Esther, already defensive. Ivy couldn't understand the influence for her attitude.

"What do I want?"

Ivy shook her head.

"I want you to cut the shit".

She barked.

"Excuse me?"

Esther chuckled, amused by her candour.

"You heard me. I know you've got something. You may as well have it plastered across your fucking forehead. What is it?"

Ivy began. Esther became argumentative, persisting that she had no idea what she was referring to, claiming to only know as much as *she* did. Ivy of course, didn't buy it.

"My boyfriend is *missing*, Esther".

She spoke, watching as her defence fell involuntarily. Esther gave in after careful consideration, deciding to throw Ivy a little bone.

"I nicked his stash. That's why I left before the police got there".

She admitted. Ivy responded with a slow disbelieving blink to indicate how she knew that wasn't all. Esther churned her attention away, staring at the chipped paintjob on the cubicle wall. Her eyes squinted and her lips pressed firmly together before apprehensively returning to the conversation.

"And his phone".

Esther released.

"You have my boyfriend's phone?"

Ivy interrogated with her eyebrows raised and her arms crossed.

"His work phone, calm down".

Esther clarified, performing an effective eye roll in condescension.

"Why, what's on it?"

Badgered Ivy. Esther explained that her plan was to review the contacts on George's customer listing. How she had been out for a drink with him that Saturday but called it a night early. She would use the phone to find out who the last person to speak to George was.

"So why haven't you?"

Asked Ivy, in an accusatory tone.

"I've had other shit to deal with".

Esther answered aggravatedly. Ivy considered the new information for a moment, demanding that Esther share the burner with her as she held her hand out to retrieve the phone. Esther forcibly rummaged through her coat pockets to find that George's burner wasn't there, assuming that it would be in one of her suitcases. Ivy adamantly refused to leave Esther's side until obtaining the phone in question. And so, they each headed to the hotel together.

Delicately sharded ice shed spontaneously from the firmament for the duration of their march when the sky calmed to an obedience after a tantrum of heavy snow. Leaving chilled residue of its cold and resistant mood. The suite felt like walking into a wooden box, deprived of airholes. A single bed lay lonely in the rooms centre, surrounded by unoccupied furniture in the form of a bedside cabinet and a wardrobe. Ivy surveyed the room before asking what circumstances lead to the use of such a dinky and interim refuge.

"Not a pleasant guest, are you".

Esther asked rhetorically. Ignoring Ivy, she inspected the contents of both suitcases inside and out, to find that George's burner phone simply wasn't there.

"It might be at Troy's. I was sure I had it in my pocket, though. It probably just fell out".

Esther explained casually before recollecting the events of the day. She'd remembered that Detective Inspector Michael Jones had stopped by, and that he'd been there for a lengthy amount of time while she was otherwise occupied upstairs with her drug paraphernalia.

Shit.

She thought to herself.

Ivy went into the lavatory as Esther walked up to the curtain, drawing them to a close. Suddenly, she spied a shadow. It cascaded across the deficient lights used for security purposes in the car park. The casting of a shapely animal. Taller than man yet postured as so. The unsightly form then flashed between the parked cars. Barely revealed by the dim glow of ineffective streetlights. As it emerged, its malnourished arms swung down to the knees while its unkempt claws grappled onto damp tarmac. Unforgiving organs of sight bulged from either socket, vacantly animated by the flickering glimmer of light bouncing from the cascading pools of melting snow. As the creature scanned its surroundings like an anglerfish, its head turned focus toward the building. Esther jolted away from the window, her back to the wall. The bedside lamp remained irresponsibly lit, luring the beast in. The scrape of overgrown claws steadily climbed upwards onto the bricked structure. The tap of teeth touched the tepid glass window. Disturbed panting, like a rabid dog, condensed the vapour from its flesh-stench breath into the cracks of the open air-vent above. Esther held her breath. Her heart, punching her eardrums with each amplified beat.

Chapter 29

What would you have done, may I ask? Now, I'm compelled to warn you. Our story will worsen before reconciliation. I'll teach you of the cursed devilment that is Teddy Toddy. What kind of monster would I be if I didn't? Pay very close attention, though. It might just save your soul.

Amongst all the excitement, I seem to have neglected poor Malcom Richard. His encounter with the beast accumulated a delectably grand outing. As you may have deducted, it had been almost a full week since Malcom originally paid his parents a casual visit. He'd planned to return to his life back in the city by that following Monday. Having had a job and an apartment to get back to. Oh, and of course, a boyfriend. See, Luke and Malcom dealt with quorums of their own. Luke was prepared to settle down, whereas Malcom still hid from his family. Intimidated by the concept of revealing oneself for the 'leap off a cliff', formally known as commitment. A secret that he couldn't conceal for much longer as Luke took it upon himself to seek out his 'on-and-off' partner, confronting Malcom for the last time with the ultimatum of a life with love or without.

The chill had thawed as the sun pushed winter snow aside that morning. Droplets clung to iced spider webs, immaturely thrown away by a clouds impatient blow. Dirt clogged the slush clumped roadsides, as the stature of snowmen came to a slow melt. It was a spring teasing sun, taunting the promiscuity of its withholding warmth. The Tavern was heated by the central system, the thermostat risen slightly to promote cosiness from the cold. Malcom, non the wiser, perched comfortably atop a barstool with his face planted afront the television as horses raced across the screen. He'd poured himself a generous portion of tea to wash down the bacon and sausage panini that his mother lovingly prepared.

"So, this is the family emergency, is it?"
A low tone voiced behind Malcom's unsuspecting shoulder. He spun on the rotating barstool to face the question presented.
"Luke?"
He gasped.
"What are you doing here?"
He asked. Luke expressed his distaste in his lover's deceit, flinging accusations of a third participant. Accusations of which, Malcom denied. Explaining the circumstances that had befallen the village, along with his compulsive drive to protect his parents.
"Then why didn't you say that in the first place?"
Luke affirmed.
"Because I knew you'd come here".
Protested Malcom. The snout of the elephant in the room filled with air, like the cheeks of a trumpeter. The tension boiled as his scalp dripped salt-soaked sweat when Violet entered the front bar. Her peripheral caught both of the boy's apprehension as she uninvitedly approached their conversation.
"Who's your friend, sweetheart?"
She asked, forcing herself into the equation. Malcom's eyes plead with that of Luke's, begging for the conciliation to remain between the two.
"Hi, you must be Mrs Richard. I just came through to sort out some paperwork with Malcom, we work together".
He lied, reaching out for a handshake.
"Oh, I do apologise. I'd offer your dad's office but Eve's using it for training today".
She blushed, performing embarrassment by her intrusion.
"That won't be necessary Mrs Richard, I have to get off now anyway. It was nice to meet you".
Luke smiled falsely, giving his boyfriend a work appropriate goodbye, for him to then leave The Tavern exasperated.

Roy had been in the vicinity, clearing a table by the booths as he watched his sons heart breaking. Frustrated by his wife's unwanted hand at play, he followed his son's companion to the car park.
"Excuse me?"
He called.
"Yeah?"

Malcom's associate answered. Roy approached him, holding a look of concern concealing admiration.

"I'm his dad".

Roy stated, pointing back to The Tavern, referring to Malcom sat at the bar.

"I'm Luke".

He replied wearily, detecting the assumption caked across Roy's expression like a rainbow pie to the face.

"Why don't you join us for dinner tonight?"

Roy offered. The lines in Luke's forehead crinkled in surprise as a grin delighted the creases of his cheeks.

"Really?"

Luke asked, seeking validation for the intention inside the invitation.

"Yeah, we usually sit down for about six-ish. The bar's still open so you can just come through this way, but I'll meet you down here anyway and walk you up".

Confirmed Roy as he headed back inside.

Luke embraced the sun's glow while clenching to the zip of his coat. A grain of hope glided from his eye before the tear stumbled onto his tight fist as he made a wish to himself. A wish that Malcom would gain the courage from his father's unconditional acceptance and approval.

Roy returned indoors, greeted by the disapproving glare of his wife.

"What are you doing, going out in that weather without a coat, you're going to catch your death".

She needlessly complained.

"I've invited him for dinner tonight".

Roy blurted, throwing away the context. Malcom jumped from his stool, frantically alert, questioning his father's actions. Roy then delicately placed his hand upon his son's hair, stroking his thumb amongst Malcom's ear to calm him.

"It's OK son".

Roy soothed.

"He's welcome here".

Violet needn't argue her husbands attempts of tyranny. Not Infront of their son. No, she would await her opportunity to retaliate. The dinner she'd concocted presented a plate of pork chops sided with green beans, carrots, broccoli, and roast potatoes. For dessert, her signature rhubarb crumble with thick double cream.

"Looks delicious".

Luke expressed, in a complimentary enthusiasm for her cooking. He waited patiently for the others to retrieve their individual servings, as some families say grace before tucking in. The Richard's did no such thing and gorged their way through the meal without so much as a *thanks, God.*

The rhubarb came with a delectable smell of a candy drop sweetness. Sleek and sticky pudding exhaled steam that crawled its way through rocks of biscuit crumbles. Cooled by the soft white ooze of rich, dairy blessed cream that pooled itself comfortably beneath the piping pink palace of dessert. The kitchen rained in heat by the gas lit oven that once deactivated, remained lukewarm.

Roy made his presence clear; his safety provided a blanket of security for Malcom from the stance of overbearing love that Violet leaked. The evening gifted Malcom with the sense that he'd no need to say it. No need to voice the words that burned his tongue with dread. His hand fell into Luke's as they held onto one another at the table. Violet watched as she sipped her tea.

Twas late when they concluded their evening and it had been a success if you would believe. Luke had wine by the plenty but felt it too soon to stay over, despite Roy's kind invitation to do so. Instead, he insisted that he stay at the hotel until morning. He could read Malcom like a book; it was clear that he wasn't ready for Luke to stay the night in his family home. Since Roy hadn't been drinking, he took it upon himself to drop Luke off. He grabbed a set of keys and the three set off out to the car while Violet stayed behind to clear up.

The world, now different, shone a little more brightly thanks to the moonlights gleaming embrace. A greeting soon withheld by a passing cloud. First transparent in its frail form, grew dense and dark as the night encouraged the emersion of the unsavoury. Pulling into the car park entrance, the headlights illuminated the moistened tarmac that copied the view of windows spread horizontally in even rows. Roy sat upfront behind the wheel as Malcom and Luke shared slurred goodbyes. Luke's hand reached out; his fingers grazed the doorhandles latch as he was just about to exit the vehicle. That's when Roy stopped him.

"Wait".

He instructed before central locking the doors in unison.

"What are you doing, dad?"

Asked Malcom, confused and dazed. His father had caught a glimpse of a usual creature bouncing off one of the puddles by the far end of the car park. Following the line of origin that reflection birthed, he witnessed a ginormous body hooked onto the buildings side. The shape of its ghastly head was silhouetted by a rooms cool light.

"I need both of you to stay absolutely quiet".

Whispered Roy as he opened the camera app on his phone. Malcom and Luke's terror quickly sobered them as adrenaline engulfed the remaining alcohol.

"Stop".

Luke spoke in a soft yet firm tone.

"Be ready to drive, I'll take the photo".

He insisted. Luke wound down the back seat window after taking his phone from the safety of his pocket. He then carefully positioned it, set it to flash, and captured the photo. A blinding light blinked, and the animal reared its disfigured head. The fear of detection had spooked it, rendering it powerless in that there moment. It leaped from the ledge and landed with a powerful thud, regaining its balance as it galloped away into the ink spilled distance. Roy instantly put the gear stick into reverse and speedily turned around to drive away.

Chapter 30

As Ivy came out from the safe confines of the hotel room's lavatory, she was bewildered by Esther's appearance. Her eyes were bloodshot with a hellish red. A lightening bolt vein coursed from her scalp to her temple as a rain of sweat soaked through her opened pores. She stood spooked, strapped to the wall beside the curtain.

"What are you doing?"

Asked Ivy, analysing Esther's body language. Esther reacted with a confused and relieved expression, peeling herself from the wallpaper. She carefully peered out of the window to find nothing was there, but an empty parking lot opposite the glass.

"What did you take exactly?"

Ivy's voice ended her inspection.

"What?"

Esther croaked in a whisper.

"From George's stash, what did you take?"

Ivy pressed. Insulted by her insinuation, Esther unlocked herself from her tremored trance.

"I'm not high".

She argued, growing impatient with Ivy's accusatory manner. She'd had enough of her hovering and questioning.

"Look, the phones clearly not here. I'll find it in the morning. Just leave, will you".

She affirmed, coaxing her out of the door.

Ivy's phone had been blowing up with the persistent nag of Cathy's concern. After informing her aunt of her whereabouts, she was instructed to wait by the entrance as Aunt Cathy would come to give her a lift home. Once Ivy had left the hotel, Esther rushed to close the curtains before forcibly dragging the unfilled wardrobe across the room to block the entirety of the window. She could omit to herself that it'd been likely, she was just experiencing visual and auditory hallucinations, but she would rather invite the monster inside than allow Ivy the opportunity to be right. Then again, the unwanted guilt rose from the pit of her stomach like an undigested chilli, burning at the back of the throat. She sent a text, asking Ivy to let her know when she'd gotten home.

The strands of her enflamed red hair withered along with the collagen in her once youthful complexion. The untimely aging that burdens those with irreversible trauma, soon to render her natural beauty to nothing but a truncated blip in her once mediocre prime. A bright rectangular glare shone from her lap as the notification for Ivy's response came through.

"Home now, mum. x"

It read. Air released from Esther's flared nostrils as she let out an exhaled sniff, humoured by Ivy's text. She then turned off the lamp and slid herself underneath the bed, scrunching up her scarf to use as a pillow and her coat as a quilt. Facing her phone screen downwards onto the carpet, she closed her eyes and tried to sleep.

Cathy's night on the other hand had only just commenced. Her worry clouded her ability to understand Ivy's point of view, so much so that their bickering progressed far too rapidly.

"What on earth do you think you're doing?"

Cathy snapped, deluded with self-appointed authority.

"Since when do I have to run it by you?"

Ivy protested inadequately.

"You know the answer to that".

She presumed.

"No, I don't. So, tell me".

Ivy demanded, seeking explanation for her aunt's audacity.

"Since people have either been killed or gone missing!"

Cathy yelled with an instant regret. Ivy remained quiet, appalled. She took in a deep breath as she arrowed an offended, disapproving glare. Cathy's guard then slopped, cascading down onto the floor, joining the intended silence previously fallen from Ivy's defence.

"I'm sorry".

She apologised. Still withholding the truth beneath her frustration, struggling with the acceptance of responsibility for her overbearing expression of concern, before giving in. Her chest dropped as though released from a great height as she threw her head backwards to look up to the ceiling. Seeking spiritual approval, perhaps from the heavens, for permission to admit her weakness.

"I'm just so fucking scared for you".

She confessed as her eyes reddened, her lips trembled, and her hands shook from a held back cry. Her eyes tried to remain closed, so to not enable tears to shed. To Cathy's surprise, her niece's arms opened wide, leading her into a safe embrace. Stroking Cathy's head as her honey pot highlights folded over Ivy's tear-soaked shoulder.

"It's OK. It's OK".

Ivy soothed in repetition.

An hour or so passed by and the two calmed from their dispute. Popcorn prepared and plated, they shared a portion, planted in front of the television. Ivy lent her aunt some comfortable pyjamas before seating themselves within Ivy's collection of decorative cushions on her bed. Her bedside ceramic lamp brightened the space, as they binge watched a British classic.

"What about Rodney then? You recon you'd have given him a chance?"

Ivy teased, shoving popcorn into her own gaping mouth.

"Well, this is the thing, He's a lovely bloke and his hearts in the right place. Just a shame he's bloody useless".

Chuckled Cathy.

"What about Del Boy?"

Ivy continued.

"What? And wonder where the money for rent is coming from, week to week? Fat chance!"

Her aunt answered candidly.

"Would be a laugh though".

She replied, lightly defensive.

"Aye, that's true to be fair".

In her spare time, Ivy liked to paint. She practiced murals along her bedroom's walls, changing the landscaped scenery she'd artistically articulated throughout the room. The most recent being that of the expanded galaxy. Imaginary planets that Ivy had invented, spread across the beautifully black of blue sifting through amethyst purple. Silver splatted stars translated through the space's colour scheme with a slate painted wardrobe paired with a matching chest of drawers. The two chatted and chomped as the late evening became early morning, both drifting to sleep while still sat upright with the TV glaring across the illustrated universe. Cathy paused for a moment as she realised something. Ivy hadn't even answered her question from earlier. She never confirmed her purpose for visiting the hotel, nor did she disclose any other participant in her outing. The unanswered query re-energised Cathy. She looked upon her sleeping niece thinking quietly to herself. Wondering, what is she getting herself into?

Chapter 31

Let's get back on track with the Neighbourhood Watch Patrol. I haven't let you know how they've been getting on have I? Deary me, my mistake. Well! As it goes, there had been a slight change of hands.
Mr and Mrs Platt took issue with their son in-law's unanticipated rejection. They simmered in their stew of bitterness, brainstorming alternate routes to take in order to retrieve their fallen fruit. If Eve would not come willingly, the two would then have to force their hand. Mrs Platt recognised that the resources fuelling Eve's independence what was stood between her and her daughter. Any plan would just be pointless if Eve suspected her mother's involvement. And so, Mrs Platt had to work discreetly. Mr Platt took an alternate approach, focusing his sights on The Taverns primary owner, Roy. Mr Platt wasn't one for a casual chat. He felt there was no need in the expressive performance of vocalising one's inner thoughts unless absolutely necessary. Mostly because he believed that people spoke far to much, regardless as to whether or not they had anything of value to say. This particular personality trait made him somewhat isolated, in a way. Not unbearably so, might I add. He sought great comfort in his solitude and lacked insecurity when opportunity arose to vocalise. One would think that this behaviour and attitude would render one's ability to know their fellow man, to nothing short of inadequate. On the contrary, dear. Mr Platts observatory skills meant that quite the opposite would take effect. Roy's position of his hierarchy's pristine power made him a particular person of interest. A power of which he would take for himself, to secure his daughters compliance.

Come Sunday, Mr Platt escorted himself to The Tavern under the pretence of gratitude towards the admirable leader. The aroma of carved carcasses, cooked to perfection, clogged the atmosphere with the promise of a delightful afternoon. Customers huddled around their numbered tables, spitting bites of chewed potatoes and meat as they bragged about their weekends. Releasing drunkard laughter as they consumed alcoholic beverages and salted bar snacks. Now, on Sundays, they would typically accompany one another for a carvery at The Tavern, but on this occasion, Mr Platt excused his wife's absence with the falsehood of an afflicted ailment. Just as he had for her lack of attendance from the church that same morning.

"Eating alone this week then, Mr P?"
Asked Roy as he wiped clean the two's usual table.
"Yes, my wife has made it clear that the further away from her that I am, the better. Thus, avoiding contagion".
Answered Mr Platt flatly.
"I actually would prefer if you spared me approximately fifteen to potentially twenty minutes while I'm here, Mr Richard. I have a pressing matter to discuss with you regarding the Neighbourhood Watch Patrol".
He requested formally. Roy asked if he wanted to speak after his meal, to which Mr Platt graciously agreed. He usually ordered the larger portion advertised, but as he was dining alone, he felt no need to prolong his visit with additional food that he'd obligatorily take longer to consume. The smaller selection proved disappointingly inadequate to his taste. The dish served as one portion of selected meat with no offer of Yorkshire puddings or seasoned sausages. It was simply the meat and whichever vegetable and potato that came displayed. Mr Platt was further perturbed to find the last of the meaty gravy had been consumed. He was reduced to pour over his insufficient meal, the tasteless goop that was vegetarian gravy. With the lack of attendance by his wife, he considered pairing the dish with a light beer. A drink of which, Roy promised to not utter a word of, as he winked at Mr Platt.

After dinner, he waited impatiently for Roy's attention.
"Sorry, Mr P. I had a customer but I'm here now. What would you like to talk about with me?"
Greeted Roy, seemingly casual.
"Thank you, Mr Richard. I appreciate you taking the time to speak to me during your working hours. I'll make it efficiently short and to the point".
Mr Platt robotically announced.

"Now, I see that you have taken on too much too quickly with the Neighbourhood Watch Patrol. That is not to undermine your efforts. It's simply an observation of your dedication to The Tavern, becoming less imperative than that of your newly obtained community responsibilities".

He continued, bluntly. Roy's response was not of offense but of relief. Mr Platt's statement held truth in Roy's overburdened chest.

"I'm retired, Mr Richard. I have the time, the ability, and the determination to distil a careful eye on the residents of our village. Therefore, I'd like to offer my services. You know how well I know the people here, their work lives, personal responsibilities, and recreational times and activities. I believe I can assist you with the provision of weekly rotas and record keeping of the equipment in use, along with the contractual obligations".

Mr Platt finished, ending his pitch. Roy's large working man's hands cupped his face before gliding them backwards, combing through his greying hairline.

"I'm not going to deny it, Mr P. You've hit the nail on the head there, to be frank".

Roy admitted, slightly embarrassed by his wavering 'hand on the wheel'.

"It would really help me out, actually. Are you sure you don't mind?"

He asked, with a slight desperation in his throat.

"Mr Richard, I would not offer if I was either uninterested or incapable of the task".

Answered Mr Platt, determined to close the deal.

"Then, yes. When can you start?"

Roy answered, offering up his hand to shake with Mr Platts.

"Excellent. If you have all of the files ready for me to return home with now, then I could start right away".

He offered in concealed excitement, accepting the shake of Roy's open hand.

Mrs Platt had been cleaning Eve's bedroom to prevent the accumulation of dust particles. The room was to be pristine for her daughter's upcoming return. After that, she moved on to tidy and clean their own bedroom. She pulled off the duvet cover, pillowcases, and bedsheet, to put on a hot wash cycle. Vacuuming the carpet before scrubbing away any stains or marks she'd previously ignored. Mrs Platt then moved onto the wooden furniture, polishing away dust and finger marks that left an unsightly residue. She opened up the wardrobe to view their clothes and shoes, just has she'd left them. All but for her husband's wellington boot. It stood slightly askew to its matching partner. She remembered the last usage of the boots, dated back a few weeks. When heavy rain sets its sights on Aviary Avenue, the Platt's tend to re-arrange their routines accordingly. Only enduring the outdoors if strictly necessary. On that occasion, Mr Platt had his yearly optician's appointment arranged. Considering his gradually declining sight, Mrs Platt stood firmly on her stance for his attendance. Fortunately so, as he was issued a new prescription. She remembered wiping scruffs of dirt from the wellingtons. Drying them from the seeped in rainwater before parallelly placing them at the wardrobes base. The other shoes beside the boots, including her own wellingtons, ankle boots and smartly polished shoes, remained untampered. So why, she considered, was that one particular boot parked amiss?

The latch within the front doors lock clinked and clonked as Mr Platt turned his key to open the door. His wife hurriedly rushed downstairs to help him unload his coat and shoes.

"So, how did it go, dear?"

Mrs Platt pestered with an enthusiastic intrigue.

"You tell me".

He smirked, presenting the papers.

Chapter 32

One, two, three, access denied. One, zero, zero, access denied. Detective Inspector Michael Jones lay in bed, fiddling with the stolen burner phone. He'd spent his evening cooped up in the office, replaying the CCTV footage taken from Dana's hair salon. Desperation consumed his peripheral. His apprehensive mind tunnelled through a vacant screen. By that point, DI Jones had collected alibi's left, right and centre along with evidence to prove each individual's statement. Every thread pulled would fray sooner or later, including that of Troy's father Zach. The social media imagery they'd posted that day aligned with the date and time relevant. Zachariah had been with his family, nowhere near Aviary Avenue. The task was becoming somewhat impossible. Find a culprit, as big as a bear and sly as a fox. His hawk eye gawked at the CCTV video. Double, no, triple checking that he'd not missed anything, before giving in for the day and returning home.

"Still no luck?"

Toby asked. He'd returned from his friend's bachelor holiday that Saturday morning, jet lagged.

"Nope".

Answered Michael, defeated.

"Why don't you just take it in tomorrow? Get it de-coded or whatever it is that they do".

His husband jabbed as he slipped out of his dressing gown.

"Because I stole it, hon. Danes is already on my back".

Michael argued. Toby joined him in bed, dropping his slippers by the edge as he folded himself into the duvet.

"Who's is it?"

He asked curiously. Michael looked up from the phone to his husband as he shrugged his bare shoulders.

"It can't be the sons. It was in a woman's coat".
He answered. Toby paused in alert, gripping hold of Michaels blonde hairy arm.
"Please don't tell me that you stole a dead woman's phone".
Snapped Toby, timidly.
"No, no!"
Michael exclaimed instantaneously.
"There was someone else in the house, Troy wouldn't say who. I just assumed he had some girl over".
He said reassuringly, convincing Toby that it's more likely to be hers.
"Question is, who's the girl?"
He added, concluding his query.

It wasn't long before they both fell to sleep. Toby was exhausted from his flight, and Michael by work. The two believed in décor being fit for purpose. They liked the odd material thing, sure, who doesn't? But, when styling their bedroom, Michael was adamant on making it a sleep educing room. All of their clothes were stored in a pantry sized closet, leaving room for a super king-sized bed. Jade green Egyptian cotton sheets engulfed the memory foam mattress. Adjustable dimming light fixtures illuminated the camomile-coloured wallpaper and the alabaster carpet's soft touch. The blackout curtains fell heavily to the floor, secluding the two from the world as they slept.

An aggressive buzz forced its way into Michaels slumbered ears, awakening him in the early hours of the morning. He discretely took the phone from his bedside table to inspect the caller details before selecting to answer, quietly climbing out of bed to sneak into the upstairs hallway.
"Hello, is this the detective? Erm, Mr Jones, was it?"
An enquiry from a woman voiced.
"Speaking".
Jones uttered.
"Mr Jones, my name is Cathy Krane. I got your number from my niece. She was in a relationship with the missing boy, George Jameson. I believe I may have some useful information regarding the case".

Morning pierced the sky with a paintball of pink to start the new week ahead. Toby once again woke up to a half empty bed, just as he had the week before. Underneath his water glass was a folded note.

A work thing came up. I won't be home late. I love you, have a wonderful day, handsome. X

It read. Toby grinned. He admired his husband's passion for justice. Michael's constantly fuelled drive to keep going, no matter how many dead ends troubled the journey.

Toby slipped the note into his dressing gown pocket as he made himself decent to travel downstairs. Sunlight burst into the house as he pushed the curtains aside and opened the latched window, breathing in the morning chill. He then opened the fridge, in search of streaky bacon and fatty sausages to fry for his breakfast butty. A week of excessive alcohol consumption called for the sanctuary that is in a full English, washed down with freshy ground coffee swirled in freshly creamy steamy milk.

Michael's Sunday morning carried out quite differently to that of his husbands. He'd arranged to meet with the woman over the telephone. Ordinarily The Tavern was the customary meeting place, but on this occasion, discretion was unusually the priority. Instead, they met at the hotel lobby's bar, subsequently empty due to the hour. Cathy was sharp in her features. She dressed for the occasion in a plain burgundy, knee length dress. Paired with a black mac, belted by the waist. Styling floral wellington boots, precautionary footwear for the remaining slush from the snow. Michael attended in another one of his casual work suits. She sat by the back of the room, ominously, as though mimicking an informant from a spy film.

"Mr Jones."

She spoke in a low tone.

"It's DI Jones, Ms Krane".

He pointed out blatantly, confidently taking a seat for himself.

"What's all this about, then?"

Jones asked, getting straight to the point. Cathy took the coat hanging from her shoulders and folded it onto the back of her oak chair, pillowed with a cherry red velvet. The bar was barely lit by the surrounding glassware sconces. A wooden panelled floor bowled across the disingenuous space. The walls were blanketed with framed illustrations of varied sceneries from petaled meadows to the vicious sea. She'd ordered a black coffee to go. Clasping onto the paper cup, she surveyed her surroundings.

"This is where she was last night".

Catchy spoke, secretively.

"Who? Your niece?"

Jones asked, confused.

"Yes, Ivy mentioned the other day how that girl, Esther Petunia was at George's apartment the day she called the police. She also said that Esther had known about him being missing, long before".

She gossiped, all knowingly.

"I'm already aware of that ma'am".

Jones sighed, realising he'd wasted his time.

"You did? Well did you know that Esther is staying here?"

Cathy boasted, seeing the suspicion develop in the detective's eye's.

"Ah, well. See Ivy wouldn't tell me who she was coming to meet last night, but I had a hunch that it was Esther, considering how persistent she was on avoiding further contact with the police until she'd gained more information".

She bragged.

"So, this is just a hunch. You don't actually know for sure?".

He questioned, trying to see the relevance.

"I know that I'm right, Mr Jones".

She snapped.

"DI Jones".

He corrected.

"What you should be questioning is why the Platt's kicked her out. They were happy to accommodate her for months. Then this happens and she's out on the curb. I bet you, they'll know what she's up to. Nothing gets by them".

Cathy finished, raising from her seat to leave, taking her stale coffee with her.

The detective journeyed back to his car. Taking a moment before fitting the seat belt, considering the new information, as minimal as it may have been. He pulled the burner from his pocket. Staring at it with focus and intent. The entryway to the hotel caught his attention as the door swung open. Esther stepped out into the cold, pulling the zip of her winter coat up to the edge of her white scarf. DI Jones watched in awe as he realised the coat she wore was the same one that he stole the phone from.

Of course, it is.

He thought to himself, styling a cocky smirk. He switched off the engine and waited for her to reach the roads edge before exiting the car to follow her. It had been a relatively bright morning, slowly darkening as it clouded with a gradually easing fog. Jones hid beneath the crevasses of liquid smoke, aided by the weather's unpredictability. Far enough to evade detection yet close enough to maintain a watchful stalk. Or so he thought. He lacked the knowledge of Esther's cautionary self-preservation, increasing in its perceptive paranoia. She, unaware that the predator was the likes of DI Jones that morning, feared her unwarranted shadow was that of the beast. Preying on her as she walked into open season.

When Esther reached Troy's door, she tried the handle. Locked, she knocked to no answer. She rang Troy, leaving text messages that stressed her desperation to enter. When he finally answered, she rushed inside, pushing him out of the way before slamming the door shut to lock it.

"Are all your windows and doors shut and locked?"

She panicked, steamrolling into the house to check for herself.

"Woah, what's, what are you doing? What's going on?"

Troy replied, waking up more rapidly so. Esther had stoked the fire to boil his adrenaline from his lazy lay-in state.

"I, I have no fucking clue".

She ranted, frantically searching for ways that the stalker could get into the house.

"I thought it was gone, I didn't, I just didn't think it would follow me. I wasn't even sure if it was real".

Cried Esther, making no sense.

"What? Who's following you?"

Troy asked, grabbing a hold of Esther's shoulders to steady her, calm her, control her. She closed her eyes and breathed in deep to release a fear-stricken sob.

"I'm next."

She spoke, wobbly. Troy, drawn speechless, questioned her tirade with a sympathetic look that begged for her to elaborate more clearly.

"It's real Troy. Teddy Toddy. The warning. It's real and it came to my window last night".

Esther eventually admitted.

"What… what is it?"

He didn't want to ask. She pulled herself from his grip, stepped slowly to face the front door. A door built by wood, protected by a key and a chained latch. A door that consequently would have proved no match. Her teeth chattered as her lower jaw quivered. Mucus streamed from her nostrils onto her upper lip as she breathed.

"A monster".

Chapter 33

A mysterious fog found its way to The Tavern. The building stood proud and still within the travelling vapour, thinning as the Sunday morning drew late. Roy hadn't slept. Barely closed his eyes, not even a wink. Unlike Violet, who had turned in early. Soon after clearing up, she was dressed for bed, tucked in for the night. Unaware that Luke had ended up staying over.

"Morning, love. I didn't hear you come in last night".
Violet greeted Roy as she scrapped her slippers across the vinyl, searching for the kettle in her newly awakened daze. He sat heavily by the kitchen table on one of the four foldable pine chairs. His veiny hands hugging a piping hot sugared tea with a splash of milk.
"Oh, wow. Sweetheart, are you not well? You look awful".
She observed, turning to face her husband after receiving no initial reply. Roy hadn't acknowledged her presence, he stared blankly into space. Not realising that the cup he held was beginning to burn his hands.
"Roy?"
Violet asked carefully, focusing on his demeanour before gently touching his forearm. Roy jumped slightly in his chair, startled. Alerted not only by his wife, but by the burning sensation of his fingers.
"Sorry love".
He apologised, rubbing his hands to self sooth. Violet took a seat next to him, cupping his burdened face into her comforting palm.
"Talk to me".
She whispered. Roy took hold of her hand and placed it amongst his lips.
"If I tell you, you won't believe me".

He replied. Roy scrambled around for a more delicate method of informing his dear wife. When it came down to it, he just had to rip the band-aid off.

"I have to show you something".

He released her hand and reached for the phone in his pocket. Luke had sent the photo to both Malcom and Roy when they returned to The Tavern. It showed an incomprehensible image of a mammal resembling that of a human's physical structure. Violet snatched the phone from him, zooming in on the creature. She slowly shook her head from side to side as her eyebrows lifted and cheeks tightened.

"I don't understand".

Violet quietly spoke, looking to Roy for answers.

"I think that's what killed Dana, Vi. And what's properly killed George too".

Luke had been up for hours. He'd managed to gain a glimpse of sleep here and there but nothing substantial. Malcom fortuitously slept well. Unconsciousness induced by the opened bottle of port left unattended behind the bar. A portion he selfishly hogged, alone in the witching hour as his family and boyfriend lay in their beds upstairs. Its stench stained his breath as he slowly awakened beside Luke.

"I've never heard you snore like that".

Luke groaned at the sight of his clumsy partner rising from the sheets. Malcom rubbed his temple aggressively as though trying to push the migraine away.

"I don't snore".

He protested in a strop.

"No, normally you don't. But you don't *normally* polish off a bottle of port, do you?"

Luke judged. Agitated by Malcom's behaviour.

Malcom chose not to indulge, brushing off Luke's snide remark and heading straight into the family bathroom. Luke excused himself and entered the kitchen to find Violet holding Roy's phone with dread painted upon her expression. He remained still, unsure as to whether he should enter or leave. Speechless and observant, awkward, and uncomfortable. That was until Roy actioned a nod, permitting Luke's presence.

"Luke took the photo. So that I could drive away".

He informed Violet.

"I'll put the kettle on. Take a seat, mate. Do you want a brew?"

Asked Roy, politely.

"Just a black coffee for me, please, Roy. Thanks".

Replied Luke. They sat quietly at the kitchen table, in a speechless state of shock. Unable to break the trance, their minds collectively waiting for an interruption, aiding cognitive thinking. Eve and Jason entered the room together, with Ellis perched upon his mother's left hip as her arms wrapped around him. Engulfed by the atmospheric foreboding, the couple paused in their steps.

"What's happened?"

Jason reluctantly asked. The sinking feeling overcame him, instinctively predicting that perhaps another life had been taken. Violet, while still holding Roy's phone, the picture on the screen, turned to her husband. They each shared a look to reinforce their alliance, in agreement that Eve and Jason should also know the truth.

Roy took out two more mugs from the cupboard. The only comfort that he could think to provide was sourced from the contents of a cup of tea. He offered his seat to Eve and Ellis as Jason took the last remaining chair.

"What do we do?"

Jason stressed, scraping his fingers across his chest. Trying to stroke his aggressively beating heart. Roy opened his lips to speak, when Eve cut him off, taking the words for herself.

"We catch it".

She answered firmly.

"If we show this picture to everyone, just by itself, were going to have a mob of angry, crazed villagers running around on the hunt. People might get hurt; lives might get ruined. So, I say, we catch it".

She confirmed confidently, reading the room for a reaction.

"Then what?"

Malcom chimed in, entering the kitchen. Styling a dressing gown tied at the waist, drying his hair with the towel in hand. They all looked to Eve, seeking a second step to her dangerous idea.

"Say, we catch it. Do we kill it? Do we call someone? Who would we even call?"

Luke added, siding with Malcom.

"What about the animal control people? Surely, they'll know what it is".

Suggested Violet, lacking in confidence.

"Yeah, there you go. Violet, we could be doing that while the lads build a strong trap. I have to watch Ellis anyway so I'll help you find somewhere that's relatively local who can handle aggressive and dangerous animals".

Eve directed, delegating tasks.

"Lads, do you think you could build something strong? Like 'keep a bear contained' strong?"

She asked, hoping that the answer would be yes, but Roy seemed apprehensive.

"Wouldn't it just break through? Even if we got some strong metal, where would we get a huge cage's worth of it?"

Interrogated Luke, sharing Roy's concern of the ridiculous idea. Violet suddenly rose from her chair in excitement, as a eureka moment enlightened her.

"You won't need to!"

She exclaimed.

"We could use the bomb shelter".

The Tavern held strong during World War Two. Roy's Grandparents built a bomb shelter underneath the beer garden. When the war ended, the trap door was covered with dirt. Once the business became Roy's, he filled out the outdoor seating area with decorative pebbles.

"You're right, love. That could work".

Realised Roy, taking a sip from his cooling tea.

"Would the lock still hold?"

Asked Malcom, trying to seek out holes.

"No, probably not but we could put some of the barrels from the cellar on top of the door, that ought to keep it in".

Roy added, contributing to the plan.

Jason's phone vibrated in his hoodie's pocket. Distracted, he read the incoming text to find it was sent by Troy. He excused himself from the discussion taking place in the kitchen, to make a private call from the bedroom that he and his wife temporarily resided in.

Jason made his pre-existing knowledge on the matter clear over the phone, proof of the evidentiary image obtained, was revealed.

"There's a fucking photo of it?"

Troy gasped, as Esther questioned the goings on in the background of the call, snatching the phone from his grasp.

"Is that true, Jason?

She begged.

"Yeah, Roy and Malcom were dropping off Luke last night."

He began.

"Who's Luke?"

Interrupted Esther.

"Some guy who's here for Malcom, I don't know. Just listen, OK? They pulled up in the car park at the hotel. Just as Luke was about to get out, they saw this massive animal thing holding onto the side of the building. So, they took a picture. The flashlight must have spooked it because it apparently fucked off in a hurry".

He finished. Esther breathed heavily down the line. Had it not been for that photo, she quite possibly would have been killed.

"Did you see it, too?"

Jason asked, concerned.

The call felt soundless for a few moments until Esther decided to hang up. She divulged in relief from the knowledge that others saw what she saw. Her mind hadn't yet untangled, but instead wove truth. Presentation of conclusive evidence delivered alleviation. And yet, she still lacked faith in her own reality.

Chapter 34

Ivy's day started with the noise polluting slam of her front door. Aunt Cathy once again had invited herself inside, causing Ivy to consider the confiscation of her key.
For fucks sake.
She thought to herself, as her aunt called to her from the next room.
"I've just been to pick up some bits and bobs".
Cathy spoke, with overspilled 'bags for life' in hand.
"You needn't bother, don't be spending your money on me".
Ivy called back, as she apprehensively removed herself from the cosy confines of her bed. Undressing from her pyjamas in order to re-dress into her outdoor clothing.
"I haven't, you owe me thirty-six, fifty".
She replied. Ivy paused to roll her eyes as her grey denim skirt pulled midway towards her waist.
"OK, I'm just getting dressed. I'll be right out".

Beneath her skirt, Ivy styled a pair of thick black, opaque tights. Along with cider orange, cotton socks to match a softly striped mustard and chocolate woolly jumper. Not before quickly applying a layer of deodorant and brushing her teeth after a flannel wash to the face and underarms. Her hair hadn't much need for great efforts of styling, with it being a pixie cut, it was rather manageable. She would typically brush it and lightly coat a holding spray to keep it neat and presentable. Though that day, she simply could not be bothered.
Entering the kitchen, Ivy found piles of groceries placed upon the countertops that she otherwise wouldn't have purchased for herself, had she carried out the shopping. The indebtedness provoked consternation as Ivy came up short.

"I haven't been paid yet. I was just going to get some basics to keep me going while the end of the month. You know, bread, eggs, milk. Maybe a couple cans of beans but that was it, really".

She explained with a regretful tone.

"Oh, it's OK don't worry about it, love".

Cathy consoled.

"I should have asked first anyway".

She added.

"Thank you, though. It was nice of you to go out of your way".

Ivy lied, annoyed by the obligation her aunt intentionally brought to her doorstep. Cathy delighted in her efforts being appreciated, hoping that her niece would feel indebted.

"How about we have some of these strawberry Pop Tarts and a nice cup of coffee? I got you the hazelnut flavour. It's instant, mind. So, I don't know how it'll taste".

Blurted Cathy, emptying the bags on to the counter, filing away the items into places that she decided they should go. Ivy watched as her aunt irrationally invaded her kitchen and its contents, contemplating her next move.

"I'm sorry but I won't have time. I have to call work this morning to discuss when I'm next in. That's if they haven't already replaced me. Plus, I've got some errands to run and stuff".

Ivy declined deliberately.

"Which reminds me, could you pass me your copy of the key? With everything that's going on, I'm going to get the locks changed. I just think it will be safer, considering George had a key and, well, you know".

She continued carefully. Caught off guard, Cathy reluctantly slipped the key from her jean pocket and passed it over into her niece's eagerly outreached hand.

"I'll be off then, sweetheart".

Cathy spoke, awkwardly. Slowly edging toward the front door, waiting for Ivy to stop her in her tracks.

"OK, then. Love you, Aunt Cathy. Thanks again".

Ivy replied, planting a goodbye kiss on her aunt's frowning cheek before closing the door behind her.

With her back to the door, Ivy listened out for the sound of Cathy's footsteps gradually declining as she descended down the stairs to exit the building. The tension released. An atmospheric clarity aired the room from the pressure to withhold her true intentions for the day ahead. But first, she was to clear away the mountain of branded goods.

"Hi, it's Ivy. I'm sure you think that avoiding my calls will make me drop this shit, but it won't. If you don't pick up or call me back, I'm coming over".

She stated, leaving a message on Esther's voicemail. She leaned on the edge of her un-made bed, hazelnut coffee in hand as she re-dialled to call, over and over. Her impatience boiled like a gas hob kettle, on the verge of an excessive screech. Ivy waited for just a few minutes, gifting Esther time to listen to the message and hopefully respond.

"Don't come over".

Esther greeted, miraculously answering the following attempt Ivy made to make contact.

"You can't push me out of this, I won't let you".

Ivy pressed, having lost her temper by that point.

"I'm not, I, It's not that".

Esther said, in an unsettling cry.

"It's real…".

She started, as a voice raised in the background, cutting her off. A hushed yell to control what she would reveal.

"What the fuck are you doing, you can't just go around telling everybody".

The voice barked.

"Who is that?"

Questioned Ivy, persistent to get to the bottom of Esther's unpredictability.

"Is that Troy?"

She badgered desperately. Rustling volumed as though the phone had been snatched from Esther's grip, it continued as faint comments were released during the scuffle.

"She's George's girlfriend".

"I don't give a shit".

The call dropped. Ivy once again was left in the dark.

The insipid kitchen chair blocked her stride as she paced back and forth. Ivy slammed her foot into the deserving chair, leaving a dent. Damaging the flimsy wall that it was theatrically plunged into.

"Fuck!"

She groaned, to an audience of furniture and utensils. Snatching her coat from the hook and leaving the flat, Ivy stormed through an unforgiving fog to the hotel. Carrying upon her back the reckoning to that of malcontent. The streets stood empty as though plagued by an eery secret. Shadows lurked behind each turn, retreating as the sun reared its lazed forefront. It disintegrated foggy smoke into a light humidity that hurt nothing more than the texture of Ivy's once soft hair. Once reaching her destination, she climbed the stairwell leading to her desired floor like that of an armed soldier. Esther's door was knocked aggressively to no prevail. The raucous that Ivy caused in her need for attention and involvement, lead to the staff having to unwillingly intervene, requesting that she vacate the premises. Threatened with the involvement of authoritative force. It was the final straw for Ivy. She'd tried time and time again to accommodate Esther, only to be pushed further away with each effort. Left with no other choice, Ivy made a call to Detective Inspector Michael Jones.

Jones had been inappropriately lurking outside of Troy's mother's home. Circling the premises for access to the two's conversation, hoping for an open window. Displaying behaviour comparable to that of a goblin. Creeping amongst the undead branches of outgrown plant life, lost to the winter's harsh climate. The awakened sunlight pierced through dissipating clouds, causing a lingered fog to rise like the pantomimes opening curtain veil. Introducing act 1, scene 1 of the beasts first puppetry at play.

Dana's back garden was nothing short of dismal. An unlevelled patio of cracked upcycled slabs. Independently glued together by her untrained hand with the use of lumped cement. DI Jones tiptoed across as though mimicking a sneaking cartoon, steadying himself against the brick of the wall. Each step, just as gentle as the last until the weight of his leathery shoe pushed a loose stone out from its crevasse. The scrape of adjusted rock alerted Troy as he stood in the kitchen, having made Esther a cup of hot tea. She sat in the living room, isolated in the box of space in which she'd sought refuge. Feeling like a mouse confined to a hole in the wall as a cat waited her escape. Keeping a keen eye on the window above the sink, Troy backed out of the room slowly to join Esther in the adjacent room. Having warned her of the potential intrusion, the two hid themselves behind the sofa. Barely taking a single breath, Esther took a hold of Troy's hand. They gripped tightly and waited quietly.

Outside, Jones carefully and discretely peered inside to find an empty kitchen. It had gotten to a point where self-awareness reared its sensical head. Already under the Chief's persistent supervision, to

be caught snooping without a warrant would inevitably result in disciplinary action, most likely removal from the case.
What good would it do?
He thought to himself. What could he possibly gain from pressing his ear against a brick wall? The instantaneous nature of his plan became more apparent with each passing moment.

Inside, the two heard footsteps travelling from the back garden through the side passage, out to the front gate. Esther listened intently, realising their error of judgment.
"That's not it, it's not the monster".
She spoke, relieved yet still unsettled.
"Who is it then?"
Asked Troy, rhetorically. Emerging from the sofas edge.
He rushed to the living room window. It's curtains still undrawn. Strolling down the pathway toward the gate was none other than Detective Inspector Michael Jones.
"Arsehole!"
Troy yelled as Jones happily walked away, assuming he'd gone undetected.
"What? Who is it?"
Esther pestered, climbing over the couch to see for herself.
"That fucking nosey bobby".
Ranted Troy.
"What? That DI Jones? Wait... So, *he* was following me?"
Questioned Esther, tripping over her own assumptions.
"Probably".
Troy snapped, indirectly at Esther. She closed her astonished gaping mouth, humiliated by her previous ramblings and theatrics.
"Sorry".
He released, authentically.
"I still believe you".

Jones returned to the hotel, assuming that Esther was unlikely to leave Troy's house. Upon entry to the carpark, he noticed a young woman pacing back and forth outside the main doorway. She appeared visibly agitated as she lit a second cigarette, having just put one out. Curiosity, as always, got the better of him as he approached.
"Excuse me, Miss? I believe we've met".
He greeted, confidently. She turned to reveal her face, confirming that it was in fact, the missing boy's girlfriend, Ivy.
"DI Jones?".

She questioned.

"I've actually just been trying to call you".

Continued Ivy. Jones' eyebrows pulled upwards to try and meet his receding hairline, pleasantly perplexed.

"Oh?".

He exhaled. Jones looked towards the entryway to the hotel, before returning his attention back onto Cathy's niece.

"Let's chat".

He suggested, gesturing for her to join him inside.

Chapter 35

What a calamity. It just doesn't add up, does it? Poor little Esther, losing grip of reality must be somewhat disheartening. Investing far too much trust in the naïve, incapable hands of young Master Troy. What did he know of the alternate realm? Nothing. He knew nothing of his mother's teachings. Perhaps had his attention been more attentive, then our fallen soul wouldn't have seeped through the cracks. Ah, but my friends, he wanted to play 'hero'. Not fully understanding what the role would demand of him. Assuming that he alone was enough to protect Esther. Why, what an egotistical and delusional mistake.

The Tavern opened for business that same Sunday, as it would any other. Business was steady. Filtering of the regulars and the odd family passing through, but nothing unmanageable. The group went about their day as per usual, or so it would have seemed. Roy & Violet worked their shifts, as did Eve while Jason took care of Ellis. Malcom and Luke however, set out to work on the plan. It required an inconspicuous approach, considering the consequences. The severity dawned on Malcom. Incorrect execution of the capture could lead to further lives being lost. It was imperative that every last detail was drawn out, leaving no stone unturned. For the inadequacy could fall on his own shoulders.

Both Malcom and Luke attended their impromptu meeting at the kitchen table with their own notebooks. Pages sprawled along the surface with sketches of the beer garden and the bomb shelter, labelled descriptively to identify the best methods to approach the entrapment.

"Meat might not be enough to lure it".

Luke voiced, concerned.

"I was thinking that too. It most likely prefers the hunt".

Agreed Malcom, leaning over the table with his hands clasping the edge as he reviewed the notes made so far.

"We need live bait".

Luke added, unsure as to what the suggestion would truly imply. The two of course understood without uttering a word that live human bait was far too dangerous.

Animal bait unfortunately wouldn't have been sufficient as they would never come to learn. See, what those imbeciles hadn't yet uncovered was that meat wasn't what the beast ate. Its palate was far more advanced. Too ostentatious for measly flesh. No, a carcase would not suffice.

"What can we use?"

Malcom asked himself aloud, puzzled. He rubbed his eyes aggressively to provoke an idea, as though rubbing a genie lamp for a wish.

"Wait, what if we record this?"

Luke blurted, interrupting Malcom's vacated train of thought, for him to respond with nothing little of a confused expression.

"This. Us talking, for like an hour or something. We leave a recording of a conversation playing in the shelter. Make it think there's people down there. As well as using meat, we just leave some of our unwashed clothes, it'll smell like people are down there".

He explained excitedly. Malcom's focus shifted to meet Lukes's anticipation.

"That might actually work".

Meanwhile, downstairs had quietened down. The lunch time rush had passed by, and the team were clearing up. Ready for the evening folk to come in, metaphorically kick their feet up for the day after a long week and drink their woes away.

Roy had a lot on his mind. Bless his little cotton socks. Although his wife shared his burdens. She too felt the crushing weight of responsibility for young Eve, Jason, and teeny tiny Ellis. Alongside her duty as a mother to her newly outed son. How was she going to protect him? Defend him from the monsters in this rotating rock. The people who deem him inhuman, call him unnatural. Treat him as a sinner and a cursed soul for his irredeemable acts of incorrect lustful urges. Sure, he was safe under their roof. Perhaps she could keep him safe within the confines of the village, but Malcom hadn't maintained his residency in Aviary Avenue. He was out there, in the world. A target for the hate of those with self-appointed moral justice. She knew what a reputation could do to a woman who 'lacked character'. The challenges it bore. The fetishising, the masculine associations and assumptions. But what of that for a man? She would consider. Would he lose the respect of his co-workers? Would he be abused in the middle of the street?

Roy too, had his own concerns. Albeit stemmed from a different root. He had always held an authoritative role within the village, as did his father and grandfather before him. The Tavern held history. It was a place of togetherness and community. Ownership of the establishment inherited an unspoken place of hierarchy, right by the very top branch. On the odd occasion, an individual or two dared to disrespect him, but it was not common practice. And doing so would have its rippling effects. Violet felt that Roy's attitude regarding Malcom was from a place of privilege. Not fully comprehending the severity of abuse that their son would be susceptible to. Having been raised in an unforgiving household herself, thanks to her boisterous stepfather, she knew how it was to be rendered powerless. It was an experience that Violet never wanted for her only son.

Roy on the other hand worried about his wife's recent performances. Identifying that she was exhibiting the attitude of intolerance herself when in fact her behaviour should perhaps represent unwavering support instead, regardless of what others may have thought. Unrelatedly, he also worried that he wasn't enough for Eve, Jason, and Ellis. That there was a chance they were better off with Mr & Mrs Platt. The fear subdued his mind, and almost his body. The inadequacy peeked once more, as it had for days. But there was work to be done, customers to serve, tables to clean, and shelves to stock. Forcibly repressing the developing depression and dread, he soldiered on with the day ahead.

'Soldiering on' was more so a challenge to Jason than he'd ever anticipated. Ellis napped in his car seat after a hefty breakfast of smashed banana, peanut butter, and a bottle of milk. Drooling in his deep slumber, as Jason drew a smile. He took a baby wipe from its wrapper and cleaned the dribble from his son's cheek.

He still resented his mother-in-law for how she handled Ellis's birth. Mrs Platt strictly forbade Jason from the delivery room as she believed childbirth is a sacred event, only welcome to women. He'd fought tooth and nail with her but inevitably she won the dispute. Poor Jason never got to witness the birth of his only child. A matter he would always regret, and an act on Mrs Platts part that he would never forgive. Having always wanted his own family, meeting Eve was nothing short of fate for him. Regardless of his age, he wanted to be a family man. Just like his father. Jason was raised in a relatively big family, with two older sisters and a younger brother. All of which became closer, following his mother's passing. He understood the importance of standing by those that you love, no matter what. It didn't matter to him, how many difficulties the Platt's threw his way. He would put Eve first regardless. And when she bore him a child, his dedication only grew stronger. The recent events contradicted this strength, rendering him mentally and physically fragile. Unaware of a way out from the intrusive thoughts and never-ending discomfort that followed his every move.

Mrs Platt had her own plans that day, that unfortunately for Jason, would include him. She loved to bake; you see. Every year the church held an Easter competition for the best spring themed cake. Submissions were expected to be three tier and contain fresh fruit. That year, she'd been preparing to structure a triple tiered cheesecake. Consisting of three alternate flavours of dark chocolate, raspberry, and vanilla ice-cream. Only the mechanics of assembling the complicated baked good to a greater height was lost on her. Fortunately, that hadn't deterred her. She sought thrill in the challenge. Her idea was to form the base with crushed, dry, chocolate biscuits and coconut butter. To then move on to make three separate batches of cream cheese filling for each of the selected flavours, having used real raspberries for the middle section. Once all of the mixtures were prepared, she lined her baking dish with greaseproof paper and filled it with the coconut chocolate biscuit crumbs. Pressing it down, until firm, before pouring the first portion of cream cheese. Starting with the vanilla ice-cream flavour. Topped it with the fresh raspberry filling to then finish off with the dark chocolate mix. She used all the remaining coconut chocolate biscuit crumbs to coat the cake in its entirety. Garnishing with the final touch of two neatly piped swirls of vanilla cheesecake filling, as a small handful of picked raspberries rested beside them. With the cream aspect of the cheesecake being so outstandingly tall, she felt it best to set her completed masterpiece in the freezer, to assure its stability.

Normally Mrs Platt would have already planned out her entry and would start prepping the prototypes around February. Alternatively, she found a beneficiary motive to start early that year. Having been up since 05:30am to bake, her cake was ready for travel by that afternoon.

Eve had been working all day. Not well, might I add. Distracted from the current events of the time, she'd been making mistakes throughout her shift. From forgetting to wipe tables and charging the wrong prices for the wrong products, to ignoring tasks and mishearing instructions. All that she could think of was the discussion from earlier. Apprehensive over her impulsive suggestion having seriously considered the consequences.

Lost in thought, she recalled the day that her and Jason were wed. Her pregnancy was beginning to show, so a fitted dress was off the table. Her mother would have been furious if Eve wore a gown that advertised her premarital relations. A white dress was still expected if you would believe. Mrs Platt aimed to take plenty of photographic proof that her grandson was in fact, not a bastard. Right before the ceremony, the two waited in separate rooms while guests seated themselves. Chatting over text, excitedly nerve wrecked.

"Your mum's just bit my head off over my wonky bow tie".

A message had displayed upon Eve's phone.

"She's your mum now".

Eve mocked in response. Regrettably so, as three dots would appear and disappear on the screen. She waited awkwardly for acceptance of her ill-timed humour.

"You're worth it".

His reply read.

She'd not chosen her dress, of course. Mrs Platt found a suitable empire gown with a lace trim. Though Eve would have preferred a mermaid fit, had her mother found her figure more appropriate.

"Eve?"

A shrill voice called, bombarding her comforting daydream. She stood leaning on the bar with a damp and soapy cloth in hand.

"Mum?"

She gasped.

"What are you doing here?"

She asked. Mrs Platt had paid her daughter an unwarranted visit as a rouse. She placed the packaged cake onto the bars end, not yet revealing its contents. Her sights, funnily enough, weren't on her offspring that afternoon. But instead, were on Mrs Richard.

Chapter 36

Being a creature of habit, Ivy stuck with the same pixie cut that she'd obtained on the fateful day that she'd met George. In fact, Ivy had actually forgotten all about him and their brief encounter by the time she returned to her flat later that same evening. Having stopped by the newsagents on her journey home to pick up a notebook and pen for her interview preparation. She became distracted by Earl, the owner. Earl was an Aviary Avenue honouree, born and bred. A local face that we all knew and loved. He was as surprised as any at the vision that was Ivy's bold new look.

"Bloody hell, love. Where's your hair gone?"

He playfully mocked. Sitting atop his backless stool behind the till. A till classically made with protruding buttons below a slim and narrow screen, resembling that of a calculator. He would 'people watch' his customers as they sifted in and out of the store. Entertained by his farming magazine subscription and the maddening vocals, heavy in bass by incorrect proximity between the microphone and its host on the radio.

"Give over, you old git".

She jokingly snarked back. They'd chat and catch up, with Earl updating her on how the family were and Ivy doing the same, mostly about her aunt and the business.

"Ah, so that's why you're wanting this job then".

Earl said, pointing out the obvious.

"Because I recon you'll miss being outside, you know. You're going to hate being stuck inside all day".

He observed, rather astutely.

"Why do you think that is? You're inside all day and you don't seem to mind".

Replied Ivy, defensive over her application.

"Well, it's like you said, love. I'm an old git. My knees aren't what they used to be, so I'd rather be in here where it's warm and I can sit down when I like".

He pointed out. The conversation caused Ivy to stay much longer than she'd intended. Without wanting to seem rude, she waited for the topic to lag. Taking advantage of the opportunity to leave, she got started on prepping for the next day.

Ivy didn't get home until gone 17:30pm. Upon entering her front door, she closed it behind her and leaned on it for a stabling comfort. Throwing her bag onto the ground beside her, she unbuttoned her jacket to let it fall from her shoulders. In doing so, she heard a crinkle from the right-hand pocket. Unsure as to what it must have been, she inspected the contents to find the folded paper pastry packaging with "Hi, I'm George" written on it, along with his phone number. Ivy had been so pre-occupied that upon finding the note, she remembered the crack on her screen. She played around with the device for a while to deduce that no further damage spread across the phone. Soon to be out of work, and unsure of the outcome that the interview would bring, Ivy felt motivated by the possibility of having the damage repaired for a reduced cost. And so, she called George.

"Hi, is this George?"

Asked Ivy, ominously.

"Speaking, how can I help?"

He responded gleefully, knowing exactly who the caller was by the sound of her voice.

"We met earlier, I'm the girl whose phone you smashed. You said to call, to get it sorted. Well, this is me calling".

She stated bluntly.

"Oh, the blonde?"

George flirted, excited to be speaking with her again.

"Can you get it fixed or not".

Ivy spat, having little patience for the playboy types.

"Sure, meet me at the repair shop in town, do you know it?"

He answered, slightly embarrassed that his flirty comment was so abruptly shot down. They met in town the following morning, relatively early by Ivy's instruction. The store wasn't even set to open until 09:00am, but since George was friends with the manager, they were let in beforehand. While the repairman took Ivy's phone into the back, her and George waited on the shop floor, browsing for phone cases and other such nick knacks.

"I'm sorry about this".

George apologised shyly. He'd picked up on her agitated state, as though she was in a rush to leave and be done with the whole situation.

"It's fine, I'm just a bit on edge today that's all".

She jittered, tapping her foot repeatedly.

"How come?"

He enquired cautiously.

"I have a job interview at noon. I've always worked in my family business, so I just don't really know what to expect".

She answered speedily, her speech fuelled by nervousness. He falsely displayed a look of dread, pausing in place to focus her attention on him.

"Well, they sit you down on an individual chair opposite from their desk".

He began, as Ivy leaned in, intrigued.

"And, if you answer one single question wrong, they pull a lever, and you fall down a pit. Right into a swamp of starved baboons".

He finished, with an impish smile. Ivy allowed herself a laugh, if just a slight one.

"So, worst case scenario then, got it".

She mocked. After the phone was back to normal, Ivy took out her purse to pay, only to be assured that the cost was taken care of. She thanked both the repairman and George for their assistance and head out to leave the store. As she opened the door to exit, George instinctively followed suit, calling after her. In that moment he'd miraculously worked up the courage to ask if she'd like to join him for a coffee or perhaps a breakfast bap from the local greasy spoon. To which her answer was, yes.

Luckily, her interview didn't end up with her falling into the hungry mouths of starved baboons. Instead, when vacating the manager's office, she bumped into none other than the 'baboon boy' himself. Both Ivy and George locked eyes as soon as they clocked one another, equally astonished at the sight.

"Wait, you were on about this place?"

George questioned, pleasantly surprised. She hadn't elaborated on the topic of her interview, during their morning coffee together as she was afraid to jinx her chances.

"Are you just everywhere now, then?"

She joked, hiding just how happy she was to see him again.

"That's it, flower. Can't get rid of me now".

He replied, expressing a cheeky wink as he got back to work.

Ivy was successful in her application and was offered the job that same evening. As the months passed by, the two became close friends. Equally afraid to confess their feelings to one and other. That is until the Christmas holidays came around. Every year the village holds a local gala for the residents to come together and watch the Christmas lights switch on. Different businesses set up their individual stalls to sell snacks, drinks, and novelties into the night. Alternatively, George had a more irresponsibly interesting idea. He'd shown Ivy the ropes in terms of the job role. Including ways to break the rules without getting apprehended. Such as, the location of the managers key for their personal toilet, so that she wouldn't have to use the public stalls. Places to hide the sale items, so that they're not all sold out by the end of their shifts. And lastly, how to gain access to the rooftop for smoke breaks. Avoiding having to smoke in the back alley by the bins.

On the night of the lights switch on, George set up two camping chairs with a pack of plastic party cups and a litre sized bottle of pop. The two stopped by the fish & chip stall and carried their food to the roof top. Counting down from ten along with the rest of the villagers. The pair peeped down below onto the high-street. George and Ivy watched as everyone chanted, five-four-three-two-one! Reindeers, angels, and stars illuminated each individual streetlamp. A great heartfelt cheer roared across Aviary Avenue. A mighty moment that compelled George to his core, encouraging him to turn towards Ivy, reading a look on her eyes that shared the same desires. He pressed his lips upon hers, taking her cheek into his wintery gloved hand before releasing himself from her kiss. They jumped as a fire work exploded from above, trickling its glowing lights before dissipating into nothing but an immemorable moment in time.
"I love you".
George expressed without regret. She froze, stunned yet thrilled.
"I love you too".

She remembered that moment. Captured in a daze while DI Jones stood by the bar, ordering their coffee's.

Chapter 37

Considering Esther's declining health and the inability to sleep. Troy left her alone to catch up on the rest that she so desperately needed. She slept on the same sofa that they'd hidden behind just a few short hours before. Wrapped in a light blanket that Dana would keep downstairs to remain cosy during the winter months.
Meanwhile Troy engulfed himself in the rabbit hole that is internet forums. Discussing the paranormal activity that he'd experienced, seeking guidance on what the disturbing riddle could have possibly meant. He detailed the tarot reading, posting photographs of the cards dealt, stressing that the unsettling card was not of his mother's collection. The majority of responses consisted of ridicule from disbelief. Claiming that his post was just mere fabrication to gain strangers admiration. Other messages were brief and ineffective paragraphs exampling their own ghostly experiences and tales of horror. As Troy began to give up hope, he noticed finally, one comment that seemed to take his circumstances seriously.
I've read about situations like this before. From what I gather, the first card may have been a kind spirit that reached out, but then it was pulled back to make way for one that's… how should I say, not so nice.
The post read. Upon further inspection, the profiles bio had written below her username, 'Kassie the friendly ghoul researcher'. Her page overspilled with article links and theories about the unknown world of the beyond. This seemed enough for Troy to believe that the reply wasn't disingenuous. He asked Kassie if there was any chance that the first card was dealt by his late mother, as she was the spirit that he was trying to reach. Kassie confirmed that his theory could be possible but warned him of the unsavoury entity that came through instead, as it could have still been lurking. She then asked for any clues regarding its activity, so to identify what kind of spirit Troy

would now be dealing with. He could remember the riddle displayed on the computer as though it was written on the palm of his hand.

The computer wasn't even plugged in, but it turned on and typed a creepy poem thing in the data coding. Teddy Toddy moves in the light. Teddy Toddy is seen in plain sight. No need for the dark, for it to embark. Into the depths of your fear in the night. Have you heard of this riddle before?

Troy revealed honestly. The entire earth coming to a halt as he waited.

Yes.

The response began. His eyes widened as his forehead folded, astonished on the edge of his seat.

It's strange though because that name 'Teddy Toddy' is associated more so with the story of a weird creature. There's a theory that every decade, a body is found completely mauled, as though by a giant bear. Investigations were carried out but nobody fitting the expected description of the killer was ever apprehended. Nobody ever knew what really happened to the victims or who did it. So, the story is that this beast, 'Teddy Toddy' killed them. I've looked into the stories before, but I wasn't able to find out what influenced the name. Maybe the spirit was taunting you, just trying to scare you for its own amusement.

The nail hit the coffin, the second he finished reading her reply. He slammed his laptop closed, accidentally waking Esther. The colour drained from his skin, as his pale lips tremored. Esther, still half asleep, tripped over the blanket to get to Troy's aid.

"What's wrong? Troy? You've gone pale".

She panicked, placing her hands on each cheek, trying to coax him to make eye contact as his vacant stare floated through her.

"Troy, c'mon, tell me".

A few seconds felt like a few minutes to him. He blinked slowly, rehydrating his crusting eyes as he brought himself back to earth. Taking in a deep breath, he released the stench of unbrushed teeth and stale coffee.

"It was mum".

He whispered. Esther tried not to take in the odour and remained close regardless.

"What was your mum, Troy?"

She provoked, rooting for answers.

"The computer. The cards. The message".

He spoke, robotically.

"How do you know? It... it can't have been. It... scared us, it intentionally scared us. Your mum wouldn't do that to you. No, there's no way she would do that".

Reasoned Esther, trying harder to convince herself, more than Troy.

"She would. She did".

He stuttered.

"When mum would try and teach me about this stuff. She would always warn me, be careful because there's some dodgy characters in their world too".

He began to explain.

"There was this one time, we were arguing about this kind of shit, and I didn't believe her. I bought one of those boards as a joke. You know those that people do, with the letters. Anyway, she was furious. Said that it's one thing not to believe her but bringing that into the house was a step too far. So, she got rid of it. Did some ritual or whatever to cleanse its energy from the house".

He babbled, getting to the point of his story. Reluctant to relive the memory that he was about to share.

"She wanted to make sure that I didn't pull a stunt like that again. So, she got a friend of hers to dress up in some scary mask with a costume to hide in the house. We were sat watching TV and her friend upstairs would be making noises, like as though an intruder was in the house. So, obviously with me not knowing that the noises were just her friend, I took a big knife and went up to look around. I checked everywhere and nothing, didn't see anyone or anything. It really got under my skin. Eventually, soon as I let my guard down, the bitch jumps out from a wardrobe. Scared the shit out of me. I almost stabbed her! Anyway, mum came upstairs, looking pretty proud of herself. And she said, do you see how scary unpredictability can be? Don't mess around with things that you don't understand".

He concluded, trying to give Esther context.

"So, we did contact her, and she gave you the answer, but she didn't want you to try and contact her again? That's why she made it scary, to put you off?

She asked curiously.

"Yeah, I think so".

Answered Troy, with an unsure confidence. Still confused, Esther asked what the riddle was supposed to mean. He then re-opened his laptop to show the conversation between himself and Kassie. Since closing the screen, Kassie had sent further information regarding the previous murders. All of which, were the same. Bodily bruising, broken bones, and the distinctive dismembered jawline. Since DI

Jones spared him from the description of Dana's death, Troy wanted to find out for himself, whether or not his mother had been murdered the same way. Though, he felt it was likely.

He stood from his seat, surveying the living room that his mum had lovingly decorated. All of the colours brought in vibrancy and light to her son's world. A space for selfishness and selflessness without guilt or pressure. He let his eyelids drop along with shoulders. Thinking carefully of his mother and the love he held for her.

"Mum, if that was you. Please, give me a sign".

He plead quietly, while Esther watched without judgement. As he spoke, a car door slammed shut from outside, shortly followed by a knock at the door.

Chapter 38

"Mrs Richard, good afternoon".

Mrs Platt forcibly greeted. Violet had been in the stock room, discussing her frustrations over Eve's poor work performance with another member of staff. The morning announcement proved too much for Violet, and so she'd thrown herself into work, focusing intently on each and every task at hand. Projecting that same coping mechanism onto Eve, bewildered by the girl's inability to complete basic jobs, proving herself incapable. Bypassing her as she stood by the bar, Violet instead approached Eve's mother.

"Hello love, I see you're feeling better. And I've told you already, just call me, Violet".

She welcomed, falsely.

"I appreciate the sentiment, Mrs Richard. However, I was not raised to refer to a married man or woman by their forename. I'm perfectly comfortable with the proper title".

Argued Mrs Platt, adamant in her ways.

"That's fine too then, I guess. What can I do for you today?"

Violet apprehensively accepted. Mrs Platt unveiled her masterpiece of a cake, slipping the plastic lid from its base as though untying a corsets lace. It stood tall and unwavering, with biscuit crumbs flaked throughout. Lit lusciously under the bars softly hung lamps as they glowed.

"Oh, my".

Exclaimed Violet.

"Mum, that's amazing".

Added Eve. Mrs Platt concealed her ego, and instead received her compliments as humbly as she was able.

"Thank you, it's just one of my practice cakes. As I plan on winning the Easter Baking Competition this year, it just made sense to begin preparations early. Considering my poor attempt last year".

She explained, self-deprecatingly.

"It's simply un-imaginable for me to consume the cake in its entirety and my husband is monitoring his sugar intake. So, if you'd accept, I'd like to leave it here. Of course, with you and Mr Richard having a 'full house', so to speak".

She finished, directing her attention to Violet.

"Oh, yeah. Thank you, we'd love to take it off your hands. I'll pop it in the kitchen now, would you help me with it, just for a moment?".

Violet replied, gesturing that the two leave Eve to carry on with her work.

"I won't be long, love. Just keep an eye on the bar for me".

She called, walking away into the back. Eve worriedly watched them begin to bond as they left her by herself. When they turned the corner, her phone began to vibrate. Having been stationed at the front of house, she wasn't able to answer. The incoming call identified as Detective Inspector Michael Jones. Once the call stopped, she checked to see if he had left her a voicemail, to which he had.

"Ma'am this is DI Jones. I'm sorry I missed your call earlier. Yes, your flat will be accessible by this Friday coming. As far as I'm aware, the sole ownership of the building has been transferred to your previous landlords next of kin. So, for any further information, you can speak directly to them. If you have any more questions or information regarding the case, please don't hesitate to call".

As Eve's shift came to an end, Jason finished up feeding Ellis and setting him down for a nap so that his wife could enjoy some peace and quiet after work. Upon entering the room, he asked if he could go and visit Troy, with the reason being that he and Esther found more information regarding the monstrous animal from the photograph.

"Ok, yeah, I'll watch Ellis. But while you're there, ask him about our flat. I got a call from that detective. Apparently, they'll be done with it by Friday, and I think Troy might be our new landlord. We need to know what he's planning to do with our home, Jason. He could fucking sell it, for all we know".

Eve panicked quietly, so not to wake the baby.

In the kitchen, Violet set the beautiful cake adequately atop the island. Taking out a little dessert dish and a slicing knife to carve herself a piece. Each layer displayed perfection in symmetry as the sharp metal glided between the flavoured variety of cream cheese. Tiny crunches voiced as it broke the crumbs apart, lightly clinking as they dropped onto the plate. Retrieving a dinner fork, Violet pierced the upper layer of cream as she slid her hand downwards to scoop every glimpse of taste into that single bite sized serving. Widening her mouth upon the fork's entry, she closed her lips, pulling the cutlery from her closed jaw.

"Mm".

She hummed, somewhat erotically.

"That's such a lovely cake, Mrs Platt".

She groaned.

"Yes, dear".

Mrs Platt thanked uncomfortably.

"May I interrupt you for a moment, Mrs Richard".

She rushed, attempting to politely remove the dish from Violet's reach.

"Oh, yeah, sorry".

Blushed Violet, as she cleared the cream from her bottom lip, to then wipe her hands on her apron.

"It wouldn't be right for me to have spoken this candidly in front of my daughter, but this cake is more so to show mine and my husband's gratitude toward you and Mr Richard".

Mrs Platt grinned.

"Being a mother yourself, you know the pressures that are associated with protecting your own. You and Mr Richard not only take care of your own son during this, let's be honest, terrifying time. You've also taken on board our daughter, and her new family".

She started, working her way into the depths of Violets anxiety.

"It's admirable, Mrs Richard. If there is anything that I, or Eve's father can do to assist you and your family. Please, we are but a phone call away".

Mrs Platt concluded, as she exited the kitchen after a job well done. Leaving Violet perplexed by her kindness.

Entering the front of house, she spotted Jason as he was just about to leave. Calling after him, Mrs Platt offered to drive him to his chosen destination under the pretence of concern for his safety. He was happy for the chance to not use up anymore petrol, considering his financial circumstances, so he accepted.

The drive was as uncomfortable as a doctor's waiting room, when there's another patient waiting that happens to be someone you know but don't want to talk to. Her car had been adjusted to accommodate for Mr Platt's disabilities. So, the passenger side felt irregular in comparison to his own car, but he didn't mind. He knew better than to start small talk with his mother-in-law. If she wanted a conversation, she would initiate one. The pair sat in silence, the only noise available being that of passing cars and the vehicles own engine.

Reaching Dana's house, Mrs Platt came to a sudden stop, giving the boy a blunt an abrupt goodbye as he stood from his car seat. Closing the car door as he looked up towards the house in front of him. Jason then turned to wave goodbye, to find that she had already driven away. After a heavy sigh and agitated eyeroll, he made his way to the front door, expressing a thunderous knock.

Earlier, back at the hotel, DI Jones had been waiting for the barista to complete their order. The warmth was humid and thick from overuse of the buildings central heating. Hotels being a place of rest and slumber, the atmospheric softness was nothing short of unusual for a meeting that held a more rigid and slightly chilled tone. Jones placed a steamed cappuccino affront Ivy's person, illustrated with a stencilled coffee bean, sprinkled with hot chocolate powder. He'd ordered the same. A tactic he'd picked up, to falsify the impression of common ground.

"So".

He broke the silence. A simplistic entry for the discussion. He took in his opponent's attire. Her scent hid a musk, one of which is familiar with that of overnight sweats. Her hair had been rushed and brushed, yet not straightened or styled. Her skin bore bare without trace of creams or make-up. She'd had a long night, and a short morning. Prime opportunity for an impatient outburst, Jones knew.

"Esther Petunia".

He grinned, reaching straight for the salt, ready for the wound.

"What's with you too, then. You both bickering over the same lad or something?"

Teased Jones, unprofessionally. Ivy breathed in an arrogant and short-lived laugh.

"Yep, good work detective, you solved the case. Do you want a lollipop?"

She snapped, sipping her coffee.

"If you have one, yeah".

He smirked, taking a confident gulp. He'd played his card too soon, as always. Pushing Ivy to leave prematurely. As she rose from her chair, he leaned back into his.

"You mentioned that you called me, Ivy. Why?"

Asked Jones, far too sure of his negotiation skills. She paused. Closed her eyes and thought. Every fibre of her being told her not to inform him of the burner. Although Esther was causing her nothing but upset, she couldn't help but feel that exposing George's life to the police could prove detrimental to his future, if they were ever to find him. Alas her mind also called for his safety. Logically, involving DI Jones was the right card to play.

"She took his phone".

Ivy voiced. He remained silent, waiting for her to finish her thought.

"She told me last night; she has his phone. If you can get it from her, you might be able to see who he spoke with or met up with last".

She released. Instantaneously anxious over her decision.

"Ok, say she did have his phone. It'll be locked, I'll need the passcode".

DI Jones imitated a self-sympathetic sigh, as though her information deemed useless.

"The code is nine, zero, five".

Ivy revealed to the detective's surprise. Concealing his excitement, he enquired as to why George would pick those specific numbers. Walking towards the exit, she called her answer as she left.

"The date we met".

Ivy vacated the building, leaving Jones to hurriedly retrieve the burner from his pocket. She headed out to the carpark, seating herself on a nearby bench. The fog had completely faded, leaving fine clouds to dilute the suns effortless light. Vomit curdled in the depth of her lower abdomen as guilt overpowered every cognitive function, demanding that she excrete her stomachs contents. She rested her elbows atop her knees, as her head hung from each shoulder. Breathing in the stench of undigested milk from the cappuccino that her body had just ejected. Sitting up to take in the fresh air circling above, Ivy drew enough strength to go back inside and confront once more, the detective on the case. Trapesing vomit onto the welcome mat as she entered, Ivy spotted him with George's phone in his grip.

"You crafty fucker".

She muttered to herself, while returning to her seat. Jones's glance darted upwards, incapable of conjuring an excuse on the spot.

"Any familiar names on their?"

Asked Ivy, in a cocky tone.

"Excuse me?"

Jones answered, lacking in understanding.

"Doubt it, since every one of those contacts are stored under a 'nickname'. You should keep me in the loop, Mr detective. I'm *very* useful".

She bluffed with a defiant confidence. Awaiting acceptance, she watched as Jones tossed the burner onto the table that separated the two. Having snatched the phone, she unlocked it to find the data had been wiped.

"You cleaned it?"

She asked, agitated.

"No, there's nothing even on it, it's useless".

He joked, laughing at his own expense for having invested so much time into what proved to be a dead end. Ivy shot her eyes into his like a bullet.

"Something funny?"

She snapped.

"I'm sure a missing person is just a rusty for you to chase at this point. But he's fucking more than that. He's a son, a brother, a friend, and *my* boyfriend. Somebody who's in danger, someone who needs help".

Her voice raised.

"Adequate help".

She added.

"Stop swinging your dick around, Jones. Do your job".

She took the phone for herself, forcing it into her coat pocket before storming out once again to return home. The next time she sought out Esther, there would be no 'brushing her off'.

Chapter 39

The scrape of leather would creak, creating sounds that one can only recognise as flatulence. Though, Mr Platt lacked the humour to consider it so. He would often lay down a blanket before taking his seat to prevent the intolerable screech. Disappointingly never having succeeded, he would increasingly show a furious scowl to those who expressed awareness of the sound. Mrs Platt knew better than to react. Though, she would often hide the smile she bore to herself.
He had perched upon his lap, the plans for the Neighbourhood Watch Patrol. Including the forms, rotas and all other additional information and ideas noted. His new position granted him access to the volunteers' daily schedules, where they would be and when. Observing the volunteers that were stationed nearby their own premises, he found two villagers names, Maisy Hogarth, and Thomas Victor. Maisy was the local librarian. She had a degree in English Literature and Language, with a free-lance business of tutoring the university students outside of her working hours. Thomas was a customer service representative for the Train Station, with additional care-taking responsibilities for the carpark, seating area and public toilets. Both individuals, were a relatively elderly pair. What they could perform in terms of self defence against a killer, I'll never know. But, they volunteered, showing enthusiasm and promise, so, they were recruited.
"I can watch my own house, thank you".
He spoke aloud to himself, altering their route on the rota. He'd rearranged the location to make it so that the pair wouldn't pass Mr & Mrs Platt's home. It would seem that his ego was far too delicate for external protection.

"How did it go with the bar maid?"

He asked his wife, looking over the back of his reclining chair. Mrs Platt had been clearing away the last remaining mess from her morning bake, ready to make a start on supper.

"I expect we'll be receiving a call from her by tomorrow, dear".

She answered sweetly, humming as she took out vegetables from the fridge.

"Well done, darling".

He congratulated, returning his focus onto the rota's. Suddenly, the landline alerted as an incoming call intruded their peaceful afternoon. Mrs Platt answered to hear Roy's voice, wavering, riddled with nerves, requesting that Mr Platt would discuss the patrol. Cautiously handing the phone over to him, she and her husband became suspicious.

Roy and Violet had much to discuss, but little time to do so. The Tavern turned out to be less busy than anticipated, giving them opportunity to leave the staff to get on with things as they went into the office to chat. Neither knowing where to even start. Violet took the reins, blurting of her disapproval over Luke and his speedy integration into the family.

"I can't keep doing this with you, Vi".

Roy groaned, coating his face in his large, dry hands.

"Protecting our son? Is that what you can't keep doing?"

She clapped back, in hysteria. Roy's hands dropped to his side, as fists began to clench.

"What are we going to do about this trap, Violet. Are we actually doing this? Because honestly, I think it's fucking stupid. There's no way that I'm inviting that thing into our home".

Ranted Roy, changing the subject to calm his upcoming rage. She could see the change in his behaviour, a stance that she hadn't seen in a man since leaving home as a teen. Violet never questioned her husband's integrity in regard to the potential of raising a hand to her. That being said, she decided to accept the change in topic as Violet had no intention of finding out if she were wrong.

"No".

Answering, nervously.

"I don't think we should either".

She lied. Roy calmed himself, relieved of the thought of them being on the same page for once.

"Ok, so, it's off. I'll call Mr P, see if we can prevent the patrol from heading out. Might as well put fucking targets on their backs if not".

Roy spat as he picked up the phone, giving Violet her queue to leave.

The bedroom clearly hadn't been cleaned or properly tidied since they moved in. Jason had used up any energy he had to focus on making sure Ellis was clean, fed and rested. Otherwise, he would usually lay flat on the bed, his eyes locked open, focused on nothing but his haunting nightmares. Eve had picked up on his standoffish persona but hadn't pestered him on the matter. Afraid that forcing him to open up would only push him away. She would wait patiently for him to approach her, which she was confident would happen when he was good and ready to do so. While Jason was out, Eve took on the bedroom herself, putting away any possessions left lying around and throwing out garbage that hadn't yet been discarded. Remaining in the work uniform, she filled the ensuite sink with soapy water. Using an unused face cloth, she dunked it into the contents of the sink and swiped the soapy cloth across every dusty surface. Including that of the windowsill, cabinets, drawers, and bathroom tiling. Once complete, she left the bathroom door open so that she could take a quick bath, while still being able to see that Ellis continued to sleep safely.

When finally ready to sit in bed, dressed in fresh pyjamas and wrapped in the duvet with the television on a low volume, an insipid knock bounced at the door.
"Hello, love. It's just me. Are you free for a quick chat?"
Violet called, opening the door. Too tired to get up, Eve stayed seated.
"What's up?"
She answered, patting the foot of the bed to offer Violet a seat.
"Roy and I have discussed it, and we just don't believe it would be safe to try and trap that weird animal thing, love. That's not to say that I don't see where you're coming from, trust me, I really do. But we have to think about what would happen if anything went wrong. You know? Like it's already killed someone, and…"
Violet trailed off, forgetting for a moment that Eve and Dana were close. Giving herself pause, she thought carefully of what to say next.
"I can't imagine how this must have affected you, sweetheart. But I know that Jason seems to think that it's his responsibility to fix it all".
She candidly pointed out. Going on to explain how none of the events were either one of their faults. The only responsibility they had was to remain safe and to protect Ellis.

"But this will protect Ellis, Vi. If we can stop it, it won't hurt anybody else".

Eve naively protested.

"The answer is no. I'm sorry, but this isn't up for debate. This is our home, Eve. This is our decision".

Finished Violet. Leaving the discussion to return downstairs, she found that Roy was visibly disheartened from his unsuccessful call.

Eve was sorely disappointed by Violets abrupt cancellation of the plan. Angry, more than anything else, actually. Familiar with abiding by another's ruling thumb, she'd learn other ways to fulfil her desires. Roy and Violet were naïve with power. Presumptuously so, assuming that their disinvolvement meant that the plan would no longer commence. Not yet understanding what Eve was truly capable of.

Chapter 40

What good is it? All know the truth, yet they won't do anything about it. Is this cowardice or is this logic? How *do* we determine bravery?

Listen to me, question after question as though your answers mattered. Fate cannot be halted, regardless of ones hope and faith. Take me for instance. I thrived, in a sense, beforehand that is. Self-awareness isn't all that it's cracked up to be. I sometimes wonder, had I never known, had I never found the truth, would my ignorance still be bliss? Or would my delusion instead have debilitated others?

Oh! Of course, where oh where are my manners? I'd forgotten all about our little leading lady, Esther Petunia. Now, you may be wondering, how much does she really know? Well, friends, she knows a lot more than you'd think.

Jason was greeted by a chain dangling between the door and its frame as Troy peeped between the gap.
"It's just Jason".
He revealed to Esther, unhooking the chain from its latch. When all were seated within the living room, the conversation never lagged, not even for a moment. Each participant spiralling with information, theories, and fears. Each updating the next with what they knew so far, trying to make sense of the whole issue. That is until Jason informed them of the plan. Having not yet heard of its cancellation, he let Troy and Esther in on the intention to trap the beast within the bomb shelter in beer garden.

"Yes!"
Troy exclaimed.
"That'll work. Let's catch the fucker!"

He yelled excitedly, swinging his fists into the air and its invisible punching bag. Esther, however, was more reluctant. She'd been in the bomb shelter before. A dark and gloomy space, home to creepy crawlies and rodent droppings. Cobwebs that'd been there for so long, even they had gathered dust. Unpleasant both by sight and smell as the musk of dirt and unfiltered air would clog her lungs. Shelves, ones filled with rations, would instead be stocked with out-dated tins of tangy fruit and undesirable meat stews. She expressed her concern of the shelters inefficiency for capture, arguing that there simply wouldn't be enough room for it, since it was such a small space. It wouldn't work and therefore endanger all the lives of those involved.

"Well, why don't we go see for ourselves?"

Troy argued, disbelieving Esther's viewpoint.

"If we mess around with the trap door now, everyone's going to see. The whole point is to do it discretely".

Jason protested quickly, trying to calm Troy's childish enthusiasm. Esther allowed herself the relief as she observed Troy's rational self, returning. Collectively deciding to discuss the matter further with the rest of those involved, the three set off out to meet the others at The Tavern. See, what Troy and Jason hadn't known was that the bomb shelter already possessed an occupant.

Esther's worst nightmare came true the day that Ivy reported George as missing. A reality that she'd been trying too desperately to deny to herself, disturbed Esther to her very core. Her close friend was likely dead, and she'd been rendered powerless. A feeling fuelled by fury after her confrontation with Mr and Mrs Platt that same evening. When retiring to her room, she'd begun to pack. The tears shed, moistened her clothing as she irrationally folded each piece poorly, to then place wonkily in the suitcase. As she packed, Esther heard an unfamiliar cluster of noises sound from outside of Eve's bedroom window. As though something large was clumsily climbing up towards it. She stood, staying still, silently. Anticipation colliding with apprehension, as she moved herself closer to the window. All of a sudden, a hand reached upwards and knocked three times on the glass. Esther didn't respond. Instead, she waited, anxious to know just who the stranger must be.

"Essie?"

The voice called, in a poor attempt of a whisper. She recognised that voice, that nickname, and now, that hand.

"George?"

She spoke, rushing to open the window to find him dangling alongside the walls brick, clinging for dear life onto the drainpipe.

"Shh!"

George hushed, as she helped him climb inside before closing the window behind him. Esther threw herself into his embrace, holding tightly. A moment she'd almost convinced herself would never happen. George pulled away slightly to face her, still holding onto Esther's waist as her hands rested atop each shoulder.

"What happened?"

She whispered, trying to read the sorrow that his eyes failed to hide. Pulling away completely, George turned to drag the curtains to a close.

"You wouldn't believe me".

He sighed, disheartened. Esther took his arm into her grasp, forcing him to meet her gaze.

"Dana was killed. In broad daylight, George. I promise, whatever it is, I'll believe you".

She begged, as he tore his arm away from her grip. Closing his eyes to shake his head, he pulled himself together.

"That's not why I'm here, Essie".

He replied, redirecting the conversation.

"I just came to tell you where I'm hiding, just so you know in case you or Ivy need me. I'm going to go see her next before I head back. I wanted to ask a favour while I'm here, though".

He clarified.

"Remember when we got pissed that time, and you tripped over that metal thing that turned out the be a door handle for a bomb shelter underneath the beer garden?"

Asked George, smiling at his reminition. Esther to let out an immature giggle, confirming her memory of the event.

"Well, I'll be in there for a bit. I was going to ask if you'd mind picking up my work phone and any left-over gear?"

He requested openly. Esther revealed that she had already retrieved the contraband earlier that day. Detailing how she'd grabbed it in a panic as Ivy contacted the authorities.

"Shit, she called the police?"

He panicked.

"We saw your apartment, George. She thinks your dead, we all do".

Esther protested.

"Well, did".

She corrected, displaying her palms, gesturing to herself. George absorbed the new information for a moment. Realising that revealing

his whereabouts to Ivy would indefinitely incriminate her. He lived a life on the edge of the law, but always respected that it wasn't a path she would ever chose to lead. Involving her would mean asking her to lie to the police for him. Jeopardising her future. The level of irresponsibility he felt about implementing her, deterred George from his planned visit that night. Instead, he simply asked Esther to wipe the burner clean, and flush the drugs. Clearly, he was perfectly comfortable to implement her instead.
"Sure, but I need something in return".
Esther bargained.
"Troy wants to go to your apartment tonight. Something to do with séance shit".
She clarified, requesting permission to use his home. George was taken aback, having not expected Esther to be involved in such things.
"Oh, erm. OK, yeah".
He stuttered.
"There's a spare key under the outdoor bin, just put it back when you're done".

Upon their arrival, Jason invited Troy and Esther upstairs into the flat where they found Malcom and Luke overlooking their notes. Evening fell along with a light rain, trinkling sprinkled moisture onto the window. Persistent in its cry for attention as it tap, tap, tapped on the glass. Successful in its plea, Esther inspected the view that such a rain would display. A disingenuous ploy to monitor any disturbances of the trap door.
"Perfect weather for a smoke".
She spoke aloud, as though to herself.
"In the rain?"
Malcom criticized.
"I'm heading out for five, just catch me up when I'm back".
She informed, ignoring Malcom's confused yet judgemental stare. The front of house was somewhat crowded. Not unreasonably so, but enough to keep Esther on her guard. The beer garden however, had cleared out due to the weather. Regardless of the fact, she wouldn't enter the bomb shelter undetected, as there stood three large windows between the seating areas inside and out. If she were to warn George, she would require a distraction.

Chapter 41

DI Jones was confronted with one dead end after another that evening. His patience thinned quicker than his hair line as loose ends would unravel while he showered. Pulling the lifeless stands from his scalp, he observed as they swam down from his reach, into the drain.
"I'm making toasties, love! Do you want one?"
Toby yelled through the closed door.
"Yeah, please! I'll be right out!"
Michael accepted, finishing up in the shower.
Toby had displayed upon the dining table, two toasted sandwiches, filled to the brim with mature cheddar and sliced bacon. He slipped in front of Michael an empty cup in which to fill. Along with the contents of a saucer, almost overflowing with freshly made coffee, placed between the pair of them. Cheddar was a 'go to' dish for his husband, often devoured when his case work hadn't gone as planned.
"You need cheering up with something cheesy".
Toby would playfully mock. Always happy to oblige.

No aspect of Dana's case added up. Nothing made sense to him. He couldn't understand how it occurred in broad daylight, with plenty of people around, but it was not detected. For there to be cameras planted all throughout the premises, yet no evidential footage. How all those within the vicinity didn't hear her scream.

"Whose red hair, was it?"
He asked himself aloud, in between bites. It had been another long and drawn-out day after having wasted his time on both Ivy and her aunt.
"Was it not his dad?"
Toby asked, trying to help.
"No, he's not a redhead. Plus, he has an airtight alibi".

Answered Michael, shooting down the suggestion.

"What about that lass, the one with the burner phone that was wiped?"

He continued to pry.

"What if it was her friend, that lad who's missing? Maybe that's why he's missing. Because he killed the hairdresser and doesn't want to get caught".

Toby babbled on mindlessly, finishing up on the burned crusts. Michael froze, connecting dot's that weren't there before.

"And she knows it, she's trying to help him to cover it up".

Michael realised, jumping to his own conclusions.

"Yeah, I mean, I'm sure the news mentioned about his build. Isn't he a tall, stocky guy? Might be stronger than he looks".

Concluded Toby, opening up a door in his husband's mind that perhaps was best left closed. Gaining another interview with Miss Petunia wouldn't have been as easy as the first occasion. But Jones knew all to well of two individuals in particular who would be happy to shed light on the kind of matters that Esther would prefer to be left in the dark.

"Who on earth could that be at this hour".

Mr Platt grunted, wafting his hand at Mrs Platt. Making her put her cleaning to a halt in order to see who'd paid them such an inappropriately timed visit.

"Oh, It's that detective fellow".

She answered, opening the door. Detective Inspector Michael Jones stood eerily confident in the Platt's hinged doorway. Water droplets pounding down behind him in the background as a roll of thunder sounded.

"I have some questions, Mrs Platt".

He began, ignoring her frustrated expression.

"I'm here to speak with you regarding your previous tenant, Miss Esther Petunia".

He introduced, expecting an invitation. Mrs Platt reluctantly stepped aside, gesturing that the detective come inside from the rain. She offered up a hot beverage, a tea to be precise. A tea with two sugars and a dash of milk.

"Thank you".

Jones voiced, accepting the brew as she passed it over to him. The porcelain cup stood on its matching dish, gifting two shortbread biscuits to accompany its beverage counterpart. As he forced his teeth into the crumbling layers of baked sugary bliss, Mrs Platt watched to see her handy work thoughtlessly enjoyed. Seating himself within the leather sofa opposite Mr Platt's chair, he proceeded with his inflicted interrogation.

Early evening became late, and the couple gladly offered up all that they could of Esther's unseemly disposition. Indicating their belief of her drug use and potential profiting of said contraband. They'd already tired of her, shortly after she'd moved in. The invitation was extended as a coping strategy for Mrs Platt, as she missed the company of her daughter after she wed. Unfortunately, Esther was no Eve.

"This is all very valuable information; I very much appreciate your co-operation".

He complimented robotically, growing bored of their rants and rambles.

"She was in cahoots with that boy that went missing, George Jameson".

Mr Platt affirmed, out of the blue. Accusatory in his tone.

"Cahoots about what? Drug use?"

Jones asked. All of a sudden, rather interested.

"Amongst other things".

He trailed. Jones waited a moment, letting the Platt's stew in their dislike of Esther, long enough to provoke the answer he'd been waiting for.

"Do you have any reason to believe that perhaps Esther and George have any relation to the murder of Dana Kirkley?"

Michael tried not to grin, putting the loaded question out into the open, like a ticking timer thrown into a crowded room. Mrs Platt subtly studied her husband's initial response. He turned his attention to her, sharing a deciding stance. Equally speechless until Mr Platt's lips unpressed.

"Yes".

Mrs Platt spat, for once silencing her husband. DI Jones overlooked them both, squinting his eyes, oh so slightly to encourage more context on their answer.

"Unlicensed pharmaceuticals make people do unspeakable things, Detective. I don't find it remotely implausible to consider that the two accidentally harmed the young woman under the influence of whatever chemicals they poison themselves with. It would explain why he's no where to be seen, now wouldn't it?".

Mr Platt added, joining forces with his wife and her impulsive answer.

"I see".

Jones nodded, agreeably.

"Well, that's all that I have to ask for now. Thank you for your time, and your hospitality".

He concluded, graciously, showing himself to the door.

Venturing outside, Michael raised his head to take in sight of a dense and greying night. Clouds, plumped and stuffed like as though feather filled pillows engulfed the sky. A thunders temper began to boil, grumbling louder and longer as the storm came closer.

Fortunately, such suspicions painted an image deemed somewhat viable to Chief Inspector Douglas Danes once receiving Jones's eager update over an impromptu phone call. Moving the investigation forward onto the authorities new unsuspecting suspects, Esther Petunia, and George Jameson. All DI Jones had left to do was to find Esther with the drug paraphernalia on her person, and issue for her arrest.

Chapter 42

Things hadn't exactly been going accordingly for dear Ivy. She'd been evading her aunts calls while stewing in her anger. Not fully sure as to where Troy resided, she thought it best to instead call in at The Tavern that evening. Assuming that Esther would have ended up there, at one point or another. Evidently correct, as Ivy spotted her by the back exit upon entry.
"You!"
She screamed, drawing in an uncomfortable attention from settled customers.
Shit.
Esther thought to herself, hearing the familiar whine of Ivy's ill-tempered tone. She'd been drenched by the rain as it gradually fell heavier. Her coat dripped uncontrollably onto the carpet, coaxing Violet to approach from behind the bar.
"Here, love. I'll put that on the radiator".
Violet offered calmly, trying to simmer Ivy down.
"No need, Vi. I'm not sticking around".
She snapped, jolting her palm into Violet's direction, as though to instruct her to stay well outside of her infuriated vicinity. Her eyes pinned wide open as though shock stricken, peering into Esther's weary expression from across the room.
"You're going to hit me, aren't you?"
Esther asked, with an awkward casualness. Ivy breathed a confirming laugh as she lifted a single foot to take a step forward. Violet stepped in her way, holding an authority in which Ivy either hadn't detected, or simply not respected, as she pushed her aside to head towards Esther. As Violet fell to the ground, other members of staff came to her aid. Roy gallantly came out from the back office when hearing of the commotion, to grab a hold of Ivy by the arm and

remove her from the building. All the while, everybody in the pub had eyes on the theatrical scene at play, with Ivy reciting profanities.

That'll do.

Esther thought, as she snuck outside and opened up the bomb shelter's trap door. The stairs on entry resembled that of an undesirable basement. Eroded from age and neglect, Esther treaded carefully as she lowered the door above her head, remaining undetected to then climb inside. The air, thick and damp, carried specs of dust that floated across a candle lit lanterns glare. The stone walls echoed her footsteps as she approached George, presumably asleep in a cold, hard corner of the room. She gently nudged him at first, so not to frighten him. The nudge was insufficient, his underweight, pale body laid practically lifeless. Esther, in a panic, grabbed him by the shoulder and shook until both eyes gradually came to an open.

"George, it's me. It's Esther, don't worry you're OK, yeah? You're OK".

She reassured, removing her coat to wrap around him. Her arms cloaked around his shoulders to share the warmth of her body.

"Essie?"

George croaked. His throat severely dry from dehydration. Lips cracked like shattered concrete and a complexion so frail that it displayed almost every vein underneath its fragile surface. Too weak to hold a conversation, George once again lost consciousness. He required medical attention, and fast.

Upstairs, the police had been contacted regarding Ivy's public dispute. The ruckus was delightfully entertaining to the youngsters and their smartphones, as a crowd gathered outside to watch Ivy be shoved into the back of a police car. Roy and Violet observed from the main door, until his phone lit up with an incoming call from Esther.

"Hiya, duck. Don't worry, bobbies have took her. Just stay upstairs for a bit if you want, have a brew. Just wait this one out".

He answered, without letting her utter a word.

"Roy, for fucks sake, listen, I need your help, it's an emergency".

She replied in hysterics.

"What is it?"

He asked, giving her his undivided attention as he walked back inside, away from the crowd while Violet followed, intrigued. Esther looked upon her close and dearly loved friend. Carrying two conflicting entities atop each shoulder. One, suggesting that she leave him where he lay, to continue holding on to the secret, thus protecting him from detection. The other, begging her to reach out for help, afraid that not doing so would cost him his life. She closed her eyes as her gut twisted and churned. Unsure as to which path would be the right choice.

"He's here"'.
She revealed, adding no context.
"Who's here?"
Puzzled Roy.
"Don't react out loud, OK? He needs to stay hidden".
Esther carried on, still not explaining herself to Roy.
"I've no idea what you're getting at, Essie".
He stated, growing in frustration.
"George".
She said flatly.
"George is alive, he's been hiding in your bomb shelter but he's sick, Roy. He's really sick and might die if we don't get him out. But he was adamant about no one knowing where he is. So, I don't know what I'm supposed to do. What am I supposed to do?"
Cried Esther, begging in a rant of desperation.
"I'll be right there".
Roy replied, hanging up the phone. Having told Violet straight away, the two agreed to close The Tavern early. They issued refunds to customers that had paid for orders unreceived or unconsumed and ushered away the punters, apologising as they herded people out. The others upstairs in the flat had heard the commotion and came down to see what was going on. Jason remained in Roy's grandparent's bedroom, keeping an eye on Ellis. All except for Eve, assumed the palaver was a result of the plan coming into action.
"What's all this about?".
Eve asked Violet, wondering if she'd misunderstood their earlier discussion.
"Not that, before you get any ideas in your head".
Answered Violet, apparently reading her mind before brushing her off as she locked the doors and closed the curtains.
"What do you mean, not that?"
Malcom enquired, suspiciously. When the coast was eventually clear, Violet requested that Eve and Luke would assist in fetching the first aid box, some dry clothes, blankets, and a jug of fresh water with an accompanying glass. Meanwhile Roy, asked Malcom and Troy to

help him with the bomb shelter, without any further explanation. The three headed down below the ground to find Esther cradling George, weeping as she held him close.

"He won't wake up".

She cried, moving out of the way for Roy to lift his body from the frozen slate. George's damp, pale and lifeless arms flopped like uncooked bacon as he rose from the floor. With Roy carrying him up the rickety, slippery steps as Troy helped to steady his balance and Luke held open the trap door.

When the police vehicle that was escorting Ivy arrived at the station, DI Jones waited patiently outside, with his stare following the car as it drove into the allocated parking space. He'd seen the theatrics while passing by, on his way from Mr and Mrs Platt's recent interview. Shaking his head at Ivy's dramatics as he returned to his office. She was placed in a holding cell, having utilised her opporture phone call to Aunt Cathy. Perched by the barred window, she clung tightly her folded legs pressed up against her chest. The walls, painted an unappealing plain paper white, framed an unreasonably weighted door that was bolted shut. A door gifted with a letterbox sized gap, allowing if not just a little insight into the hallway and its passers-by. Her clothes, still wet, pushed against her skin. Aiding gravity in its attempt of sinking her further into the pit that was rock bottom. Ivy felt dehumanised. As though everybody that could help her to find George, simply just wouldn't. DI Jones no longer sought need in Ivy's involvement with his investigation. Considering her failure to compose herself.

Her Aunt Cathy finally arrived, paid any outstanding fines in relation to Ivy's arrest, and took her home. Taking her soiled clothing to place into the washing machine, before cooking her a serving of toad in the hole with mash potato and gravy. As they dined, Cathy watched her niece eat in a daze. Ivy chewed without blinking as her mind wandered elsewhere. She was thinking of how it may have been time to decide. Decide as to whether or not she should continue in her pursuit of George, regardless of the restrictions consistently presenting themselves along the way, or to give up. To accept that the love of her life had passed, and that if she were to uncover anything, it would never be enough to bring him back.

"I think you should stay with me for a while, sweetheart".

Cathy suggested carefully, bringing Ivy out from her trance. She had little left in her to fight anymore. Scraping up a piece of diced sausage topped with mash-soaked gravy, she looked up to her aunt in defeat.
"Ok".

Chapter 43

Mr Platt, though irritated by his wife's instantaneous decision to answer before him, was pleased with the outcome of the detectives visit that evening. His opinion of Esther hadn't started with any level of admiration, unlike Mrs Platt. They'd met just about a year prior, on a Sunday service after the communal wine. The sermon had concluded his weekly preach and the members of the church scattered off into their cliques to chat before heading off on their separate ways. Mr & Mrs Platt enjoyed their visits, and so would occasionally stay from the beginning at 9:00am, right up until 11:30-12:00pm. Mr Platt would accompany the other fathers, speaking of the recent news, housing market, cars, or construction. Battling in an unspoken rivalry of 'masculinity'. Whereas Mrs Platt's friends would talk about their husbands, the dissatisfaction in their submissive marriages, always ending on a note of compliance in relation to the subservience of their imbedded beliefs. On that particular Sunday, a young woman had entered halfway through the preacher's speech, taking a seat quietly by the back. Eve hated attending, but guilt overpowered her. As was the way. Afterwards, her mother's friends would invite her to chat, though she always had an excuse at the ready to vacate the church. No matter how trivial.

"What a beautiful colour".
Eve said, complimenting the lonely young woman, as she rushed away from her mother.
"Excuse me?"
She asked, caught off guard.
"Sorry, I was just noticing your hair".
Apologised Eve, politely.
"I'm Eve".
Introducing herself.

"I'm Esther".
She replied, awkwardly.
"Nice to meet you, Esther. I'd love to stay and chat, but I have to head out".

Eve rushed, speed walking away. Slightly bewildered by the hasty conversation, Esther looked around the room to see people in their selective groups, most of which were looking in her direction as they spoke amongst themselves. She was clearly the topic on everybody's mind, uncomfortably so. Feeling like a fish out of water, she decided not to stay and followed suit. That is until Mrs Platt caught her attention. She was a petite lady, small in stature but not in might. Dressed in a perfectly suitable floral maxi dress, buttoned all the way to the neckline. Mid high heeled, closed toe shoes completed her ensemble, along with a matching cream coloured handbag hung over her left shoulder.

"I don't believe we've met".
She stated plainly, reaching out her hand to shake with Esther's.
"That girl you just spoke with is my daughter, Eve. My name is Moira Platt. I prefer to be referred to as Mrs Platt though, might I add. And your name is?"
She enquired bluntly.
"Esther, Ma'am. I'm Esther Petunia".
She answered, accepting the handshake offered.
"Do you live locally?"
Quizzed Mrs Platt, knowing already what the answer was.
"No, I lived in the city".
Esther answered vaguely.
"Lived?"
She continued to press. The church was very much her and her husband's territory to her own perception. The girl instantly intrigued her. She mindfully questioned her intentions, having interrupted the sermon halfway through with her lateness. Turning up alone with no explanation. Such an occurrence would send tongues wagging. What she would come to learn was that Esther had taken off on a whim to turn up in the village, through no prior plans or preparation. The only link being that of her previously made friendship with George.

"Where are you staying?"
Asked Mrs Platt, critically.
"I've just been staying with my friend for a few days. He's great company but I'm still on the lookout for a flat".
Esther answered, honestly. The thought of an unmarried women, living alone with a man was a concept, far too disgraceful for Mrs

Platt to accept. She excused herself to request her husband's permission to rent out the room, previously occupied by their daughter. Suggesting that such a sacrifice would be that of their lord's work, and they would likely be rewarded for their generosity. Additionally, the extra income would have been put to good use. Esther watched Mrs Platt speak to her husband from across the room. A stocky fellow, sitting comfortably in an electric wheelchair. Dressed in a light grey suit, matched with a plain white shirt and black tie. His upper hair thinned, leaving a hairless dome with a moat of grey strands stretched from ear to ear around the back of his head. Glasses incorrectly worn, resting on the very tip of his nose to shelve his wrinkled eyes of hazel. They spoke for a few minutes, leaving the young woman to wait by herself in the pew, until they came to an agreement and approached her as a united front.

"Hello, Miss Petunia. My wife and I have just been discussing your current living arrangements".

Mr Platt began, without so much of an introduction. Esther was somewhat offended. She'd entered the church with the hope for a sense of peace, having had a difficult transition in her life. She wasn't typically religious. But that being said, most aren't until their darkest hours. That morning, Esther couldn't have possibly imagined that walking into that particular church would then rope her into an unanticipated tenancy with two perfect strangers.

"I'm sorry, sir but I don't feel comfortable discussing my living arrangements to any further extent than general chit chat. I don't even know who you are".

Protested Esther, getting up to leave.

"Oh, my apologies, Miss. My intention was not to intrude. My wife came to tell me that you were looking for a flat. And though we don't know of any flats available right now, we do actually have a room to rent. You see our daughter recently married and moved out with her husband and new-born. We have no use for that room and so we were considering renting it out. I was simply going to ask if you were interested. But you don't need to decide right now. If you'd like time to think it over, just come back for next Sunday's service, and we can discuss it further".

Mr Platt clarified, easing Esther's concern. Having listened to his reasoning, she thanked them both with caution before leaving the premises.

"This better not cause any problems".
Mr Platt snarked under his breath.

"She's just a young woman down on her luck, darling. It'll be nice to have another girl in the house again".

Mrs Platt reassured, happy to be getting her own way.

"You've got a week to find out more about this 'woman'. Make sure we're not inviting some jezebel into our home".

He snapped, returning to his chat with the other men.

Well! Esther obviously took the offer. Mainly because George's studio apartment wasn't exactly spacious. Mrs Platt grew increasingly dissatisfied with the disgraceful reality that was Esther. Feeling robbed of her rewards for being such a good Samaritan. Oh dear, how sad. Her faith hadn't deterred, however. Still engrossed with the belief that gratification for her loyalty would soon be reaped, as she persisted to regain her daughter's residency into their home. Blissful denial of Eve's own intentions, completely blind to the act of self-preservation, she herself was about to perform.

Chapter 44

Esther woke in an unfamiliar bed within Roy and Violets bedroom after falling asleep by George's side. Violet had changed his clothes, having removed the icy stale T-shirt and jeans to replace them with Roy's winter buttoned up pyjamas. A set he'd received for Christmas, with Rudolf printed across the long sleeve top to match a pair of bright red bottoms. The radiator had been on for hours to warm him as he lay wrapped in a fifteen-tog duvet with a filled hot-water bottle by his feet. Esther took the first watch. Making sure he was still breathing, and that his body temperature regulated, which eventually it did. She sat up, resting by the edge of the bed, inspecting the room surrounding her. It was clear that Violet had the last say on the room's appearance, taking charge with her decorative influence. The wallpaper coated the space with illustrated lavender plants, setting the colour scheme for the rest of the layout with tones of beige, lilac, and subtle splashes of pastel lime green. The blackout, plain plum curtains were drawn closed. The only light source being that of a bedside table lamp. As she stood, Esther heard the bedding rustle behind her as George miraculously awakened. His eyes had crusted along with his mouth, releasing a foul odour as he spoke.

"Essie? Where am I?"

He panicked, forcing himself to sit up in a struggle.

"Woah, it's ok, we're in Roy's flat".

Esther soothed, handing him a glass of water.

"Don't' worry, they're not going to tell, OK? You're safe, I promise".

She reassured, watching him devour the drink he'd been given. Once consumed, he returned the glass to Esther and resumed his previous position, tucked up comfortably within the quilt.

"You look after me, don't you".

He thanked, appreciatively.

"I try".

She replied with a smile, pleased with his gradual recovery. Esther left him waiting as she entered the kitchen to retrieve something to eat for them both. Malcom and Luke were in their bedroom, while Eve and Jason were seated by the table after letting Roy and Violet use their room to get some well needed rest. Leaving Ellis in his crib along with them.

"How is he?"

Asked Eve, concerned.

"He's awake, thankfully. He's had some water, but I figured I'd get him something to eat. Something mild that won't upset his stomach".

Answered Esther, rooting around in the cupboards and the fridge before deciding to make a simple dish of scrambled eggs on toast.

Troy stayed for a while when they brought George inside originally but returned to his own home after noticing that Esther had fallen asleep. He'd spoken with Eve and Jason regarding the premises inherited. Jason respectfully suggested that if Troy wasn't to sell, he and Eve would contribute to the upkeep. Advertising that they would do all that they could to help run it. Fortuitously for the couple, Troy couldn't possibly imagine being rid a company that he watched his mother work, day in, day out to lift off the ground. The salon meant the world to her. He had no intention of selling. Troy was extremely grateful that Jason and Eve cared almost as much as he himself did and was happy to keep them as tenants.

The clock displayed the late hour of 3:01am, making Esther feel obliged to tread carefully, so not to wake the others. Jason took himself into the living room to rest on the sofa in front of the television, whereas Eve stayed up, speaking with Esther as she cooked herself and George some breakfast.

"Do you want some toast putting in?"

Asked Esther, taking Eve into consideration.

"No thanks, I don't have much of an appetite at the minute. I'm quite happy with my tea".

She answered. Eve had been fiddling on her phone, scrolling through social media and the news during her relentless sleeplessness. Placing her device onto the table, giving Esther her full attention.

"So, he was never missing? He's been hiding in The Taverns bomb shelter this whole time?"

She asked inquisitively.

"Yeah, it's insane isn't it. But I mean, I get it. I would have probably done the same".

Esther replied, defending Georges bizarre behaviour. Eve slightly nodded in agreement, continuing to sip her tea as Esther cooked. She inspected her phone, checking what apps she had left open to close them all before locking it once again. Deciding that she had nothing left to distract herself with, Eve joined Jason on the sofa. Watching whichever shows were on at that time.

What seemed like an hour passed by as Esther updated George on her recent discoveries. Detailing how she herself had come into contact with the same ghastly monster, only it didn't manage to reach her. Sharing how Roy, Malcom and Luke had also witnessed it and even captured a photo as proof. All while reassuring him that Ivy had been kept completely out of the loop, and away from any danger. As George became relieved from the news that he no longer stood alone in his strive for survival, he sat up with his back against the headboard to eat the scrambled eggs and toast with Esther. Distracting themselves by watching videos online from her phone which she'd propped up between them both on the bed. Failing to contain their laughter at the shenanigans that went on within the videos they enjoyed.

That is until the sound of a car door slammed shut from outside, triggering George. Causing him to lung forwards to grab the phone. Stopping the video and instructing Esther to remain completely quiet.
"What's wrong?"
She whispered, as quietly as she was able, as he pressed his hand against her mouth to silence her.
"It's here".

The two quietly snuck into the other bedroom to wake Roy and Violet before entering the living room to find Eve still awake. Violet gently lifted Ellis from his crib so not to wake him, while Roy discretely pulled open the attic door to help them climb up. With Violet and Ellis going first, following afterwards were the others until only Roy, Esther and Eve were left.

"If it doesn't find anybody, its going to look in there".
Eve spoke, very sure of herself.
"Why would it? How would it even know that it's a doorway?"
Roy argued quietly.

"It'll smell you".

Esther realised.

"We'll smell like an open buffet, hiding in there all together. And if Ellis wakes up, we're all dead".

She pointed out, agreeing with Eve. They paused, if just for a moment as they realised the severity of danger that they were in. Esther stepped forward, setting her sights on Roy's distraught expression.

"I'll kill it".

She spoke with an aggressive and arrogant authority.

"What? No, it'll rip you apart".

He responded, worriedly.

"I'll set it on fire. It won't come for you then".

She put it bluntly.

"And light the place up along with it".

Argued Roy, pulling Eve towards the step ladder to forcibly coax her into the attic.

"You've got a sprinkler system set up for if there's ever a fire in the building. It'll be trapped outside".

Esther argued, trying to keep her annoyed tone to a low volume.

"You know that Eve's right. If it gets inside, it'll kill all of us".

Battled Esther, eager to be heard.

"You've all got families to take care of, Roy. Please. Just, let me do this".

She finished, watching the frown on Roy's face release into a defeated, heartbroken gaze. He looked up towards the attic entryway, the space now filled with everybody that he cared about, all except for Esther. He wanted her to be wrong but unfortunately, she wasn't. Roy solemnly nodded in acceptance, taking his first regretful step onto the ladder as he climbed upward, closing the hatch behind him. Esther, deep in anxiety, riddled with adrenaline, exhaled her profanities.

"What the fuck am I thinking?"

When hearing the drag of claws across the beer gardens concrete, Esther rushed downstairs in search of a bucket. The largest one she could find was in the cleaning supplies pantry next to the office. Rummaging around in Roy's desk, she found hidden in the bottom draw, a box of matches by a taped-up pouch of tobacco. She quickly took multiple bottles of whisky, vodka, and rum to empty them into the bucket before returning upstairs, carrying the excessively heavy bucket of booze. Back inside the bedroom, Esther listened intently, trying to figure out whereabouts on the premises, the monster had wandered off to. She heard the creak of rusty joints as the trap door to the bomb shelter opened, pulling the curtain to peep ever so slightly as it went below. Once underground, she quickly turned off the bedside lamp so that she could get a clear view without it noticing her so easily. Sliding the window open fully, keeping the bucket nearby, ready to throw. She then emptied the matches onto the windowsill, resting them beside the box. Providing her future self, the opportunity to quickly light a backup, if the first didn't catch. She had mere seconds to assure that everything was at the ready as she stood by the ledges edge, awaiting her fate.

Chapter 45

Detective Inspector Michael Jones had endured hours, stuck inside of his office, contemplating the case. Researching into Esther's background and her possible link to the crimes committed. Confused as to why the Platt's would practically take in a stray from the city.

There was little information about Esther, as though her general public profile had been intentionally reduced, significantly. Social media posts displayed by the family members had some pictures of her, but they looked like old photos. DI Jones presumed she'd become estranged, for some unknown reason. His assumption leaned toward her use of illegal contraband. Not having caught her with the drugs on her person as of yet, he'd heard of her addictions.

Pulling them up on the data base, he obtained the families contact information. The late hour obstructed the task of reaching out. Deciding to wait until the following morning, DI Jones shut down his computer, packed up his desk and set off to drive home. His phone overflowed with notifications of missed calls and voicemails from Cathy Krane. After hearing the first one, he deleted the rest and blocked her number. The voicemail was of her yelling furiously over the arrest of Ivy and stressing his incompetence. Questioning as to why Esther Petunia hadn't instead been arrested. DI Jones's narcissism was far too imbedded into his ego to allow his way of thinking to be considered anything but astute. One mistake after another didn't imply failure to carry out the task at hand for him, it simply meant ruling out each theory as it came to pass.

On his drive home, he spotted something in the dark of night, creeping toward The Tavern, lurking into the back of the premises. Parking up by the side of the road, he stepped out of his car to inspect the suspicious activity further. As he entered the beer garden by the back gate, he heard the clang and crash of shelves beneath his feet. It was as though someone was pottering around underground.

"Psst"
A noise sounded, coming from above. As he looked up, he found Miss Petunia practically hanging on the ledge of an open window. Her skin, sheet white with an expression drenched in horror.
Run.
Her eyes read.

The noisy cluster from below abruptly came to a holt. DI Jones ignored her perceived instruction. Curiosity cloaked his judgement as he wanted to see who was hidden down below. She ducked down for a moment to retrieve what he thought looked like a heavy bucket, and then rested it on the sill beside herself. He watched, confused.
What on earth is she up to now?
Jones thought to himself, tiring of her shenanigans. She fixed her gaze, like a hunter on prey. The person underneath the ground then reached out their hand, clutching onto the concrete to lift themselves out from an opened trap door. A hand with loose skin draped from the bone with yellowed claws, chipped and clogged with grime. He froze in disbelief as what followed, was the sight of a being so unimaginably contemptable. Jones, instantaneously regretting his disposition, paused. Unable to move, to speak, to blink.

The creature quickly caught wind of Esther's familiar scent. And so, it slowly turned its predatory head. Locking its empty, soulless eyes directly onto her.
"This is it".
She released, in a frightened gasp. As though to say goodbye to her own life. It leaped onto the brick and began to climb, reaching out an undernourished scaling arm forward. One after the other as it creeped toward her. Its mouth filled with the teeth of a leviathan, salivating at the sight of its next meal. It's monstrous protruding spine barely hid beneath a slab of shedding skin. Its eyes were ghostly, empty, like clear marbles, bursting with milk. A figure deemed slim, clung to sagging skin that dragged from the knees and elbows.
Esther pushed the bucket forwards, forcing the weight of the pooled liquor out of the opened window, dousing the monster's vision completely. A wail screeched, a sound like no other vocally protruded from its widened jaw. The drenching only further aggravated it, as its muscles tensed, regaining its focus on the climb. Esther hurriedly

tried to light a match, scraping the red tip speedily across the igniter as it lit for a moment just to dissipate in a flash. Throwing it aside, she attempted with another, only for it to do the same. The creature reared its head from the base of the open window, displaying its sharp and deadly grin as it relished at the sight of Esther fearing for her life. Until suddenly she was grabbed from behind. Two human hands cupped onto each forearm as her body was pulled backwards and then thrown to the floor across the room. Her head slammed upon impact, causing her to lose focus momentarily. Looking up, Esther saw the blurred shape of a woman, seemingly rushing to grab what was left of the unused matches. Taking a step back, one hand was held outwards possessing the little box. With a dry match in the other, the two paired for a final attempt. A tiny flame set ablaze. Floating in the air as the woman threw the spark directly toward the entering evil, just as the creature began to crawl inside. For a split second, time stopped. Esther took what she anticipated to be her last breath.

A blinding light exploded from the windows ledge as ferocious flames burst uncontrollably. A heat so powerful, it burned what air was left in the room. Esther choked on the smoke as the mysterious woman dragged her weakening body out from the flat. The creature, screamed in sheer agony as it failed to continue its climb into the building, falling chaotically onto the ground outside. It's body, jolting in a fit of despair, as though screaming for relief. Its screech, at first sounded animalistic. Like the beg for death, released from the vocal cords of game as its skinned.

DI Jones hadn't taken a single step out of place. Paralysed on point, he listened. He listened to its call, it's final plea for the end. Hearing nothing else but the monstrous abomination, suffering. Until those haunting sounds slowly became what couldn't be mistaken for anything else, but the spoken words of man.
"Help!"
It cried.
"HELP!"
It repeated, over and over and over. DI Jones observed in shock. Its body began to disgustingly mutate into what appeared to be human form. Jones rushed to the beer gardens hose pipe, previously wrapped neatly by the outdoor plants. Turned on the tap and hosed down the scolded body sprawled along the concrete.
To the detective's dismay, it was just far too late. To no surprise, extinguishing the flames hadn't prevented the creature's demise as

the twitch of its muscles spasms eventually came to an end. A carcass lay lifeless amongst the tables and chairs within The Taverns beer garden. He remained motionless. Holding the hose pipe which continued to flood the ground beneath his feet, as water soaked through ill prepared footwear.

Chapter 46

A blaze erupted; an inferno of flames spread across The Tavern. Fire engines set up around the front of the premises, accompanied by incorrectly parked police vehicles. An aggressively powered force of water excreted from a nitrile rubber tube, extinguishing the burning brick effectively and efficiently. Fire fighters surveyed the perimeter for potential survivors and an ambulance awaited on standby. The smoke violently escaped upwards into the apprehensive clouds, coughing with toxins, rearing to pop. A heat so unbearable, leaving even the human skin of the living to smell of cooked meat. A crowd gathered promptly. The roads were sealed off as news presenters arrived at the scene. The people watched in worry, weary for answers, wondering about the whereabouts of those who resided within. Amongst the crowd was the familiar face of Mrs Platt, unaccompanied and alone as the fire slowly came to a calm, before being completely defeated by its elemental counterpart.

Earlier, her and Mr Platt lie in bed. They'd retired early, shortly after the detective's departure. A nightly breeze descended through the thin, uninsulated walls leading to the use of double layered duvets. Equally reluctant to waste additional resources on utilities when body heat can be effectively preserved through the use of blankets, regardless of environmental temperature drops, so they thought. Mrs Platt was unable to relax, thawing gradually as she shook from the cold that remained in the lifeless room surrounding her. Mr Platt had no such trouble. He'd dropped the moment his head hit the pillow, leaving his wife to toss and turn as she made her efforts to rest. Counting the hours as she lay wide awake, 23:00pm soon became midnight, and then 1:00am to 2:00am. Eventually she accepted that the night wouldn't allow her slumber and instead used her time to think of her daughter and what actions to take next in order to bring her home. Just as Eve's name appeared in her mind, it then propped up on her mobile as she received an unexpected call. She slid her index finger across the screen to answer when she heard speech in the background. Her daughter's voice was present, but more so as an accidentally overheard conversation. Only, my friends, it was not accidental.

As the fire came to a stop, there was a sense of relief throughout the crowd. Though they felt that the worst was still yet to come as no survivors were yet revealed. The police did however uncover an unlocked vehicle parked discretely near the back of the building. A black hatchback, filthy with ash and specs of rubble. When searched thoroughly, an envelope was discovered within the glove box. A general piece of mail associated with an overdue bill for a repaired tyre, addressed to a Mr Michael Jones.

"I'm here at the well-known and well-loved local hot spot, The Tavern. Centred in what was once a quiet and peaceful village. Now appears to be a prime target for some pretty gruesome crimes. Just over a week ago, the body of a brutally murdered victim was discovered on the rooftop of a hair salon. The police still have not provided any suspects as of yet and claim that the investigation is still ongoing. Tonight, a devastating fire has caused severe disruption for the residents here as flames spread throughout The Tavern, currently owned by a Mr Roy Richard who inherited the business from his father. Running it alongside him is his wife Mrs Violet Richard and their son Malcom Richard. None of which have yet been accounted for by the authorities as the rescue services are still currently searching for survivors. Locals informed police that another family were in fact living on the premises. As well as Malcom Richard's close friend, Luke. Who according to witnesses, was staying temporarily to visit. We haven't a confirmed surname as of yet for the friend that was staying with them. But the family also living in the flat upstairs with the Richard's family, were Mrs Eve and Mr Jason Murphey, and their infant son, Ellis. All of which, also have not yet been found. The premises is sealed off, with locals surrounding the area as they watch to find out if the people who may have been inside the building, have survived and are hopefully unharmed".

The news reported, exploiting the tragedy as it unfolded.

Eventually there was a development. A body was recovered from the rubble, pulled out from the scene in a zip tight black bag, and escorted by the emergency services. The news anchors went wild for the story, like dogs eager for a treat. Pushing their way through the villagers to gain a better camera shot, hoping to be the initial reporting body.

"A victim has been recovered, I repeat, someone has been found. There's speculation as to who the individual is, an identification of the corpse is still to be revealed".

They'd report, thrilled by the progression of the story's tragic nature. Concealing their excitement to falsify their respect for the victim and their family. Just in case.

Mrs Platt tried to call Eve, just as she had over an over again since the events took hold. Each time being sent straight to voicemail. Familiar faces blocked her view of the scene as they forced their sympathies and support. Pressure to perform appreciation increasingly grew tiresome for Mrs Platt, until she'd finally had enough.

"Please, contain your excitement people. Please do not suffocate me!"

She yelled, verbally pushing them into an intimidated step backwards.

"May I suggest that we organise ourselves. They could be searching through the rubble for hours".

She began to tear up, the tremor in her speech preventing an end to her intended sentence.

"She's right".

Henry, the local butcher, spoke up.

"If Roy and Vi were here, they'd tell us to get our shit together".

He valiantly announced.

It was as though the weather specifically selected not to adhere to the tone. As morning graced us, the waking sky illustrated its once vacantly grey pallet with a rupture of baby pink and butterscotch shades of orange calmed yellow. A cold only weakened by the warmth of the gradually strengthening sun. Cheerily cascading natural light over the heart-breaking weep, contagiously spread throughout Aviary Avenue.

"We seem to be having a change of activity throughout the village here. The majority of locals have left. By the looks of it, they're heading back to their homes whereas some are directly going towards the community hall. There have been murmurings of setting up a food and beverage station there, so were presuming people are bringing in home made snacks or food produce from their own personal stores. Everybody is coming together, preparing for what might possibly be a very long wait, to find out what has happened. To see how the fire was caused and who, if anyone, managed to survive".

Chapter 47

It was a quite beautifully decorated bedroom. Walls of plain, clean white reached down to a sandy shaded carpet. An easily assembled pine bed frame carrying a queen-sized mattress, centred across the left side of the room. Independently woven dream catchers, detailed with glossy beads and dyed feathers hung lightly by unpainted thread. A wheeled clothes rack, supporting the variety of tops and trousers, dresses and skirts, cardigans and scarfs that made themselves at home upon it. A tie-dye bed spread of cornflower blue blended with raspberry pink, once again brought comfort to Troy as he tried to sleep. Shortly after leaving Esther with the others, he reunited with Dana's memorabilia for another lonely night within his empty house. His mother was everywhere. But yet, no longer anywhere. She was in the things she'd left in the hallway. The shoes left untied, the jacket unzipped and the necklace on the nightstand. Her very essence plagued the air. Troy choked on his grief into the early hours, a new routine as it seemed.

His slumber, never dreamless, had become a place of despair. His mind played tricks and games, teasing Troy with the image of his dearly departed mothers' corpse. Forcing him to relive the moment, only amplified by his imagination and trauma. Awoken by sirens and alerted by the distressful disarray coming from outside and people exiting their front doors, heading towards the high-street. Troy rushed to get dressed after inspecting the goings on from the bedroom window and followed suit. He needn't ask what happened, as the blaze's smoke had already reached exceeding hights.

"No!"

He cried, distraught, running with all the strength and speed he was able to muster. Chaotically barging through the gathering crowd, locking eyes on to his target until reaching the foreboding yellow tape, blocking further entry.

"Woah, son. Stop there, now. Can't go past this point, I'm afraid".
An officer instructed, raising his arms to prevent Troy's passage.
"My friends are in there. Did they get out? Are they OK?"
He begged, trying to gain a better look behind the officer blocking his view.
"No one's come out yet. Just let us do our job, son".
The officer carried on, shooing the boy away.

Troy fell to his knees. An exceeding wail elated from his soul as he wept triumphantly, watching the flames burn the last of those whom he held dearly. He was the only one left in the world. The life he had before, perished. Troy closed his eyes to pray. Pleading with God to reunite him with his late mother. Asking if only he could be with her again. Mucus streamed from his blocked nose, mixing with tears as he gasped for the relief of death. Then, he felt a warmth upon his shoulders as he looked up to see Henry. Flickering light of apocalyptic orange and crimson red danced amongst a face of concern. Placing his oversized raincoat over Troy, to blanket him from the winters early chill.
"It's going to be OK, lad".
He spoke, in a dense and powerful voice.
"You're not alone".

The last use of the community hall had consisted of a Neighbourhood Watch Patrol meeting. The foldable table was out with remaining stains of tea or coffee, left undealt with. The chairs, sloppily 'put away' as three piles of stacked stainless steal seats cluttered the entrance floor. Before, the sirens of services alarmed outside, passing the facility along with the news anchors in their branded commercial vans. Roy raided the storage pantry for the unused patrol equipment packs in search for a battery-operated torch. Managing to obscure at least three, he brought them back into the main hall where the others waited within the dark of early hours.
"Let there be light".
He whispered.

They'd thankfully escaped with their lives, but nothing else. All their memories melted by forceful flare of flame. DI Jones kept watch by the window, discretely concealing himself behind the 80's themed curtains that styled the miniature kitchen. Returning to the room, he observed everyone before him. Roy was fiddling with the batteries of his torch as Malcom avoided Violets persistent attempts to cradle him. Luke kept himself calm with breathing exercises as he clung to the loose jeans on his knees. Eve, breastfeeding Ellis as Jasons arms wrapped tightly around his wife's shoulders, his head leant against hers. And finally, Esther, still catching her breath, sat legs crossed on the lineal beside an undernourished, but awake, George.

"Right".

The Detective Inspector raised his voice, indirectly requesting the groups undivided attention.

"Let start with you, Esther".

He began.

"Let's not".

George protested. Encouraging an expression upon Jones's face that could only be construed as a personal offence.

"Excuse me? Do you know who I am?"

Jones stomped, displaying his entitlement. George rose to his feet, if somewhat slowly due to his decrepit health.

"You fucking saw it".

He blurted.

"You know you did! So, what now?"

Asked George, rhetorically.

"She saved your fucking life, mate. Don't forget that".

He finished, taking back his place beside Esther.

"Besides, if you really think that we had something to do with any of this shite, then why did you come here to hide with us?".

Roy piped in, defensively.

"You know what we're hiding from. You know why we can't just wait out in the street. It'll find us".

Malcom helped, standing by his father.

"It won't".

Jones replied, shortly with a flat attitude. He could feel the power of authority start to shrivel. Not only questioned by the defiant civilians, but also internally ridiculed by his own fragile ego. A once 'sure of oneself' loyal associate of the law, compelled by truth and justice, now begrudgingly bested by a case, not even he could master.

"It's dead".

He uttered. An answer met with unspoken hints of denial and disparagement.

"You saw it die?"

Asked Eve, as Ellis still rest upon her lap. Jones felt compelled to remain conscientious of what to reveal and what not to. Acceptance of the validly of said beast's existence alone was incomprehensible.

The people within the room, of all the monstrosities they'd endured, still wouldn't believe the transformation that took place upon the creatures' final moments. With sorrowed eyes lost in focus as he contemplated his answer. Jones revealed all that was needed with an unadorned nod.

Michael Jones. Now, what can I saw about him? He had his moments, lets be fair. Not the most competent at his role, but not completely imbecilic, not really. It didn't take him long to realise that he could just as well become a suspect for arson as anyone else in the room, considering the hour, and knowing that it wouldn't be long before his car was discovered. He understood the system. What he could or couldn't get away with, the boundaries that he could push without too severe a consequence. This unfortunately, was far more out of his depth than he ever could have expected. The body would soon be identified by any glimpse of DNA left unscathed. Meaning that he hadn't witnessed the hunt of an unruly animal, but a murder of a cursed human. He would need an alternate theory, one that would sell, one of which Chief Inspector Douglas Danes would buy. Yes, friends, what he needed was a decent story.

After a few hours passed, the doors slammed open. In poured the villagers packing with sandwiches, pies, crisps, and chocolate snack bars along with some juice and plastic cups. Chit chatting loudly amongst themselves until reaching the main hall where each individual person dramatically came to stunted halt. As the lights switched on, revealing a sight of all those that the village feared were lost. Mrs Platt, perplexed over the pause, pushed her way to the front. Eve passed Ellis over to Jason, buttoning up her blouse as she stepped slowly towards her mother. Skin stunned with shock framing eyes of unanticipated fury. Mrs Platt reached her arms outwards, welcoming her daughter to take hold. Everybody watched as mother and daughter reunited. The moment their hug locked; the crowd released a theatrical cheer. A celebratory cry so loud, they failed to hear the words Mrs Platt uttered. Her crinkled, over-lined lips closed into Eve's unwilling ear. A hot and moist, coffee reeked breath released words of a threatening note.
"I know what you did".
She said, releasing Eve with a smile of presentable affection.

Chapter 48

The year was 1990. The commence of 'The good decade'. An era of live-audience sitcoms and alternative rock. Audacious fashion trends swept across the UK along with boy bands and "Beanie Babies". The women wore tight skirts and cropped tops exposing their belly bars, dancing provocatively at concerts and night clubs. Life ran riot as did the youth of its time. With his Twenty fifth birthday on the horizon, Theodore Todd planned a big birthday bash.

His wife had fallen for his reckless grace originally, but the honeymoon period had strayed. He'd formally known her as the "girl next door". The delicate and desirable beauty that every boy in town had dreamed to obtain. She was a girl with honour, decorum, and intellect to herself. A prize, a score, a doll to place on the commemorating shelf to the boys. And so, she kept herself to herself. This is until the likes of Theodore Todd came along. Misguidedly unaware of the games that men play of trickery for conquest.

Moira saw it all. She saw the girl with a single braid stood outside the barbers, how he stroked her cheek and made her blush. She saw the bright-eyed blonde sat by the canal on his picnic blanket, her caressing his leg as he fished. Within the year, there'd be eight in total that Moira had seen but never spoke of. Her husband's advances often proved too fruitful, more consistent than she was prepared for. His deceit provided her with the solitude she preferred. Trapped in an inescapable and regrettable marriage, she prayed that her husband's upcoming birthday would in fact, be his last.

She stored cleaning chemicals and materials underneath the kitchen sink. A consistently moderate space with sand countertops that were always cluttered by a glass cutting board, kettle, and other such things. Window cleaner, multi-purpose spray, washing-up liquid and the fabric softener stood attention in the cupboard. Additionally, the essentials for Theodore's car were under there too. Moira experienced serenity in the company of those chemicals. You see from the very beginning of the day, right up until the end, she was to relieve any sense of control and autonomy over to her husband. Her friends were accessories. Their company was obtained for the inexpensive presentation of delightful domesticity, costing her nothing but her authenticity and sense of self. No one to hear her, even if she deigned to vocalise her truth. She hadn't possessed the authority, not even over the food she was to prepare and engorge on. Moira did, however, get to choose the ingredients to precure.

"Evening dear, how was your day?"

She greeted politely as her husband returned from work. His profession was like that of most men of his stature within the village. The conclusion of 'Thatcher's Briton' brought on a new dawn for the working class. Many still scorned from its iron fist, sought what employment they could through factories and manual labour.

"Exhausting. When's dinner?"

Answered Theodore, uninterested in her invitation for a conversation.

"I've made the pancake mix that you wanted. There's some beef and veggie stew, that'll be ready in about ten minutes. I've used half of the mix for some giant Yorkshire puddings, then the other half I'm going to fry for dessert and serve with your favourite, lemon juice and sugar drizzle. Is that alright?"

She explained, trying to coax his pleasantly tolerable side.

"Aye, that sounds grand, love. Call me when it's done".

He answered, accepting the proposed meal. Taking a bottled beer from the refrigerator, her husband then made himself comfortable within the family room. Sitting with his filthy feet, slummed on the coffee table. Unwinding in a factory uniform brimmed with the stench of dirt and must. A face greased with sweat from his working man's brow.

Moira stared upon her husband with a delightful thought that brought her smile to reach each ear. Lemon juice is particularly zesty, she knew. A perceptively chemically sharp and bitter taste. One of which could perhaps conceal another unsavoury ingredient.

It was a small victory for Moira, and extremely short lived. Theodore Todd didn't go down so easily. She assumed he would simply drop and that would be that. She didn't expect that the poison wouldn't actually be the culprit to finish the job, but instead would be his tumble down the stairs when retiring to bed with an 'upset stomach', practically snapping his spine in two. A beautiful thing, she was. Dressed for the occasion, though he'd clearly not noticed. A black velvet midi slip under a cropped charcoal and ash grey floral cardigan. Closed toe, low heeled formal footwear with black opaque tights. Her hair appropriately groomed in a low bun with a natural make-up look, all pulled together with a cherry red lipstick. Bowing her head to pray, Moira respectfully brought her hands together and knelt before her husband's unmoving body.

"Dear Heavenly Father, please forgive me for I have sinned".

The other side wasn't at all what Theodore had in mind. Raised with the threat of eternal damnation in an infinite inferno or bargained with the blessed brightening bliss bestowed upon one by the creator. To his surprise, he was nowhere. Nowhere at all. No physical form to reel, no atmospheric temperature or light, nothing but the thoughts racing through his mind. He was an entity of sorts, locked in limbo. His fate not quite decided.

"Where am I?"

His soul voiced, bewildered and afraid.

"Where do you think you should be?"

Another voice asked. Sophisticated, smoky, sexy, and smooth. Poor Theodore Todd didn't know how to answer, how could he? He wasn't sure if he was dreaming, hallucinating or perhaps just couldn't open his eyes.

"Allow me to make things a little clearer for you, Teddy Toddy, my friend".

The voice began to clarify. Playing sadistically with the man's loosening mind.

"Your physical form has deceased. Your spiritual form, however, is still very cognitive".

It explained vaguely.

"So, what does that mean? Am I… is… what is this? The afterlife?"

Theodore panicked, unable to comprehend the reality of his own death.

"Yes, deary. This is what happens next".

It answered, straight to the point.

"It can't be!"

He cried, devastated by the sudden truth.

"Please!"

He begged.

"Please, there must be something I can do. Please, let me go back! This, this can't be it, this can't be it".

Wept Theodore's soul, crushed by his untimely departure from earth.

"Well... I could let you go back".

The voice teased, dangling a fruitful yet forbidden apple.

"But it comes at a price".

It revealed, bargaining its hidden intentions.

"Anything".

Theodore answered, almost immediately. The empty space drew soundless. Unable to detect the passing of time, he waited, forcing patience in himself for an anticipated response.

"See, the fact that you're here means that the afterlife has retrieved a fresh soul, yes?"

It began.

"Yes...".

He agreed, directly with an obedient compliance.

"So, deary. If you were to leave, you would need to replace that soul's vacancy. If you can manage to replace it, I'll give you... what? A decade? How does a decade sound?"

It promised, happily and sillily in a casual ease.

"What do you say?"

Moira was lost in thought, begging her lord for redemption over the disobedient act of a condemned sin. Coming to her senses, recognising the severity for her actions as she stood above her husband's motionless body.

"What have I done?"

She asked herself quietly, seeing herself finally for the murderer that she was.

"What have I done!"

She screamed, falling to grace upon her knees, pulling her husband's corpse onto her lap to cradle the weight of his head.

"Theodore? Sweetheart?"

She cried, as though to revive him with the simple call of his name.

Eventually, Moira rid herself of the strength to utter another breath as she laid herself onto the carpet beside him. Her face touched his as she closed her eyes, hoping to join him, wherever he may be. Each lay in the deathly silence of their family home. Lifeless, by the bottom of the staircase.

Chapter 49

So, there you have it. I'm sure I covered everything. Haven't I? As you've probably guessed it, Detective Inspector Michael Jones assisted with fabricating a more realistic story to his superiors. Considering how revealing his knowledge of the real events that took place wouldn't have boded well for his reputable stance within his role. See, that's why everybody thought that we had a crime wave of suspected gangs or delinquents attacking innocent civilians and committing arson. Though the police took some convincing when it came to young George. Fortunately for him, due to Esther's unwavering loyalty, they weren't able to collect any proof of his unfavourable business dealings.

Ivy, however, knew George all too well to believe such trope. After the news had spread that he was found alive, she went to visit him. Perched by his hospital bedside, she stayed morning, noon, and night until his eventual recovery. Not once forcing the conversation of what happened, not until he'd regained his strength fully. No, it wasn't until they'd reached his apartment, ready for residency once again. A team of crime scene cleaners had dealt with the splattered blood beneath the floorboards. It was a Saturday, funnily enough. Though his time, unlocking the door, George checked the vicinity with caution, having learned vigilance the hard way. He threw his keys onto the countertop, just as he had the last time that he'd set foot in that same apartment.

"You, OK?"
Ivy asked softly, closing the door behind her.
"Yeah".
He lied, fronting a non-cholent grin as he sniffled. She stepped to him calmly, pressing her palm delicately across his cheek.

"I know you're not. It's alright, though. You don't have to be right now".

She soothed, planting a kiss onto his forehead.

"You can tell me when you're ready".

Ivy whispered, showing her willingness to wait for the truth.

"Tell you what?"

George replied, caught off guard, slightly confused.

"Tell me what really happened, sweetheart. I know you had to lie to the police, I get it. But you know, I'm not the police, you can tell me".

She explained, not really understanding the atmosphere building.

"That is what happened. Someone broke in. I don't know who, I didn't see who it was".

He replied defensively, inadvertently pushing her away. Ivy took a step back, crossing her arms as she darted George a low browed look of disapproval.

"I know you've been through a lot. I do. But George, I almost lost my mind trying to find you. I thought you were dead."

She began, trying to control her temper.

"Don't you respect me enough to tell me the truth?"

She asked openly, unaware of the weight such a question carried. Not realising that the answer determined the very future of their relationship. What was the boy to do? He had mere moments to collect his thoughts. To decide his fate. Admitting the truth meant the reveal of Esther's handy work to conceal his whereabouts. Allowing Ivy to know that he actively chose not to visit her the same night he'd been to see Esther. That he'd entrusted her with his livelihood, but not Ivy. Alternately, he could have continued to lie, letting the relationship die on a hill built of mistrust and manipulation under the pretence of protection.

"Well?"

She badgered.

"What's it going to be?"

Esther had packed her things and moved out of the hotel suite, not long after the fire was put out and the police took everyone's statements. Troy insisted that she stay with him. Not only because he couldn't afford the mortgage by himself, but also because the isolation had become too much for him to bare. Gifting Esther his own bedroom, so to upkeep the preservation of Dana's memory through maintaining her bedroom as it was. A space he still heartbreakingly slept and wept in. Only now, he wasn't so alone. He'd also re-opened his mother's salon, May and Olly went back on to work full-time once things had calmed down. Troy managed the company, setting Esther on as a part-time receptionist. A position she felt gave her the financial stability that her writing was forever insufficient in, though the repetitive nature of the job often proved challenging.

Troy wasn't the only one to inherit a new business, as Roy and Violet took for themselves an early retirement, passing The Tavern to their son. A proposition he'd not always been so keen to precure, but after having almost lost his parents, Malcom felt a sense of responsibility to take the wheel. Especially with the workload set with restoring its structural integrity after a considerable amount of damage.

You'd think a night so catastrophically life threatening, would force Violet to gain a new perspective on her recent attitude and expressed behaviour regarding her son and his 'friend'. But no such luck as it would seem. Though, she managed to keep a tight lid on her opinions when Luke would visit Malcom. Especially on Sundays, family picnic day. Which soon began to include Luke, whether she liked it or not.

That particular Saturday, on the same afternoon that George had moved back home, Esther and Troy were closing up the shop. Carrying out the last-minute checks after having cashed up. All equipment was unplugged, lights switched off and the doors were locked before setting the alarm and pulling the shutters down. The promise of an upcoming spring had birthed the surrounding blossoming trees. The early evening breeze was no longer warmed by a soon to be sleeping sun. Usually on days where they'd started their shifts at the same time, it made more sense for them to carshare. That morning, Troy had driven his mum's car, parking it around the back of the building, so to not block the entryway for customers. It'd been a long workday, fully booked with just a short ten-minute break for lunch. The two strolled in silence, too tired to converse. The back road by the salon was slightly concealed by nature. Overgrown hedges and weeds clogged the pavement, partially hiding the vehicle from passers-by.

As they reached the end of their walk, a car door slammed shut behind them. Esther stopped in her tracks, still triggered by the sound. A man's voice yelled from behind. She turned to see George approach from Ivy's car as he'd come out from the passenger's side. Upon hearing his voice, Esther ever so slightly let down her guard.

"Essie, are you alright?"

He asked, reading her alarmed expression.

"I heard the car door".

She explained, still unsure.

"That was us, we're parked just there, look".

George replied, reassuring her. Neither Troy, nor Ivy understood the significance of that specific sound. Relieved that the threat was nothing but her mind playing tricks, she asked the two, what lead to their unexpected arrival. George and Ivy shared a tense look of conflict. His eyes weary with the fear of regret, hers fuelled with a determined curiosity.

"I want to see it".

She blurted blatantly.

"See what?"

Asked Troy, not sensing the tone. Esther read her meaning instantaneously, judging by the severity of her expression and disposition towards George. And so, she pulled out her phone, searching through her gallery for the photograph that Roy had sent her weeks prior.

"Holy fuck".

Exclaimed Ivy, in disbelief as she took in the ghastly image presented before her.

"Wait, so is that what you saw when I was there? Why the fuck didn't you warn me?"

She snapped, irritated by Esther's 'selfishness'.

"Excuse me, I fucking tried. You accused me of being high! Besides, I texted you. Asking you to tell me when you got home. I wouldn't have done that if I didn't give a shit".

Esther pointed out, recalling the conversation they had.

"Well, if you'd shown me".

Ivy argued, unreasonably.

"I didn't have a photo! Should I have asked it to pose for one?"

She defended herself.

"Alright, alright, can the pair of you pack it in, please".

George lost his patience.

"That's it OK, Ivy, that's the truth. We knew the police wouldn't believe us, since you'd already gone to them with this… which I'm not having a go, obviously I get it. I'm grateful that you wanted to help. But I'm just saying, if I came to you, you'd have to lie to them, or you'd have told them the truth. Then they'd have sent you off in a straitjacket".

He exclaimed.

"I really am sorry that I didn't come to see you, I'm sorry that I lied. I know that I've hurt you. I genuinely thought I was doing the right thing. Looking back now, it's clear that I was wrong".

George stumbled on his every thought.

"I love you, Ivy. I'm sorry".

He apologised authentically. It was a lot of information for the poor girl to take in all at once. Obviously, she loved him. But, friends, is love really enough?

Chapter 50

What's that? Oh, what happened with the others? Well, Mr Platt's body was identified after it had been recovered from the fire. There were murmurings that he set the blaze alight, motivated by jealousy over his daughter having chosen the Richard's to take refuge over her own mother and father. Oddly enough his wheelchair was never discovered. It was assumed to have burned, but it did seem odd that not even a shed of its remanence was left. Nothing could be proved, in that respect.

For those secretly involved, all concluded that the beast must have engorged on Mr Platt before appearing at The Tavern, conjuring the theory that as it burned, all that was left to uncover was what remained inside. Silly really. Maybe they knew that their theory held no promise, or perhaps they just opted to repress the hell they'd encountered.
Though her husband's reputation had taken quite the blow, Mrs Platt still expected everybody who knew him personally within the community to attend the funeral. She made that perfectly clear when calling each and every guest invited, to ask them individually for a direct RSVP. Most recipients expressed some reluctance, but nothing of which Mrs Platt couldn't efficiently nip in the bud. A respectable affair, she desired. An honourable send off, for an honourable man. A final act of dedication from his most loyal companion. The ceremony was to be carried out within the church. She'd had a few weeks to arrange the event due to his remains being held by the morgue, whilst undergoing investigation upon original discovery. It wasn't until the case had closed that Mr Platt's death was ruled as a tragic accident. With a little nudge in the right direction by Detective Inspector Michael Jones, of course.

No expense was spared as the ceremonies scent was to be induced by fresh white roses, appropriately placed throughout the main hall. The pews had been cleaned, along with the floors and drapes. Even the stain glass window of the mighty Ark was washed and polished for her husband's last farewell. Everything had to be perfect, she felt. Her way of an apology for having not protected him in his final hour.

Eve was expected to find sufficiently suitable temporary care for Ellis, so that her and Jason could attend the funeral.

"He'll only fuss, and cause disruption".

Her mother stated, disinviting her grandson from the event. Things had been uncomfortable between mother and daughter since her father's demise. See, Eve came to learn in her early adulthood, that her parents' perception of respect was more so associated with compliance, obedience, and fear. Since having met Jason, her understanding of respect came to be that of mutual ground. An acceptance of each other's boundaries and an effort to assure the other can feel comfort and safety in one's presence. No longer believing that respect should be 'earned' but instead given freely. To be revoked, only when proved necessary. A concept considerably alien to her mother. Eve understood, her recent behaviour was yet to be reprimanded. A punishment she grew wearier of with each passing day.

Jasons mental health improved, slowly but surely. A never-ending struggle, I'm sure. With his wife's unwavering support and the maternal instinct to be the father that his son deserved, Jason attended an appointment with his local GP. He'd been referred for cognitive behavioural therapy and prescribed a mild dose of anxiety medication to reduce further risk of regular panic attacks. Eve would tell him the truth one day, about who her father really was, and the depth of deception enforced on her to conceal such a dark and evil secret. One day, when he would be stronger and therefore more prepared for such knowledge.

Working late nights as a delivery driver, no longer served Jason. The guilt that weighed down on him for so long over Dana's loss, would ease ever so slightly as each week passed. Keeping up on his word, both he and Eve helped Troy to maintain his mother's company. Jason was able to enrol onto an online business management and accounting apprenticeship, as he worked part-time at the salon. Eve took a more creative approach, implementing her newly explored interest in interior design. Harnessing her developing skills to spruce up the properties outdoor land as a memorial to Dana, with the use of a beautiful garden for customers. A summer seating area for people to wait for their appointments or a place to relax as their hair treatments set. Eve shaded a built-in patio with pine wood panels. Blanketed by free-willed ivy leaves, lit aglow with a string of miniature bulb shaped fairy lights. All centred in the entrance garden of planted hedges, seasonally survivable all year round.

As the ceremony was about to commence, the guests respectfully remained seated. Quietly chattering amongst themselves, waiting for the sermon to enter. Copies of a pamphlet that Violet had put together were distributed amongst attendees. Displaying a photograph of Theodore Todd Platt in his prime. Mrs Platt had selected a snapshot from his younger years. Whereas the easel stood afront the coffin had the image of Mr Platt in his seniority rested upon it. The stern and serious man. A scowling smile blended into a rippling layered chin. Greys would whisp from his crinkled eyebrows amongst a clean-shaven face. A suit, most appropriate attire for the occasion. Its bright white shirt locked up by a correctly fastened tie. Brought in with a sleek black dress jacket, drawing the attention towards a costly tie pin placed between the third and forth button.

Jones sat uninvited by the back pew. Persuaded by obligation and curiosity. A neatly stacked pile of programmes was placed atop a cabinet upon entry, framed by two adjacent single lit candles. The picture of a young man, a hard-working man. Vainly strands crept from the crevasses of his eyes. Skin, tight and un-worn, un-weathered. Light and porcelain and plain. Slenderly built with muscular undertone, concealed by an oversized polo shirt, most likely his past professions uniform, Jones assumed. A man of stature and grace, hansom and holy. With slicked back, luxurious locks of flaming red hair.

Eve and Jason were seated beside Mrs Platt right at the very front, after having left Ellis with Luke for the following hour. The Richard's shared a bench with Esther. Their hearts feeling as darkened as their formal ensemble.

"If Eve hadn't pulled me out that night, it could've been me up there".

Esther spoke delicately, locking her glance onto the coffin perched peacefully.

"Thank fuck she did".

Roy replied, wrapping his arm around her shoulder as he sat to her left.

"But we can't be thinking about, *what if*".

He suggested, pulling her in for a hug before releasing his arm from her person.

"We're all still here, love. That's all that matters now".

Violet added, finishing her husbands thought. Esther agreed with a single nod of the head. They sat in a respectful silence for a moment or two, as Roy watched Esther's face of weariness.

The service commenced and the room dropped to a deafening silence. The sermon introduced his speech with biblical references and dramatized cliché's. He spoke for the duration of fifteen minutes before inviting Mrs Platt to the front, to say a few words. She'd prepared what to say, holding onto a stapled collection of notes, handwritten.

"My husband hadn't the most obviously desirable qualities that one looks for in a companion. He wasn't comical nor was he conversational. He was instead, significantly earnest. Solemn yet profound. Considerate, but not blatantly so…"

She stopped, clearing her throat.

"My husband loved me. He loved our daughter, Eve".

Mrs Platt went on, darting a disapproving glance, subtly so. One of which, only Eve had picked up on.

"We all wish for our loved ones to go peacefully when it comes to their time".

She paused again, this time, unable to catch her breath.

"I..".

Mrs Platt stopped. Eve could feel everybody's eyes. Expecting her to stand and comfort her mourning mother. She didn't know what to do, how she was supposed to react. She froze, awkward and uncomfortable, as her mother stepped down to return to her seat. Placing herself next to an 'uncaring daughter'. A murmur scattered amongst the crowd, judging Eve for her lack of attentive nature. Detecting her discomfort, Jason took a hold of her hand.

"It's OK".

He whispered. Assuring that his wife didn't feel so alone. The sermon returned to his previous position to thank Mrs Platt for her efforts and concluded the service. The drapes were closed as a symphony by Skeeter Davis sounded on an old timely record player. A classically harmonious song. Lyrically blissful in both its beauty and its horror. As the attendees rose to scatter, Moira stubbornly stayed seated by her lonesome. Locked inside the room that's emptiness echoed with the ache of a shattered self. She sang, patiently waiting for her Theodore to awaken. Just as he had once before.

The End.

Ah, that was a nice little happy ending for you, wasn't it? Everybody is grand. It all turned out fine. There aren't gangs and delinquents running rabid throughout the village, so you needn't trouble yourself with any concern. Your visit will be delightful. I assure you. Oh, and don't you worry about my old friend, Teddy Toddy. I won't be sending him back like I did the last time. No, I'll be keeping a close eye on him, and on my favourite little village, Aviary Avenue. Just as I always have.

What's that? So, who am I? I thought you'd never ask! Well, evidently, I don't really have an official name, though I'm referred to as a number of things. We've met, actually. You may not recall. We became acquainted that morning you'd woken up, questioning whether or not you should have. That night you'd drank too much, staring at your empty glass, wondering if you even wanted to see the sun rise once more. The times you've questioned your life's worth, its purpose, its point.

My job is to test human nature. To push a person to their absolute limit in order to uncover their truest self. Figure out if their redeemable qualities, qualify them for redemption. A decider, of sorts. "The judge, the jury, the executioner". The captain of lost souls, burdened by unexpected defeat.

So, go! Live your life. Make good decisions. Make bad ones. Your choices are confined to your mortal realm, obviously. You may as well enjoy them whilst you still can.

Printed in Great Britain
by Amazon